Seven
Deadly Zins

Also available by Nancy J. Parra

California Wine Country Mysteries
A Case of Syrah, Syrah

Perfect Proposals Mysteries
Newlywed Dead

Bodice of Evidence

Engaged in Murder

Baker's Treat Mysteries
Flourless to Stop Him

Murder Gone A-Rye

Gluten for Punishment

Seven
Deadly Zins

A CALIFORNIA WINE
COUNTRY MYSTERY

Nancy J. Parra

CROOKED
LANE

NEW YORK

Published in the United States by Crooked Lane Books, an imprint of The Quick Brown Fox & Company LLC.

Crooked Lane Books and its logo are trademarks of The Quick Brown Fox & Company LLC.

Library of Congress Catalog-in-Publication data available upon request.

ISBN (hardcover): 978-1-68331-871-2
ISBN (ePub): 978-1-68331-872-9
ISBN (ePDF): 978-1-68331-873-6

Cover illustration by Jesse Reisch
Book design by Jennifer Canzone

Printed in the United States.

www.crookedlanebooks.com

Crooked Lane Books
34 West 27th St., 10th Floor
New York, NY 10001

First Edition: January 2019

10 9 8 7 6 5 4 3 2 1

This one is for my family and friends, who put up with the time it takes to write a book.

Chapter 1

"When are you going to put my winery on your tour list?" my friend Tim Slade asked. Tim owned a winery south of my Aunt Jemma's winery in Sonoma County, California. He was a tall guy with a slender build and blond hair. He often stopped by my aunt's tasting room to hang out and discuss the wine business.

"I didn't know you wanted me to do that," I replied. "I thought you didn't like people."

He shrugged. "I've changed my mind. When's your next tour?"

"I've got a group tomorrow," I said. "I'm taking them up to the sculpture garden at the Sonoma County Museum. Then we have a tour of the Charles Schultz Museum, with stops for wine tasting on the trip up and back."

"So squeeze my winery in," he said.

"Your place is south of here," I stated.

"And your point is?" He leaned against the tasting room's walnut bar, awaiting my answer. I had poured him one of Aunt Jemma's zinfandel wines, which he'd swirled before taking a delicate sniff and tasting it.

"The point is, I would have to go out of the way to bring

1

them by your place. I can plan a tour for next week that goes south." I had started my Off the Beaten Path wine country tours to highlight the wonderful hidden gems in Sonoma County. It was perfect for anyone who loved wine tasting, arts, or outdoor activities. My business had picked up quite a bit lately, and I was enjoying finding new places to bring my customers.

"Next week." He pressed his hand to his chest as if he would have a heart attack. "You're killing me."

"I usually plan a tour for a specific group," I said. "For instance, the group I'm taking out tomorrow are all cartoon fans and want to see the Charles Shultz Museum. It's tough to compete with Charlie Brown and his friends."

"Are the people who take your tours likely to join wine clubs?" he asked. "Because I can find someone to dress up as a Peanuts character if that'll bring in people who'll join the wine club."

Wine clubs were the main business for smaller wineries like Aunt Jemma's and Tim's. After a tasting of a variety of local flavors, the sommelier would offer the tour group exclusive memberships in the vineyard's wine club. Customers would pick monthly wine selections and get free tastings for the year. It encouraged them to come back, buy more, and hopefully bring a friend.

"I don't think I can fool them by driving south and showing up at your winery to see you in a Charlie Brown costume," I said. "That said, you finished picking grapes this week, right?"

"Yes," he said. "Why?"

"My Thursday group is filled with enthusiasts interested in the process of making wine. You can show them your vats and your lab where you test the sugar content."

"That might work," he said with a thoughtful nod. "Would

there happen to be any investors in your group? I might be in the market for a sponsorship."

"Wait a minute," I said. "I thought you were happy as a sole proprietor."

"You do know how to make a little money with a winery, don't you?" he asked.

"Why don't you tell me?

"Start with a lot of money," he said and saluted me with his wine glass before taking a sip.

I laughed. "Very funny."

"Taylor, I've been looking for you," Aunt Jemma said as she pushed through the doors to the tasting room. She appeared to float over to me—her colorful caftan brushed the floor so low, you could barely see her feet.

Aunt Jemma was my mother's sister, and when she'd had a heart attack in the spring, she'd convinced me to move to Sonoma from San Francisco, to look after her. In reality, she was healthy as a horse and only had a symptom if I talked about how my boss from San Francisco kept calling, trying to get me back to the city and my high-paying job in advertising.

Aunt Jemma was also a bit of a character.

"What do you need?"

"I have a séance scheduled for this evening, and I was wondering if you wouldn't mind joining the group."

"Okay," I said with a tilt of my head. "Why?"

"My psychic, Sarah, couldn't make it. You have good energy. I thought you could stand in for her."

"If Sarah isn't going to be there, who is leading the séance?"

"I could," Tim said and shrugged. "My girlfriend, Mandy, knows a psychic who taught me a few tricks."

"I think you need to stay out of it, young man," Aunt Jemma said. She put her hands on her hips. "You'll scare the ladies away with your antics."

"Antics? I never . . ." He attempted to look affronted, but it didn't work, and I burst out laughing.

"Tim is trying to convince me to take one of my tours down to his winery."

"I'm trying to get some notoriety for the smaller, scrappier vineyards," he said and raised a blonde eyebrow. "You should back me on that."

"I agree we need better marketing," Aunt Jemma said. She turned to me. "You were in marketing, right? Can't you do some kind of social media something to help us out?"

I made a face. "I was in advertising, and I thought you all were working with the other bigger wineries in the region, to share the wealth."

"We are," Aunt Jemma said with a shrug. "But Tim's winery has some of the oldest zins in the USA. That's something you could tell your tour groups."

"Here, here," Tim said and raised his glass.

"That's the best part of my business," I said. "Really, trying to get people to see beyond the commercial wineries and look at the great Northern California art, hikes, parks, and smaller, quirkier wineries."

"Quirkier?" Tim asked.

"Well, Aunt Jemma's place is famous for its previous owner being a witch, and now we offer séances."

"Ghost hunting is all the rage," Aunt Jemma chimed in. "Oh, I know, we could set things up as a haunted winery. Bring out those new-fangled cameras and recorders, and have a few great investigations."

"So that's what the séance is really for?" I asked. "To draw in spirits so you can get people to pay you to do ghost investigations around the winery?"

Aunt Jemma's eyes sparkled. "You could use your contacts to get us on television. We could do one of those ghost hunter shows, and then people would be coming out left and right to visit and buy our wine." She placed her hands inside her sleeves. "We all know that once they taste it, they'll buy. We simply need a hook to get them into the tasting room."

"Here's to a hook," Tim said, lifting his glass again. He swallowed the contents and motioned for more.

"Are you driving home?" I asked.

"Mandy's picking me up," he said. "She had some kind of thing in town."

"What is Mandy up to now?" Aunt Jemma asked.

"Who knows," Tim said with a shrug. "She's always trying some trendy diet or New Age spiritual guidance. Last week she declared she would only eat non-soy tofu."

"Wait," I said, "is that a real thing?"

Tim shrugged again. "All I know is I'm not eating it."

Tim was so much into gourmet cooking that he had spent a month in France—twice—to take classes at Le Cordon Bleu cooking school.

"I hardly think tofu is food," Aunt Jemma said. "I can't imagine soy-free tofu being a staple in any diet, let alone mine."

"As long as I can cook," Tim said, "I'll make anything that pairs well with wine."

"Hmm," I chimed in, "I wonder what wine would pair well with soy-free tofu?"

"I imagine that would depend on how it's cooked," Aunt Jemma said and tapped her chin. "A rosé perhaps, or a pinot grigio if it's cooked with garlic."

The door to the tasting room opened, and Mandy came in, looking flushed and rosy. I had to admit I was a little jealous of her. She was a year younger than me, and California blonde. She was all of five foot two inches and lucky to weigh one hundred pounds. She wore leggings and a tunic top and over-the-knee boots. Tim had found her on an online dating site about a year ago. She'd moved in with him on their third date. And why not? She had gone from struggling actress to pampered woman of the house, and Tim had *three* houses.

When he said you had to start a winery with a lot of money, he wasn't kidding. He'd made his fortune in the original dot-com boom. He was ten years older than me and inclined to dabble in whatever struck his fancy.

"Hi all," Mandy said and gave Tim a kiss on the cheek before she climbed up on the bar stool next to him. "I just came from this seminar in Sonoma. Dr. Adam Brinkman was the speaker."

"Him again?" Tim asked and poured himself more wine. "That's the fifth time in three weeks."

"I like him," she said and thrust her lower lip into a pout. "He has some great ideas for spiritual healing. I went down to Orange County to see him a few months back. He took the entire auditorium full of people on a guided meditation and then started healing people. The man is gifted."

"Healing people?" I asked as I poured her a tasting of the pinot noir.

"Yes," she said, and her eyes went round with wonder. "This woman came in on crutches and left practically running from the room. It was a miracle. I've never seen anything like it."

"I was running from the room as well when I saw how much that nuttiness was costing me," Tim said.

"It was worth every penny," Mandy said without skipping a beat. "I closed my eyes and felt this warm healing energy flow up from my feet to the crown of my head. Then there was this angelic voice that told me I was destined for fame and fortune."

"Wow," I said and gave Tim a suspicious look. He shrugged.

"I know," Mandy said, her eyes wide. "That's when I knew I had to convince Dr. Brinkman to come to Sonoma. I told him all about our town. He was interested, so he came up here and fell in love with the area." She raised her chin proudly. "Now all I have to do is attend the next five sessions, and he promises I'll learn how to follow my destiny."

"Your destiny?"

"You know—my spiritual path."

"Your spiritual path is fame and fortune?" Aunt Jemma asked.

"Yes," she said. "Dr. Brinkman thinks that all any of us need to do is to change the way we think, and all our dreams will come true."

"Change the way you think?" I asked.

"Yes, what you think goes out into the world. Transforming your thoughts transforms your life so that you live your destiny . . . your true life."

"And you change your thoughts by doing what?" Aunt Jemma asked.

"By thinking positively. It's called the law of attraction. You

7

attract what you believe. I believe in fame and fortune, so I'm sure it will come my way."

"Interesting," Aunt Jemma said. "Do you think you can change your destiny?" Her expression was one of wonder. I felt like mine must have been one of disbelief.

"Yes," Mandy said.

"For only fifteen hundred dollars a session," Tim said with a snort.

"Well, it costs money to learn how to change," she said. "But Dr. Brinkman says if you follow your dreams, you can earn back more than triple what the sessions cost." She leaned in and waved her wine glass. "He thinks I'll be a natural to teach others about the miracle of positive thinking. People will look up to me—me, Mandy Richards."

"So will you be traveling the world?" Tim asked.

"What? Oh, no, baby," Mandy said and leaned into him. "I'm going to star in Dr. Brinkman's videos. The residuals will be fantastic."

"Here's to the power of positive thinking," Tim said and touched his wine glass to hers. "I'm positive I can get Taylor to schedule some of her tours to visit our winery."

"Oh, how fun!" she said and turned to me. "Timmy's appellation needs more exposure."

"That way I can finish the remodel of the house," Tim said, "and keep my Mandy happy." He winked at her, and I rolled my eyes.

"I've never heard of Dr. Brinkman," Aunt Jemma said and frowned. "Where is he from?"

"He's from Los Angeles," Mandy said. She opened her purse and pulled out a flyer. "One of my actress friends told me about him. He's done amazing work with some very famous people. See?" She handed Aunt Jemma the paper.

"Huh." Aunt Jemma pulled out a pair of purple reading glasses and studied the paper. "He does séances."

"Oh please," I said and took the paper. "We don't have the kind of money he would want to do a séance."

"I guess that means *you'll* have to help me tonight, then," Aunt Jemma said. "See you at eight. Oh, and wear something mysterious. Bye, Tim—good luck, Mandy." She left me shaking my head.

"Are you really going to run a séance?" Mandy asked as she sipped her wine.

"I'm not going to run it," I said. "All she needs is an extra body for a full table. I can sit and hold hands for a while."

"While wearing something mysterious." Tim raised his right eyebrow. "That's something I'd like to see."

"Don't hold your breath," I said.

"Come on, Timmy," Mandy said as she put down her wine glass, took his hand, and pulled him to his feet. "Let's go home. I need to do my homework before the next seminar."

"Let me know when you schedule the wine tour," he said. "I'll try to have something special for them to see."

"I bet you will." I wiped down the bar top and prepared to close the tasting room. Tim was right. He and Aunt Jemma put a lot of work into the local wine organizations. The least I could do was schedule a tour or two for his winery.

Chapter 2

"Oh, Taylor, there you are," Aunt Jemma said. "Do come in—we are getting ready to be seated."

I was wearing a maxi dress and sandals. It was the closest thing I had to Aunt Jemma's flowing caftans. I hoped I looked mysterious enough. "Hello, I'm Taylor." I introduced myself and took my seat at the small round table. There were four other ladies there to make a table of six. Aunt Jemma had set up the séance in the library just off her family room. There were two winged-backed chairs and an end table and floor lamp on one side of the room, and a small desk, where Aunt Jemma did the paperwork for the winery, sat on the other side. In the center was the round séance table. It was big enough for six chairs to go around it, yet close enough we all touched knees, if not hands.

"Taylor, this is Marion Wells, her sister Susan Applegate, Kelly Blue, and Jeanne Fellow. Ladies, my niece Taylor."

"So nice to meet you," Marion said. She was a handsome woman with champagne-colored hair. "We're here to try to reach my father, Buddy Jones. He promised that if we did a séance on the anniversary of his death, he would come back and tell us something very important."

"I love that we get a girls' night, good wine, and a little fun," her sister Susan said with a wink.

"Okay, ladies," Aunt Jemma said. "Please be seated while I light the candles."

They pulled out their chairs and took a seat. Aunt Jemma lit candles around the room and turned off the lights. "All right, let's hold hands. Please, whatever you do, don't break the circle. If you do, the energy will be lost."

We all clasped hands with the persons beside us. Suddenly, the tablecloth moved as something landed in the middle of the table. Jeanne shrieked and I jumped. The surprise was my cat, Clemmie.

"Clemmie," I said as I stood and grabbed my silly orange and white cat I've had since college. "I'm sorry, ladies. She likes to be the center of attention."

"Oh, no need to apologize," Marion said with a chuckle. "I have four cats at home. I know how curious they can be."

"Daddy loved cats," Susan said.

"Maybe Clemmie knew he was around and wanted to say hi," Jeanne said.

"I'll be right back," I said and left the room. I knew I would hear about Clemmie later. Aunt Jemma liked to pretend she was annoyed with Clemmie, and Clemmie liked to pretend she didn't like Aunt Jemma, but I'd walked in on them at lunch one day. Clemmie had been sitting on the table sharing Aunt Jemma's tuna fish salad.

"You are one naughty kitty," I said and carried Clemmie into her favorite bedroom and closed the door. "Stay in here until we're done, and I'll get you special treats."

Clemmie jumped out of my arms and stalked off to go into the closet.

"I wish I could be hiding in here with you, too," I whispered. I closed the door and turned to find someone standing behind me. I might have screamed a little.

"Oh, I didn't mean to scare you," my best friend, Holly, said. "The door was open, and I let myself in. I thought you were locking your doors these days."

"I thought we were too," I said and gave her a quick hug. "You look good." Holly was an all-American beauty with long brunette hair and a figure to die for. She was also very good with makeup and fashion. She told me once it was because she worked at La Galleria, an art gallery. It seemed in the art business, being as fashion forward as possible was expected by her boss and her customers. Frankly, I think she would have worked at a dress shop if it gave her something to dress up for.

"Thanks, so do you," she said and motioned for me to twirl. "What's the occasion for the maxi dress? Don't you usually wear jeans?"

"Aunt Jemma's holding a séance and wine night."

"A séance? I've never been involved in one of those. Is it okay if I come and watch?"

"You don't have to just watch," Aunt Jemma said as she came up behind her. "We're reaching out to Marion Wells' father. He always loved a pretty girl. I imagine he would love to come visit if you were here." She put her arms around Holly and me. "Let's go start the séance." She turned to Holly. "My psychic canceled on me, and I'm leading this thing without much outside help. You two lovely ladies will draw every male entity for miles. Surely we'll be able to get something out of Buddy Jones."

"Cool," Holly said and kissed my aunt on the cheek. "I always wanted to be in on a séance."

We walked back into the room. Someone had poured the ladies tall glasses of wine. My nose told me it was likely a zinfandel.

"The girls are going to really draw the old man back to this dimension," Aunt Jemma said. "Alright, gather 'round the table and hold hands. Please, let's all take a deep breath. Breathe in and ouuuuut."

We all did as she asked for the next three breaths. Then Aunt Jemma went into séance mode. The routine sounded like something straight out of a movie. At one point, I opened one eye to see if anyone in the room was buying my aunt's shenanigans. Everyone, including Holly, seemed to be really into the dramatic questions and vague answers. I loved my aunt, but I was pretty sure there were no ghosts in the room.

"Ladies," Aunt Jemma said after the last question was asked and answered, "I'm getting a message that you need to go the First National and check a safety deposit box."

"Oh, a safety deposit box? Really?" Marion asked. "Wow!"

"Thank you, Buddy Jones, for taking the time to visit us today," Aunt Jemma said. "You can go with love. Ladies, breathe in and out." We did. "Now open your eyes." Aunt Jemma clapped her hands and brought the lights up. Her guests smiled at each other. "Okay, you can let go of hands and enjoy your wine."

The ladies shook off the session and took a swig or two of wine.

"I have some snacks in the kitchen," Aunt Jemma said. "Taylor, come help me. We'll be right back, ladies."

We walked out of the library, through the family room, and into the large gourmet kitchen. There were two trays of crackers and cheese on the granite countertop. "Why did you tell them to go to First National Bank?"

"I called around," Aunt Jemma said. "There were no accounts in Buddy Jones's name but there was a Eugene Jones. So I went to the library and did some digging. According to the census of 1920, Eugene Jones had a son named Buddy. I connected the dots."

"Won't they need a key?" I asked.

"All they'll need is a death certificate or two," Aunt Jemma said. "I've put them on the trail; now let's see how they follow it."

"You had this rigged from the start," I said and picked up a platter.

"What was rigged?" Holly asked. "Oh no, don't tell me that little show wasn't real. Oh, I was so looking forward to talking about how cool it was that you channeled that man."

"It's theater," I said.

"There are clues for the ladies to chase," Aunt Jemma said. "I like to think of it as a fun way to give an investigation report."

"Oh, are you an investigator?" Holly asked.

"I've done my fair share of research," Aunt Jemma said. "Plus my psychic friend advised me to do some before a séance. It's what she does."

"Wait—I thought that psychics were able to talk to the dead," Holly said.

"A good psychic *does* talk to the dead," Aunt Jemma said. "I was lucky enough to know Marion and Susan, and I knew why they wanted the séance."

"You knew they wanted to speak to their father?" I asked.

"Yes," Aunt Jemma said. "When Sarah—my psychic— called to tell me she was sick, I knew what I had to do."

"So she knew that the ladies needed to get the message about the safety deposit box," Holly said and grabbed a platter of canapés.

"Yes," Aunt Jemma said. "So, see? They did get a psychic reading."

We walked back into the den.

"I'm so excited to see if there is a safety deposit box at First National bank," Marion said.

"I'm sure there is," Susan said. "Why else would Daddy tell us to go look for it?" She smiled. "I can't wait to see what's in it."

"It might be a lotto card," Jeanne said. "You could be million-dollar winners."

"As long as it's not expired," Marion said in horror. "What if it's expired?"

"I'm sure it's not a lotto ticket," I said.

"Maybe it's a family heirloom," Holly said. "Like something from *Antiques Roadshow*."

"I'm sure Daddy wouldn't keep an heirloom from us for that long," Susan said. "Would he?" she asked Marion.

"Daddy could have kept all kinds of cool things from us," Marion said. "That man was kooky the last twenty years of his life. I swear he had dementia."

"Well, you'll have to call and tell me what you find in the box," Aunt Jemma said and put her tray down on the table. "For now, how's the wine? Does anyone need a refill?"

"I could use one," Jeanne said. She lifted her empty wine glass.

I went to the sideboard and grabbed the carafe of zinfandel and poured her half a glass. Then I added more to everyone else's and sat down. My puppy, Millie, came running into the room just then. Millie was a tan cocker spaniel that Aunt Jemma's winemaker, Juan, had found abandoned in the far vineyards. Our best guess was she was five months old. I'd had her for two months now and loved every minute of it.

Clemmie, of course, had other ideas. I think she loved Millie. She definitely loved to pounce on her or sneak up around a corner and bat her on the nose. Millie would give chase, and Clemmie would jump up on the counter and grin at her.

"Hey, baby," I said as she jumped on my lap. "Who let you out of your crate?" I had put Millie in her crate while the ladies were here for the séance. I didn't want anyone to be distracted—by the puppy sneaking under the table and scaring someone. Séances could be touchy things.

"I let her out," Holly said. "When I went into the kitchen, one look at those sweet, sad, brown eyes, and I was done."

"It's okay," Aunt Jemma said. "We were done with the serious part of the evening and on to the party part." She lifted her wine glass. "Right, ladies?"

"Right!"

Chapter 3

Tim's winery was on a two-lane stretch of road along with five other little places. When I say little, I mean each had twenty or thirty acres of rolling hills and carefully cultivated grape varieties. Some of the vineyards simply sold grapes to other wineries, but a few had little wine-tasting barns and a lush lawn for people to come and picnic. The road was lined with tall oaks, and the air smelled sweetly of grapes.

It was Thursday, and I'd brought my tour, as promised, to check out the business of a small winery.

"All right, everyone," I said as I drove my trusty VW van down the road, "this is a hidden little area that grows the best zinfandel grapes. The wonderful part about wineries that are smaller is that the wines are small batch, and carefully cultivated and blended to bring out the flavor of the region."

This tour was a group of six entrepreneurs who were looking into investing in wineries by buying up small ones, or estimating the value of the business. In other words, these people had money to burn. Oscar Webb, the leader of the group, had a passion for small business and wine, and had found me via my website.

"What types of events do these small vineyards do to bring in customers?" Oscar asked. "Are tours like yours common?"

"Good question," I said. "In order to compete with the larger wineries, they offer events like summer concerts and bring in local bands. They may offer a scenic area for weddings and have connections with local caterers. Others offer seasonal events like hayrack rides in the fall, yoga classes in the summer, and Christmas events during the holidays."

"Do they make most of their revenue from the event space or from the wine?" Marsha Scott asked.

"It depends on the winery," I said, answering as honestly as possible. After all, the wineries didn't pay me, although it didn't hurt to go to the appellations and get their recommendation or endorsements. "The better the wine, the more money they make from it. You will find some of the best winemakers at these small vineyards. You will also find quite a few newbies who are still on the learning curve. The advantage to being on the learning curve is they think outside of the box and create some original blends that boost their brands."

"Are there any wineries that are run like start-ups?" Marsha asked.

"There are two in this appellation," I said. "Running River Wines and Iron Fist. They're run by small groups of investors experimenting with lean and agile business models. That said, most wineries are run as farm businesses. They are in the farming category for taxes and other advantages."

"Huh," Sam Heath said from the back of the van. "I didn't think of wineries as farms. I always saw them as microbreweries. Do any of them have booths at farmer's markets, fairs, or festivals?"

"There is a county wine festival in Sonoma," I said. "It is an opportunity for all the regional wineries big and small to produce samples of their wares. I do know that some of the locals attend farmer's markets regularly."

"Have any of them tried social media to promote their wine clubs? You know, Facebook ads, Instagram, or Twitter?" Robert Gillespie asked from the back seat.

"That's an interesting question," I said. "I'm not familiar with their marketing methods—that would be a great question for Tim Slade, the proprietor. I've set up today's tour at Tim's so you can see the behind the scenes activity of a small winery."

We pulled into Rock Paths Winery. The drive took us over a culver, and half a mile through grapes, to the top of a hill, where Tim's house stood. Just before you reached the mid-century modern ranch, the gravel drive split off, with a sign saying, "Welcome. Wine tasting this way."

"This certainly is a hidden tasting area," Chandra Crammer said.

"Tim has plans to move the wine-tasting area closer to the road so that people can see it from the street. But there are issues such as restrooms and water accommodations. Right now this setup encourages private events such as family reunions."

"He has a bocce ball area?" Oscar asked as we came around the side of the hill to the parking area.

"And a picnic area with a horse-shoe-throwing pit," I said.

"Does he do weddings?" Chandra asked.

"No," I said. "The previous owner was fine with the winery being an event setting, but Tim is looking to take it in another direction."

"Does he have any old vines?" Robert asked. "I'm particularly interested in grapes from pre-prohibition."

"Yes, he is lucky enough to have some of the only old vines left." Parking the van, I turned to my group. "This is a great opportunity to see how a small vineyard uses all the resources it can to make small batch wines."

As we got out of the van, Tim came down from the main house on top of the hill.

"Welcome to Rocky Paths," Tim said. He shook hands as people introduced themselves.

Oscar was a stocky man in his fifties, with salt and pepper hair and high-end jeans and dress shirt. He wore Italian shoes and oozed money. Marsha was shorter than me and wore chic casual clothing. The diamonds at her ears and fingers left no guess as to what kind of money she had.

Robert looked like he was from the 1980s, or maybe he just liked the preppy look. He looked around as if unsure how a farm worked. It made me wonder if he'd ever done anything more than drive through the countryside on his way to the beach.

Peter and Sam were young and thin and barely lifted their eyes from their cell phones. They had hipster beards and dark glasses. Finally, Chandra seemed out of place with her bright red hair and denim dress.

From my point of view, they all had money to burn. Which made them the perfect word-of-mouth candidates for my tour.

Tim's eyes lit up as the group was clearly of investor quality. "Let me give you the grand tour," he said. "Follow me." We walked back down the drive to the lines of vines. "The grapes are watered through a drip system that comes from the well on the vineyard. They grow all summer, and we just finished harvesting last week. Next week we'll take all the fallen leaves and prune the vines back. The leaves and branches will all be chipped into mulch and used to nurture the vines through the winter." He paused. "Nothing is wasted."

"What types of grapes do you grow?" Oscar asked.

"What varieties work best in this area?" Robert asked.

"Do you use a press to mash the grapes?" Chandra asked. She smiled at Tim. "Or do you stomp them?"

He snorted. "We don't stomp them. When I bought the winery, the main crop was pinot noir. Two years ago, I added fifteen acres of new zinfandel to mix with the old vines. This is my first really productive year for the mixed zins." We walked around the side of the hill where the house and garage sat, until we were behind the house. "Pretty much all the vines you can see from here are mine. I have a small team come out, and we work long hours to cut the grapes. Follow me to the wine barn."

He took us to a huge white barn. To the side of the building, under a covered area, were five or six large white vats that were six feet tall. The air smelled distinctly of grapes and fermentation.

"Ladies and gentlemen," Tim began, "we bring the grapes in from the vines and wash them. Then we sort them to cull any that look wrong, and remove the stems. See these vats? They have been sterilized and made ready for the grapes. Once the grapes are clean and sorted, we put them through a fruit press to release the must."

"Must?" Marsha asked.

"It's the juice," I said.

"We then vat the pressed fruit and juice, add wine yeast and a little sugar and filtered water from the well."

"And then?" Robert asked.

"Well, then we wait while it ferments. We have to open the vats up twice a day and stir them." He pulled out a stepladder and took a wide paddle off the wall. "It's usually me who turns the vats. I like a hands-on approach." He winked at Marsha. "Come in closer—it's okay. Get a good look, and sniff the vats. You see, we want to turn over all this stuff that floats to the top. I usually turn once at ten in the morning and then again at ten at night."

We all edged in close to the vat. I stood on my tiptoes and peered inside as Tim climbed the ladder. He stuck his paddle in and pushed down on the grape skins that floated to the top. Then he stirred, bringing up the denser juice. The second stir took my breath away as I saw something that made me gasp and freeze in horror.

"Is that a hand?" Chandra asked, her eyes wide.

"Where?" Robert asked. "Oh, crap!" He jumped away from the vat.

"There's a head," Marsha said with horror.

Peter and Sam looked up from their phones.

"It's a body," Oscar noted, strangely calm.

We all looked at Tim. He seemed startled by the man who bobbed up from the bottom of the tank. "Okay," he said. "That wasn't a planned part of the tour."

Sam snapped photos with his phone while Robert ran out of the vat area to be sick.

"Do you think he's alive?" I asked.

"Mateo," Tim shouted.

"Yes, boss?" An older Hispanic man came running up.

"We need to pull this guy out of the vat," Tim said, and he looked as if he were going to climb over the ladder and into the vat.

"Wait!" I said. "If this is a crime scene, you'll contaminate the evidence."

"I'm not going to sit here and wait while a man drowns," Tim said. "Mateo, get a ladder."

"How are you going to get him out of the vat?" Oscar asked.

"There's a scaffolding over there," Tim said and pointed to the other side of the vat. "Pull it over here."

I rushed to the scaffolding. Marsha, Chandra, and I pushed it until it was right beside the vat. Suddenly Tim jumped in the vat, and the grapes and juice spilled and splashed out as Mateo followed Tim.

"Nine-one-one said the police and ambulance are on their way," Peter said. "I sent them my GPS coordinates."

Tim and Mateo worked together silently, treading juice and turning the man so that his face was above the liquid. Grape seeds and skins stuck to their bodies, coloring everything in the vat purple.

The scent of yeast and grape juice mixed with a darker scent. I watched in horror as they pushed, pulled, and tugged the man up and out of the vat and onto the scaffolding.

"I'll go down to the road and direct the ambulance," Marsha said. She looked very pale, and I thought it was probably a good idea to get her out of the shed area.

"Chandra," I said, "why don't you go with her?"

"Okay," Chandra said with a nod. She entwined Marsha's arm with hers, and they left through the front.

When I turned back around, Tim was on the scaffolding. He tilted the man's head back and cleared his airway before starting CPR.

"No pulse?" I asked.

"None," Tim said grimly and banged on the man's chest. I helped Mateo out of the grape juice mixture. The man was a few inches shorter than me, but very sturdy. He climbed down the ladder.

"Do you have any blankets?" I shouted up at Tim.

"In the tasting room," he said as he counted pushes.

I left them in the shed and rushed into the tasting room. Tim's sommelier, Stacy Randolph, was there, cleaning wine glasses. Luckily it was mid-morning, and they didn't have a room full of tasters.

"What's going on?" Stacy asked. "You look white as a sheet."

"Tim said you have blankets in here."

"Yes," she said and put down the glass and the towel she was using. "What's wrong?"

"Tim just pulled a man out of a fermenting vat," I said. "Mateo is shivering."

"It could be shock," Stacy said. She opened a cupboard and handed me a stack of blankets. "I know first aid." She followed me out of the tasting room back to the wine barn.

Robert sat outside on the grass with his head in his hands. "I'll never un-see that," he said over and over, and rocked himself. I handed Stacy a blanket and pointed to Robert. She nodded and went to put the blanket on his shoulders.

I hurried into the barn. Tim was still on the scaffolding, and it shook under the weight of the compressions as he did CPR. "Hang in there, Tim," I shouted up at him. "Help is on the way."

Mateo sat on a bale of hay and beat his chest as he shivered. I put a blanket tightly around him and squatted down to look him in the eye. "Are you okay?"

"I'm fine," he said through gritted teeth that chattered. I wrapped a second blanket around him.

"It's probably shock," I said. "Try putting your head between your knees."

I looked up at Tim, who worked fiercely, trying to revive the man. "I can hear the sirens," I said. Then I took another blanket, threw it over my shoulder, and climbed up far enough on the scaffolding that I could reach Tim's shoulders and dropped the blanket around them. He continued to work hard at CPR, and I could hear the man's ribs cracking.

"I'm with you, Tim," I said and reached through the bars to put my hand on his back. "I'm with you.

Chapter 4

Sheriff Hennessey was the first to arrive on the scene. He didn't have Marsha or Chandra with him, so I assumed they stayed at the end of the drive to continue to direct emergency responders.

"Taylor, what's going on?" he asked as he entered the barn and looked up at Tim and me. My heartbeat sped up a bit at the sight of him. There was just something about his action hero good looks that attracted me. I swallowed down my reaction.

"Tim and Mateo pulled this man out of the vat," I said. "Tim's been doing CPR for over fifteen minutes."

"Stop," Sheriff Hennessey said.

Tim froze.

"Is there a pulse?" The sheriff pulled me off the scaffolding. His hands on my waist were comforting, and the easy way he lifted me off was distracting. He didn't seem to notice as he climbed up next to Tim.

"No," Tim said, his expression uncertain.

I watched as the sheriff pushed Tim aside and checked the man. "He feels like ice. I think he's been dead for a while."

"So, my CPR?"

"Not ever going to save him," Sheriff Hennessey said, his expression grim. "Why don't you climb down and sit next to Mateo. I'll call the coroner."

Tim muttered something dark under his breath and climbed down. I helped him to the hay bale and tucked a second blanket around his lap. The ambulance pulled up next, and two EMTs got out.

"Stop!" Sheriff Hennessey said as they stepped toward us. "This guy is dead. I've called the coroner. All you two will do is further contaminate my crime scene."

"Don't you think you should let the professionals check him out?" one of the EMTs called.

"Listen, I know you can't pronounce him dead. All you'll be doing is wasting your time trying to revive him and taking him to the ER, where any doc in their right mind will pronounce him DOA."

"Is he stiff?" the second EMT asked.

"No, but he's dead cold," the sheriff said as he climbed down. "Hand me that blanket." The young EMT had a medical kit in one hand and a blanket in the other. "I'll cover the body until Doc Abernathy can get out here. I've already put a call in to the station."

"Are you sure you don't want one of us to check him out?" the EMT with the name tag "Mathews" called as he passed the blanket over.

"I'm sure."

Mathews shrugged. "It's your call, Sheriff."

Hennessey climbed back up the scaffolding and covered the body. I sat next to Tim and held his hand. "It's going to be okay."

"I lost a whole vat of wine," Tim said. "My best grape blend."

I patted his hand. Tim could be a smart aleck, but he wasn't intentionally selfish. "You're in shock. Do you know the guy?"

"I didn't get a good look at his face. All I could think about was how the heck I was going to remember everything from my CPR training. I mean, you take the training and then never think of it again. Right?" He looked at me. "I didn't want the guy to be dead."

"No, no one wants that," I said.

"Did you recognize him?" he asked me.

I shook my head. "He was pretty purple and, I think, a little bloated." I cringed at the thought. "I think it was a good call to stop the CPR. You tried. You really tried."

"I'm not sure I did it right."

"You did," I said. "They say you'll crack ribs if you do it right."

He put his hands over his face and rubbed his face. "A man is dead."

Mateo sat beside Tim, silent, tears running down his face.

"Hey," I said and stood. "Ron, er, Sheriff Hennessey?"

"Taylor?" he replied. I thought I caught a glimpse of heat in his gaze before he settled his expression into cop mode.

"It might be a good idea for the EMTs to check out Tim and Mateo."

"Right," he said. "Go out in a straight line, and be careful not to disturb too much,"

I helped Tim to his feet. He shuffled out of the shed, and I helped him to the back of the ambulance. Then I went back to help Mateo, and we followed the same line out. By the time I got both men to the ambulance, Marsha and Chandra had walked up the drive. Two more police cars arrived with their red and white lights flashing. Deputy Bloomberg and Deputy Hanson got out and huddled with the sheriff. A white van showed up, and an older man stepped out.

"Who's that?" I asked Mathews.

"The medical examiner, Doc Abernathy," he answered and went back to checking Mateo's vital signs. I watched the coroner walk into the barn, followed by a younger man wearing a black jacket that said "CSI."

"Taylor," Marsha said and called me over to where she and Chandra stood.

"Thanks for flagging everyone down," I said.

"I tell you what, this has put me off wine for a while," Chandra said. "Maybe forever."

"Tim likes to say that no known human pathogens can survive in wine," I said with a half-smile.

"Not exactly comforting," Chandra said.

My cell phone rang. "Excuse me a moment," I said and walked away as I answered it. "Taylor O'Brian."

"Taylor, it's August Smith. I thought you had a tour scheduled for my winery this afternoon," said the voice on the other side of the line. "We had a picnic planned?"

"Oh my gosh, I'm so sorry, August," I said. "There's been an incident at Rocky Path Winery. We'll have to reschedule."

"Is everyone alright?" August asked.

"Not everyone," I said. "Listen I can't talk about it, but I'm sure the details will be out later." I looked back at the group that I had brought to this disaster. They milled about in various stages of shock and uncertainty.

"Your tour group is investors, right? Will you be rescheduling?"

"I don't think they are going to be coming back any time soon," I said.

"Darn that Tim," August muttered. "It's just like him to keep all the investors to himself."

"This isn't about Tim," I said. "Listen, I have to go, but I will take another tour through your winery soon."

"Will they be investors?"

"I can't promise," I said. "This was my first such group."

"Well, we'll take what we can get, I suppose. I'll talk with you soon."

"Okay, bye," I hung up the phone and dialed the two other places we were supposed to tour and let them know we wouldn't be coming.

"Is everything all right?" Stacy asked as she came up behind me.

"Yes," I said, looking at the empty parking lot of the tasting barn. "It looks like the police presence has killed your work for today."

"I really don't think it's good to have any tasting near a crime scene."

I frowned. "Did you see the man? Do you know who he is or what he might have been doing on the property?"

"Deputy Hanson asked me that same question," Stacy said and hugged herself. "I didn't see anyone besides Tim and Mateo and Mandy today."

"Mandy's here?" I asked and looked around.

"She left when I opened the tasting room," Stacy said. "I think it was around nine. She has a day job."

"Where does she work?"

"She's got a couple of jobs—one is the office manager for a realtor. Do you know Jeffery Hoag?"

"No," I said. "Is he the realtor?"

"Yeah, he's around our age," Stacy said. "He moved here from San Jose."

"Strange for him to get into real estate up here if he's never been here."

"He's got a group of investors backing him," Stacy said. "He was out visiting all the little wineries in the area. I think he was taking notes on which ones had the best views. You can make more money off of resorts than you can from wine, you know."

I winced. "I didn't think any of the families would sell out."

"They had a meeting last week," Stacy said. "I'm not an owner, so I don't know what was said, but Tim came back pretty darn upset."

"Is that why he asked me to bring people by his winery? Is Tim in financial trouble?"

"That's a good question," Sheriff Hennessey said as he stepped in behind me. I turned toward him.

"Do you think Tim had anything to do with this? Because I highly doubt it. The man jumped into a vat of must and skins and pulled the guy to the scaffolding and then did CPR for twenty minutes."

"I'm simply asking questions," Sheriff Hennessey said. He was a handsome man with neatly cut brown hair and gorgeous blue eyes. We had a bit of a history. A few weeks ago, he'd given me the impression that he'd like to have dinner with me, but he never really asked. It felt awkward standing next to him now.

He might be square-shouldered and buff in his khaki uniform, but I could tell he was all business. The problem was, today I didn't know when he wasn't in work mode.

"I don't know anything about Tim's state of affairs," I said. "Do you know who the dead man is?"

"He hasn't been identified yet," Sheriff Hennessey said. "Why don't you tell me what happened?"

I recounted everything that had happened from the time I'd parked the van and let my tour group out, to the moment that the sheriff had showed up.

"That's everything?" he asked as he took notes.

"Yes," I said. "Do you know what the cause of death is? I mean, I didn't see any obvious bullet holes. Did he drown?"

"Doc thinks it might be blunt force trauma," the sheriff said.

"Oh," I said and blew out a long breath. "So he didn't drown."

"We'll know more after the autopsy."

"Sherriff," one of the deputies called out to Ron.

"Excuse me," he said and left.

Stacy came up to me. "Is everyone all right?"

"Yes," I said. "How's Tim doing?" I scanned the now crowded drive to find my friend still covered in purple grape juice and sitting on the back edge of the ambulance.

"He's taking it pretty hard," Stacey said. Stacy was a gorgeous brunette, fresh out of college, and working her first full-time job as a sommelier. Tim liked to surround himself with pretty women and said it didn't hurt the business any to hire them. The thing was that most of the people who came wine tasting were much older than struggling twenty-somethings. She looked over her shoulder at the sheriff. "I take it Sheriff Hennessey thinks Tim had something to do with this murder?"

"Oh, I don't think so. Why would Tim ruin an entire vat of grapes and then pull the guy out and spend twenty minutes attempting to resuscitate him?"

"I didn't say it made sense," Stacy said with a shrug. "I still think he suspects Tim." She tugged on the ends of her hair. "I can't work here anymore. My dad is going to flip when he hears I'm involved in a murder investigation, or worse, that my boss is a suspect in a murder investigation."

"I'm sure your dad will understand," I said, patting her shoulder.

"No," she said and eyed me with concern. "He's going to be upset I stayed this long." She leaned into me. "Listen, I don't want to tell Tim I'm quitting. You're his friend—will you tell him?"

"That you quit?"

She winced. "Yes?"

"I think you should be a grown-up and go talk to him," I said. "He's an understanding guy."

"I know," she said and chewed her bottom lip. "That's why it's so hard to tell him, you know? Because he's nice, and I'd hate to hurt him."

"I'll walk over there with you," I said, "but you have to talk to him."

"Fine," she said. "But I'll blame you if he starts crying."

"He won't cry," I said and took her hand. I pulled her toward Tim. The poor man smelled of yeast and grape juice. "Oh boy, I hope that doesn't stain."

He sent me a brotherly half-smile. "I'm going to have to watch out for the purple people eater."

"Stacy has something to say," I said and pushed her forward.

"What's up, Stacy?" he asked.

"Listen, Tim, I'm going to have to go now. There's no way my dad is going to let me work for a murderer."

"Wait—what?"

"There was a murder just a few yards from where I was working. He's not going to let me come back. And he's going to be very angry that I haven't left already."

"Aren't you a little old to be worrying about what your dad thinks?" he asked.

"I've got to go," she said and took off her apron and handed it to him. "You know where to send my paycheck." She walked off.

He watched her in silence for a moment. "Well, you know what they say . . ."

"What?" I asked.

"Good help is hard to find."

I patted him on the back. "Holly and I can help fill in until you hire someone new."

"Thanks. I might take you up on that. I think it might be a few days before they let me have my winery back."

"It is a crime scene," I said. "I can tell you that it takes longer than you think to process it."

He ran his hand over his hair. "Do you think the same thing that Stacy thinks?"

"What's that?"

"That I'm a killer." He shrugged. "I know I have killer good looks, but . . ."

"But I don't believe you'd harm anyone," I said. Picking up a towel, I brushed grape skins off his shoulders. "I mean, look at you. You jumped right in to save the guy. A killer wouldn't do that."

"What if I was jumping in to save my grapes?"

"A little late for that, don't you think?"

"Yeah," he agreed and tussled grape skins out of his hair

with another towel. "That was probably the best batch of zin since I took over the winery ten years ago."

"You should change the name of your winery from Rocky Path to Deadly Zins." I teased.

"I have more than seven of them."

"You better hope murder isn't one of them," Sheriff Hennessey said as he walked up.

"Not this time, at least," Tim replied. "I don't have any reason to kill a man."

"Let's hope not," Sheriff Hennessy said. "For your sake. What about you, Taylor? What do you know about the people on your tour?"

I tilted my head in confusion. "The guys on my tour? Why? They got here with me."

"I'm working on getting a clear picture of what happened," he said.

"Oscar Webb called me and asked me to do a tour of smaller wineries in the area. He and the rest of the group were thinking about investing in wineries and wanted a good look behind the scenes at a local place."

"I see," he said.

"Tim asked me to bring a group by his winery, and I thought this would be the perfect one. Like I said, they came with me. I really doubt they had anything to do with the murder." I crossed my arms over my chest.

"Perhaps, but what do you really know about them?"

"They are businesspeople who have money, and they are up from San Francisco for the day." I shrugged. "What more should I know about them?"

"I don't know. Maybe you should check and make sure you

aren't hauling around a murderer," he said, his eyes suddenly concerned. The flash of emotion left as fast as it arrived, and he was back to wearing his flat cop look.

"I'm a businesswoman," I said. "People pay for a tour, and they get the tour. I can't do a background check on everyone."

"Hey, Taylor, when can we go?" It was Peter. "I can call an Uber if this is going to be longer."

"Have you given your statement?" I asked and pointed to the sheriff.

"I talked to the other dude," Peter said and pointed his thumb over his shoulder. I saw Deputy Bloomberg taking notes and asking questions as well. "Sam and I have been hanging around for over an hour. We didn't even get any wine."

"Not that I want to drink any right now," Sam said.

"Is it okay if they go?" I asked Sheriff Hennessey.

"I have everyone's information," he said with a nod. "You should probably take your people home."

"I'm out of here," I said and held back the urge to salute him. "Call me, Tim."

"Don't worry. I will."

Chapter 5

"What happened?" Aunt Jemma asked as she came out of the house to watch my latest tour group sadly crawl into their cars and drive off.

"We didn't get any farther than Tim's winery," I said and picked up Clemmie to stroke her back.

"I'll have a talk with him about high-jacking your tours. I mean, you didn't have to take them to see him. You were doing him a favor."

"He didn't highjack the tour," I said. "He was showing us how he stirred the vats, when a body popped up to the top."

"Oh my goodness!"

"He and Mateo jumped in to try and save the guy, but he was pretty dead."

"Well, I suppose there are worse ways to go than drowning in a vat of wine."

"I'm not sure he drowned," I said and walked into the house, where Millie jumped up to see me. Clemmie leapt out of my hands as soon as the dog reached me. I sometimes wished they would just get along.

"What do you mean you don't think he drowned?" Aunt Jemma asked as she followed me.

"Sheriff Hennessey was questioning everyone, like he did during the last murder," I pointed out. "He also got a closer look at the body than I did. I suspect he knows something."

"So you think someone murdered a man and tossed him into Tim's vats?"

"I think Sheriff Hennessey thinks so," I said. "Like I said, I didn't get a good look at the body. I have no idea who he is. All I could see was purple skin and bloating."

"Any hair color?"

"It was purple too. I suppose it could have been blond or white or gray. I don't think it was black."

"It could also have been red," she said and tapped her fingers on her lips. "So a mysterious man of unknown age and features floats to the top of the must vat when Tim stirs it. That must mean the man found his way *into* the vats between ten at night and ten in the morning."

"Yes," I said and felt my mood brighten. "That's right. Tim stirs the vats twice a day, so there's a twelve-hour window for someone to have gotten into the vat."

"I highly doubt the man was murdered and then hours later put in the vat," Aunt Jemma said. "Dead bodies are difficult to move. You've heard of the term 'dead weight,' right? It means that—"

"I know, I know—a dead person is super heavy," I interjected. "I can't imagine picking up one hundred and eighty pounds and lifting it over my head to toss it in a vat." I petted Millie while Aunt Jemma poured us both glasses of wine. "It took two strong men to drag him out of the vat."

"That means it was most likely a man who killed the dead guy," Aunt Jemma said and handed me a glass. "That's a good place to start."

"To start what?"

"The investigation."

"What do you mean 'the investigation'?" I sat down on the big overstuffed leather couch so that Millie could come and sit by me. "Why would I care about the investigation?"

"Well, surely you're going to help Tim figure out who did this thing on his property," Aunt Jemma said and took a seat on the cabbage rose–covered, winged-back chair across from me.

"I am a bit curious," I said and leaned toward her. "I want to know who the dead man was and how he ended up in the vat."

"Dead man?" Holly asked as she came in through the back door. "What dead man? Are you okay?"

"What are you doing here?" I asked and got up to give her a hug.

"I was working in the tasting barn," Holly said and poured herself a glass of zinfandel. She was dressed in the classic black skirt and white shirt that Aunt Jemma asked of all of her sommeliers. "Aunt Jemma is training me in the ways of wine so I can do a proper job at the art gallery."

Holly worked full time at La Galleria, a contemporary art gallery specializing in Northern California artists. Just last month the gallery had showcased a lovely young artist who helped me investigate another murder that happened on one of my tours. But that's a different story.

"I'm taking a class at the community college too," Holly said. "It can't hurt to understand wines and everything. It's sort of expected, considering where we live."

"I'm surprised you haven't taken one sooner," I said.

She blushed. "I wasn't interested until Jeremy."

"Jeremy?"

"Yes, Jeremy Rentz," she sat down next to me. "I met Jeremy at the art gallery. He came in looking for local artists to highlight in the resort he'd just bought."

"What resort is that?" Aunt Jemma asked.

"The Timbers," she said. "You know, down around the hot springs. Anyway, Jeremy was telling me that he was remodeling the old place to bring it more in line with a five-star hotel and resort, with the hot springs as a draw and the old Spanish Mission architecture."

"Do I know this Jeremy?" Aunt Jemma asked.

"I don't think so," Holly said and sipped her wine. "He came up here from Monterey a few months back."

"What's he look like?" I asked. I walked over and lifted Clemmie off the countertop and stroked her fur.

"He's about six feet tall and thin, with shiny blond hair cut sort of preppy, and vivid green eyes." Holly sighed a little over his eyes.

"I bet he's handsome," Aunt Jemma said.

"Yes," Holly said. "He sort of looks like a movie star, and he made a bundle of money on a couple of start-ups and is moving into the resort business."

"I didn't know you were dating anyone new," I said, raising an eyebrow and sitting back down on the couch near my wine glass. Clemmie squirmed because Millie was nearby, but I kept petting her, and soon she settled down into a superior look as the dog was left to find pets elsewhere.

"I didn't tell you because it was all *too* new," Holly said.

"But then he suggested I take a wine class with him at the community college. We go together every Thursday night, and—well, as part of the homework we need to work at a tasting barn."

"That's where I come in," Aunt Jemma said.

"Yes," Holly said. "Aunt Jemma is allowing me to work in her barn a few hours a week to understand the local flavors and see some of the business side of a winery."

"Does this Jeremy have a wine bar at The Timbers?" I asked.

"He does," Holly said. "He's redoing everything and is going to put in a very high-end wine list and Kobe beef steak house."

"That's pretty expensive." I sensed Clemmie was done with sitting in my lap and let her go. "Sounds like something Tim would like."

"Jeremy knows a Michelin two-star chef and has promised to let the man create whatever he wants for the menu."

"Wow, that is high end," I said. "Sonoma is a small town. Do you think there will be enough people to keep a place like that in business?"

"I believe there will be," Holly said. "We're going to do some serious advertising and cross promotions."

"We?" I asked.

"Yes," Holly said. "I've talked to my boss about cross-promoting La Galleria and The Timbers. I've got a meeting set up with the Chamber of Commerce to see about creating a wine festival to correspond with the opening of The Timbers."

"That is gutsy," I said. "There are some people on the board of directors at the Chamber who are really influential."

"I can help you as well," Aunt Jemma said. "I have some influence with those folks. I've been a member of the Chamber for over twenty years, and I've attended every one of their monthly coffees to network."

"I knew I could count on you," Holly said.

"Are you doing all this to impress Jeremy?" I asked. "He must be a heck of a guy. I don't remember you putting so much effort into a relationship before."

"I think I'm in love," Holly said with wide eyes.

"Wow," I said and gave her a hug. "That's fantastic."

"And quick," Aunt Jemma added.

"I think it was a classic case of love at first sight," Holly said. "Anyway, I've got a lot to learn if I want to help out at The Timbers and get everyone at the Chamber of Commerce to agree to hold a festival in time with the grand reopening of the remodeled hotel. That's why I'm so glad that Aunt Jemma let me work in the tasting barn."

"You might be able to pick up a few extra hours out at Tim's place," I said and sipped my wine. "His sommelier walked out today."

"Oh no, that's terrible—why?"

"She said her father wouldn't let her work right next to a crime scene."

"Are you talking about Stacy?" Aunt Jemma asked. "Her father is Senator Randolph. Can you imagine how he'd be if his daughter was part of a murder investigation?" She stood. "Now, ladies, I'm making grilled salmon and salad for dinner. Who wants some?"

* * *

Aunt Jemma was a grill master. She had learned from an old boyfriend who was a chef. He'd taught her everything there was to know about how to prep and grill all types of foods, from appetizers to entrees, to desserts. I loved her simple grilled salmon with garlic and lemon pepper. After dinner, Holly went home to get ready for her evening work at the gallery and I was in my bedroom in the poolhouse beside Aunt Jemma's big house. The poolhouse had a small living area and kitchen-ette, a full walk-in closet, one bedroom, and a bathroom. I sat curled up on my couch, working on my laptop, while Clemmie sat on top of the breakfast bar and batted at Millie as the puppy raced around underneath her, trying to get her to come down and play.

My phone rang and I saw it was Tim, so I answered it. "Hey, Tim, how are you?"

"I could be better," he said. "Your friend Hennessey has me on his suspect list."

"That's crazy," I said. "There is no way you would kill someone."

"Trust me, if I had, I wouldn't have put him in a vat of the best grapes I've grown since I bought the winery. Whoever did this is sabotaging me."

"Do they know who the dead man is yet?" I asked gently.

"It's Jeffery Hoag," Tim said.

"Wait—where have I heard that name before?" I asked. "Do you know him? Was he a friend or something?"

"He was Mandy's boss, the realtor," Tim said. "I had no idea he was even in the area. The last I'd heard, Mandy said he was working a big deal in Monterey."

"How did he get from Monterey to your winery?" I asked and pursed my lips. "Does Mandy know this?"

"I don't know," Tim said. "She said he was going to be in

Monterey this week, and she would have more time to work at the steak house."

"Wait—now I remember: Stacy said you went to a meeting and came back not too happy with this realtor. What happened?"

"Hoag and Senator Randolph are trying to push new zoning through. I suspect he's influencing the local of the Food and Drug Administration to do their due diligence on the wineries just to hassle us. Personally, I think Randolph's mad because I didn't contribute to last year's campaign. Now that he's won, he's harassing the people who didn't support him."

"He can't do that, can he? Use his influence to get back at you?"

"He can certainly try," Tim said. "Anyway, I didn't even know Hoag was on the property, let alone toss him in a vat of my best grapes."

"Why do the police think you were involved in the killing?" I asked. "I mean, it's not like he was scheduled to meet with you. Was he?"

"No," Tim said.

I frowned. "Then why does Ron—er, Sheriff Hennessy think you might have had something to do with this man's death?"

"He said I had motive," Tim said, and I heard the roughness of his hand on his beard as he rubbed his hand over his face.

"What motive?"

"Apparently, a lot of people knew I was upset at that meeting."

"Just because you were upset doesn't mean you killed the man. It's not like you threatened him."

"I might have . . . I don't know. I was mad."

"What exactly did you say?"

"I don't know, I might have said something like he was too stupid to live."

"That's not a threat. This is all a big mistake. Everyone knows you wouldn't hurt a fly. You have an alibi. Stacy was there,and Mandy was with you, right?"

"No, Stacy didn't come in until nine thirty this morning," Tim said. "And Mandy stormed out last night over something I said."

"What did you say to make her storm out?"

"She's so darn emotional," he said forcefully. "I might have said something about her new guru. She takes everything so seriously."

"New guru? You mean Dr. Brinkman?"

"Yeah. She never sees these guys for the con men they are. Seriously, it's all a kind of pyramid scheme. I mean, don't get me wrong—Mandy's a pretty girl and all, but if you needed an international spokesperson for a real business, wouldn't you get a Hollywood actress with a following, who needed more exposure? Some of those actresses make one or two movies and disappear. They would be perfect for a gig like the one Brinkman is talking about. Not real estate office manager Mandy."

I winced. "Please don't tell me you told Mandy that."

"What? It's the truth."

I sighed. "Was she gone for the entire night?"

"She went to her sister's house," he said. "Or her mom's."

"Was Mateo around?"

"Mateo has a family. He's a good guy, though. Gets here around seven most mornings and works till dark if I need him to. I gave him the weekend off of turn duty. It was his daughter's birthday."

"So you have no alibi."

"I was on my own property," he said with an edge of frustration. "What the heck do I need an alibi for?"

"And you had no idea anyone else was on your property?"

"Look, we have a big sign, "Wine tasting." People drive up all the time. They come and go."

"Wait," I said. "Where's his car?"

"What?"

"This Hoag guy." I stood and started pacing. "He's not your neighbor, right? So where's his car? You would have seen his car, right?"

"Yeah," Tim said. "I didn't see a car. There's not one on the property. I mean, I didn't look over all the acres, but if he drove up to inspect the place, he should have parked in the tasting room lot."

"Tell Sheriff Hennessey to go looking for his car," I said. "He'll listen. He doesn't like things that don't make sense."

"Let's hope that's true."

Chapter 6

Sonoma might be famous the world over for its wines and wineries, but it really is just a small farming community. Like many small farm towns, it has its layers of society, with the bankers, the large landowners, and the business owners—all members of the country club. The Chamber of Commerce is run by lawyers, judges, and local business owners trying to capitalize on their reputation. I joined the Chamber of Commerce to get my company on the website and in the tourism brochures.

It was Friday morning, and I was in town for a workshop on ramping up your local networking. The Chamber offered workshops for everything, from start-up information to inventory and budgets. I crossed the street to enter the Chamber's Mission-style building.

"Hi, Taylor," Missy Simpson, the receptionist, welcomed me. She sat behind a tall, round counter. Behind her was a short wall, papered in beige and white stripes with a grapevine border. Like a lot of small-town receptionists, she dressed in a business casual blouse and slacks. Her short blond hair was buzzed close on one side and long on the other, to show off the rows of earrings she wore.

"Hi, Missy," I said. "I'm here for the workshop."

"Of course," she said. "Candy is setting up now in the conference room down the hall to the left. I have your badge and packet." She pulled out a packet of paper and a "My name is" badge. "Help yourself to coffee and bagels. Restrooms are on the right."

"Thanks. How's Ned?"

Ned was Missy's horse. When I'd joined the chamber last month, we'd spent a good two hours catching up. Missy had told me that the horse she had gotten when we were juniors in high school was still alive and practically her best friend. She had gotten him for riding and to help with chores on her father's large winery. But in his old age, she mostly rode him for pleasure.

"He's good for an old man," she said with a bright smile. "Thanks for remembering."

The doors behind me opened, and a woman who appeared to be in her late forties walked in. She had short, impeccably highlighted hair and wore a sheath dress with matching jacket. "Hello, Missy," she said with a perfect smile. "I'm here for the workshop."

"Good morning, Bridget," Missy said. "I have your badge and packet."

"I'm attending too," I said and lifted my packet to emphasize what I'd said. "I'm Taylor O'Brian."

"Bridget Miller," she said and shook my offered hand. Her hands were small and her manicure perfect. There wasn't even a scuff on her shoe. It made me feel a little like a secondhand rag doll.

I was wearing a simple maxi dress and sandals. At least I'd painted my toenails a nice color to match.

"What do you do?" I asked out of curiosity. I imagined she ran an accounting firm or something that needed a lot of precision.

"I run a wine country tours business," she said with a shark-like smile. "Nice to meet my competition."

I tried not to react, but I might have stopped short for a brief moment. "Really—how nice."

She pulled out a slick business card. It read, "Quirky Tours—the original wine country tours, with two daily tours."

"Huh," I said as I read it. "I'm sorry—I haven't heard of Quirky Tours."

"I started the business in June," she said.

"And two tours a day?"

"Yes, my business really took off. I have two pink buses, drivers, and tour guides. I've made a wonderful splash. How about you?"

"I'm not quite at the two-bus stage, but I'm not doing too badly."

"Oh, good," she said. "I thought perhaps the murder that happened on your tour might have dampened your business."

"Any publicity is good publicity," I said and raised my chin a bit.

"I suppose that's true," she said. "Funny how my business grew twenty-five percent during that time." She patted me on the shoulder. "If you'll excuse me, I've got to talk to Anderson Phillips. I've got a tour group interested in touring his business to see how wine gets made."

I watched her as she walked up to Anderson and hugged him as if they were old school chums. Which they could have been since he looked to be her age. Anderson owned one of the larger privately owned places in the country. I'd been trying to get Anderson to return my calls about a tour for the last two months.

It was disheartening to know she had two tour buses and was expanding her business.

"Isn't she great?" Karen Green, chamber marketing manager, said. "She started in June and has already visited all the wineries in the county. I've heard nothing but praise for her tours and her connections. She's bringing in real wine enthusiasts and has driven wine club memberships up nearly ten percent across the county."

"Wow," I said. "That's a statistic."

Karen nodded. "All of the winery owners just love her."

I took a deep breath. "Right."

"Oh," Karen said, turning to me. "Don't worry—there's plenty of room for your little business. That's why you're taking this class, right? To learn how to network? All I'm saying is that you should keep an eye on Bridget. Learn from her. Her business is growing like gangbusters."

"With pink buses," I muttered.

"She really tapped into the female market," Karen said. "She's designing a girls' weekend getaway, and I hear she's working with Rose's Day Spa. She is putting together a package called Days of Wine and Roses. Fun, right?"

"Right," I said, shaking my head, but I caught myself in the nick of time and changed it to a nod.

"Oops, there's Mrs. Turbine. If you'll excuse me, I need to go talk to her about her plans for expanding."

I put my packet down on a seat at the end of the second row and went to get coffee while Bridget worked the room like a pro. She handed out business cards and smiled, shaking hands as if she were a contestant for Miss America . . . and was winning. She didn't even trouble herself to look my way. I didn't think to bring business cards. Right now, everyone in the room had her business card in their hand or placed on their packet. It was networking 101, and I'd fallen down on the job.

"Taylor!" Holly came into the room and waved at me. "Where are you sitting?"

"Second row," I said and pointed. She put down her things and came over to get coffee too.

"How's Tim?"

"He's worried," I said and sipped the bad coffee, wincing before putting more sugar in it. "He thinks he's Sheriff Hennessey's number-one suspect, and he doesn't have an alibi."

"What? Why would he be a suspect?"

"The dead guy was Jeffery Hoag," I said, and we moved to our chairs.

"That realtor Mandy works for?"

"I'm not surprised to hear Hoag was killed," George Wash said. "Hoag's the one who was pushing Senator Randolph into rezoning our area. I think it was his idea to sick FDA inspectors on us."

"FDA inspectors for wineries?"

"They're supposed to inspect any food producer, but they usually give us a pass because wine is not produced like cheese or anything like that. Anyway, lately anyone who's opposed the rezoning has been subject to a surprise visit from the old FDA. It's harassment."

"Oh boy, like that's not going to cause a fuss," I said sarcastically.

"The entire appellation is up in arms," George said. "They can't inspect us as if we're making yogurt or something. Last time they got up in arms, they came out and fined Bill Paddock for having a barn cat roaming around the barrels. It's a barn, for goodness sakes."

"I'm going to talk to Senator Randolph about this ridiculousness," Bernie Pere said as he came over and sat down with our group. Bernie and George were the best of friends. Bernie ran Bakes and Cakes Bakery and George ran the Sonoma Wine Tasting Room.

George snorted. "I wouldn't waste my time with that. The man is all about Senator Randolph. I have no idea how he got elected."

"Maybe we should all be like Tim Slade. I heard he murdered some guy for insulting his wine," Bernie said. "My grapevine tells me Taylor was there when they found the body." He gave me a pointed look. "Did you see anything?"

"Tim didn't kill anyone," I replied.

"Oh, I wouldn't be so sure," George said. "That man will get into it with anyone. He's not afraid to speak his mind."

"Speaking your mind and getting angry enough to take a life are two different things," I said. "Besides, none of you were there to see Tim try heroically to revive a dead man."

"All right, let's get started, shall we?" Candy stepped up to the front of the class. "Please take a seat. Today's seminar is ramping up your local networking. I'm Candy Bushart and I'll be your facilitator today."

I took my seat and glanced around to see Bridget. She sat in the front row to my right.

Working for the marketing and advertising firm in San

Francisco, I'd been skilled at networking. But for some reason, when it came to marketing my own brand, I was struggling. I grabbed my phone and hit the Notes app. It was time to put my knowledge and experience to work for my own business.

Step one, I typed into my notes, was to understand that we had different audiences. It was pretty clear that Bridget was catering to the wealthy suburban mom who wanted to get away with her friends. My audience was a bit more eccentric. I catered to people who wanted to see the real wine country for all its hidden art, history, quirky museums, and small wineries.

I frowned. Karen had said that Bridget's tours were bringing in wine buyers. Her demographic was joining wine clubs and making large purchases. It was difficult to compete with that. My tours were business outings, team building, club outings. They were more geared for people who wanted to know the real Sonoma County. That meant they were more than wine lovers; they were hikers and artists and enthusiasts.

That was the real reason Anderson and others of his statue weren't taking my calls. Although I had a lot to offer the people who booked my tours, I didn't have much to offer the wineries or other businesses that we toured, beyond a bit of publicity.

It was something I was going to have to figure out, or Bridget would knock me out of the market all together.

* * *

"Well, that was dull," Holly said as the workshop broke up. "It seemed pretty much like networking for dummies. Did you get anything out of it?"

We walked toward my car. "I learned I had competition I didn't know about." I pointed with my chin toward Bridget as she left, walking side by side with Anderson. "Did you know about Quirky Tours?"

"No," Holly said. "When we did a competitive analysis when you first started to think about your business, she wasn't on anyone's radar."

"Now she has two buses running two tours daily," I said. "That's a lot of growth."

"You can do that too," Holly said. "People like your California experience with the VW van. You've said it yourself: Sonoma County is more than just the big wineries like Anderson's. Let her have those. Stay quirky—it's the Northern California way."

A crowd on the corner caught my eye. "What's going on over there?"

"Maybe someone famous is in town," Holly said. "I heard they were scouting out areas for a movie."

"Movie?"

"Yes, some Ron Howard film," Holly said. "Hey, you don't think it's Ron Howard, do you? Come on." She put her arm through mine and pulled me toward the crowd. Holly was tall but even she couldn't see through the throng of people. She jumped up to catch a glimpse over the crowd.

"Is it Ron Howard?" I asked.

"No, it's some old guy I don't recognize. He's dressed in some kind of white outfit . . . like someone from India."

"It's Dr. Brinkman," the man in front of us said. "I understand he's a gifted spiritual advisor to Hollywood stars. Have you heard of him or the Brinkman method and the law of attraction?"

"He's the guy that Tim's girlfriend, Mandy, was talking about," I said.

"What's the big deal?" Holly asked.

"What's the big deal?" The man sounded affronted. "You obviously haven't heard him speak. It's life changing." He pulled two tickets out of his pocket and pressed them into our hands. "You have to attend one of his seminars. I'm Bruce Warrington, and I'm one of his disciples." He studied us. "I see you don't believe me now. Go—you'll be thanking me later." He turned and pushed his way through the crowd to join Dr. Brinkman.

"Okay, that was weird," Holly said as we looked down at the tickets. They had a time and date stamp for Tuesday at 7 P.M. and a price of $199. We looked at each other at the same time. "One hundred and ninety-nine dollars?"

"That's crazy," I said.

"He just gave them to us," Holly said with a frown. A stretch limo pulled up, and the driver came around and opened the door. Then it left and the crowd dispersed around us. The crowd was mostly women, but a few men were debating the merits of the guru's marketing.

"Excuse me," I said to one of the men walking by us. "Are these tickets real?"

The young man stopped and looked at the ticket. "Sure," he said. "You must have been one of the lucky ones. Those are VIP tickets. Worth every penny if you ask me."

I looked at Holly. "I guess I need to do some research into this guy."

"He seems to have quite the following," Holly agreed as we walked to my car. "But why give us expensive tickets for free?"

"I don't know," I said and pulled out my phone. "Maybe Mandy knows something." I dialed Tim. "Hey, Tim."

"Taylor," Tim said, "I'm a bit busy right now. I've got a truck coming in with grapes I purchased to replace the vat I lost. Can I call you back later?"

"Oh, sure," I said. "I was looking for Mandy, actually. I don't have her phone number."

"Listen, the truck is coming up the drive. Mandy works part-time as a hostess at the Japanese garden steak house on Twelfth Street. She's running the lunch shift."

"Oh, that's right. Is she doing okay?"

"As best I can tell," he said. "She never got as many hours as she liked at the real estate place, so she supplemented her income with this other job. Good thing, what with Hoag's death and all. It's only lunch a few times a week, but I hear the tips are good."

"Thanks, Tim. We'll go see her. Good luck with the new batch of grapes, and stay out of trouble."

"New batch of grapes?" Holly asked.

"He's replacing the vat that was ruined by the murder." I took Holly's arm. "Do you have time for a fancy lunch?"

"Why? Are you buying?"

"Sure," I said with a smile. "Come on. Tim said Mandy is working the lunch crowd at the Japanese steak house."

"Wow, I've always wanted to have lunch there," Holly said. "I heard it was fantastic and just as fantastically priced."

I winced. "Maybe we can just have appetizers."

Holly laughed and put her arm through mine. "Maybe Mandy will give us the house special." We walked to the Japanese steak house. It wasn't terribly crowded as it was two in the afternoon and most of the lunch crowd was already gone. We stepped out of the bright sunshine and into the cool, calming atmosphere of the high-end Asian restaurant.

"Taylor," Mandy greeted me as she came out from behind

the hostess desk. She was dressed in a black pantsuit. Her long blond hair was pulled back, and her makeup was expertly done. "What brings you here?"

I gave Mandy a hug. "Hi. I was looking for you actually," I said. "I heard about your boss. Are you all right?"

"Yes, yes, I'm fine. Jeffery and I weren't that close. He was gone a lot on business. Who's this?"

"This is my best friend, Holly."

"Hi, Holly," Mandy said. She studied us both. "You didn't just come here to check on me, did you?"

I felt the heat of a blush rush over my cheeks. "We saw a crowd on the street and went to see what was going on. We think it might have been all about your guru."

"Dr. Brinkman?"

"We think so."

"Some guy named Bruce gave us these," Holly said and lifted up her ticket. "We were wondering why."

Mandy pulled the ticket out of Holly's hand, read it, and smiled brightly. "You are so lucky! These are great box seats. That is awesome. Listen, do you want to stay for lunch? I can seat you. I'm still kind of on the clock," she whispered to us.

Holly was reading the menu. "Um, I think we'll skip this time."

"I fully understand," Mandy said. She leaned into us. "This place is for businesspeople who are bringing important clients for a meal. I have a break coming. Why don't you meet me at the coffee shop on the corner?"

"The Beanery?" I asked.

"Yes," she said. "I'll be over in a minute."

We stepped back out into the sunshine. The Beanery was

literally on the corner a half a block from the steak house. "Well, so much for Japanese," I said.

"Did you see the prices?" Holly shook her head. "You couldn't sit at a table for less than a hundred dollars a person."

I winced. "I bet that's how they met."

"Who?"

"Tim and Mandy," I said. "Tim loves gourmet meals. I bet he went in there for the Kobe beef and came out with Mandy on his arm."

"It must be nice to have made all your money in a start-up," Holly said.

"Someday we'll eat like that too," I reassured her as we stopped in front of The Beanery.

"What if I don't want to?" Holly said with a twinkle in her eye. "Seems such a waste just for a meal. I never did understand the whole wining and dining clients. I'd rather give the money to charity."

"You are a pure heart," I said.

"Who will never be wealthy," Holly said with a laugh. "I've had some people in the art gallery who are so rich it oozes out of their pores, and you know what?"

"What?"

"They don't seem any happier than you and me."

"Then we are very lucky girls," I said. "Come on—I said I'd buy you lunch. How about a sandwich bagel?"

"Only if it's tofu," she said.

"I'm sure they have vegan."

Chapter 7

"So, tell me, what did the guy who gave you the tickets look like?" Mandy asked.

"Like he was in his thirties, maybe. With brown hair, dark eyebrows, and green eyes."

The barista came over and delivered our chai tea lattes. "Here you go, ladies. Your sandwiches will be out in another minute or two."

"What did you say his name was?" Mandy said.

"Bruce something," I said and drew my eyebrows together. "He said he was a disciple."

"Oh my, that's Bruce Warrington. You ladies are really lucky. He's the driving force behind Dr. Brinkman's lectures here in Sonoma. The story is that he heard Dr. Brinkman speak in Berkeley and begged him to come out and do a retreat at the Mission. He's a true believer. Why, it was Bruce who gave me my first ticket."

"Your first ticket?" I asked.

"Oh yes. After I heard Dr. Brinkman speak, I had to go back. Once you go, you'll understand."

"Wait, you paid two hundred dollars to hear him speak a second time?"

"No, actually, I've paid nearly a thousand dollars," she said and sipped her tea. "And let me tell you, it's been worth every penny of Tim's money."

"Tim's money?" I asked.

"He gives me whatever I want," she said with a smile.

"Sure, but a thousand dollars?" I had to ask. I could only imagine Tim rolling his eyes and handing out five one-hundred-dollar bills. It was what Tim did. My friend could be very generous, but he could also be very demanding.

"He said it was worth the investment," she said smugly. Then she leaned in toward us. "Seriously, if Bruce gave you tickets, you should go. Dr. Brinkman has journeyed all over the world, studying the words of wisdom. He says the universe has a purpose for us all." She put her hand on mine. "He can help you find your purpose."

"I think my purpose is to show off the secret corners of California wine country," I said with more confidence than I'd felt after finding out that Bridget Miller was far more successful at it than I was.

"Of course you *think* that," Mandy said. "But wouldn't you rather know for sure?" She turned to Holly. "What if you were to learn that you were actually prophets? That your true role in the universe was to enlighten people? To be activists for change for the world?" She nodded toward our tickets. "You were chosen for a purpose. You should attend and find out what that is. Trust me, it will rock your world. I should know—I've been called for private sessions with Dr. Brinkman."

"Oh, that's right," I said. "He wants to make you his worldwide spokesperson."

"Not worldwide," she said solemnly. "His United States spokesperson. It's a great job offer."

"What does it pay?"

"It's simple really," she said. "I pay him a thousand up front, and then he shoots the videos and trains me to give compelling speaking engagements. Then, with his marketing, I will be on a platform where I will sell out conference rooms. He promises that within the first year I can make upwards of half a million dollars. I know that you will be able to do the same if you follow his advice."

"Wait—you have to give him money first?" I asked. "It sounds like a scam."

"Oh no, it only covers the cost of the video and training. Think of it like school tuition. You pay, get trained, and start to earn."

"A half a million dollars a year and I could eat at the Japanese steak house every day if I wanted," Holly said.

"Your sandwiches," the barista said and set our bagels in front of us.

"Are you eating lunch?" I asked Mandy.

"Oh no, I have to watch my figure. They say the camera puts on ten pounds." She patted her nonexistent stomach.

Holly dug right into her egg salad sandwich. I had tuna salad on my bagel, and we both had a small bag of chips.

"When I'm rich, I'll hire a dietitian and a personal trainer," Holly said as she chewed.

"Not that you need one," I said with a smile. "I do have one question."

"What's that?" Mandy asked.

"What is the deal with Dr. Brinkman? Why do people treat him like a rock star? You should have seen the crowd. I didn't know there were that many people not working in the middle of the day."

Mandy laughed. "You are too funny, Taylor. Those people have all taken Dr. Brinkman's seminars. They adore him. You will too, once you go see him. Trust me, you'll fully understand." She glanced down at her fitness device. "Oh my, look at the time. I've got to get back to work. I'll be there tomorrow night. Will I see you there? I promise it will change your lives. What do you have to lose? You have the free tickets."

"Sure," Holly said. "I'll be there. I'm up for any excuse for a girls' night out."

"Taylor?"

"Why not?" I said and picked up my sandwich. "Curiosity is a good thing, right?"

"It never hurt a soul," Mandy said and stood. "Bye, ladies— see you at the seminar tomorrow."

We watched her walk out.

"Promise me one thing," I said to Holly.

"What's that?"

"When we go to this seminar, don't drink the Kool-Aid. Okay?"

Holly laughed. "I won't if you won't."

"I'm only going because I'm curious," I said. "Not because I have a thousand dollars to invest in getting rich."

"I'm going for the pure entertainment value," Holly said. "After seeing your aunt Jemma in action with her séance, I know better than to believe anyone without the right research."

"Oh, research," I said. "That's brilliant. I don't have a tour today, so I'm free to dig around and see what I can find out about this Dr. Brinkman."

"Why don't you give Chelsea a call?" Holly asked. "She gets paid to dig around into the backgrounds of shady characters."

"Brilliant," I said.

Chelsea McGarland was a friend of Holly's and now a good friend of mine. She wrote for the *North San Francisco Chronicle*. She had earned her job by helping me catch a killer last month, so I knew firsthand how good her investigative chops were. Right after lunch, I would give her a call and get the wheels rolling on finding out as much as I could about Mandy's guru and why anyone would give away two $200 dollar tickets to go see him.

* * *

My phone rang later that night when I was sitting on my couch in the poolhouse, researching quirky places for tours in Sonoma Valley. "Hey, Tim, what's up?" I asked as I picked up my phone.

"Taylor, who was your lawyer? You know, the one who helped when you were under suspicion of murder."

"Patrick Aimes."

"Do you have his number handy?"

"Sure," I said and frowned. "I'll text it to you. Why? Are you all right?"

"No, I'm not," he said. "I've been charged with murder and have turned myself in. I really need a lawyer."

"Oh no, Tim," I said. "Whatever you do, don't say anything without him present, okay?"

"I can remain silent," he said. "You on the other hand . . ."

I shook my head at the poke. "Thankfully, I'm not a suspect. I'll call Patrick."

"Thanks, kid," Tim said. "You know how much I hate germs. This place is crawling with them."

"That's why you like wine."

"No human pathogens can survive in it."

I hung up the phone and dialed Patrick. Holly and I had gone to school with him; he'd been in her older brother's class, and so darn handsome.

I'd been reunited with him last month when I'd found myself under suspicion of murder and Aunt Jemma had called him in to help guide me through the legal process. Unfortunately, I was a bit more stubborn than most and kept going against Patrick's advice. He stuck with me through the process, though, and helped save the day a time or two.

I'd offered to take him out for drinks after that, but I'd never gotten around to calling.

"This is Patrick Aimes," he answered.

"Hi, Patrick—it's Taylor O'Brian. Thanks for picking up the phone."

"Hi, Taylor. Is everything all right?"

"With me, yes," I said. "With my friend Tim Slade, not so much."

"What's going on?"

"We found a dead man floating in one of Tim's grape vats. It turned out to be Jeffery Hoag, Tim's girlfriend's boss and a realtor that Tim got in a public fight with over zoning. Now Tim called me to say he's been arrested and asked that I call you for him."

"Where's he being held?"

"At the sheriff's office," I said. "Can you take his case?"

"I'll see what I can do," Patrick said. I could hear him get up, and it sounded like he was putting on his shoes.

I suddenly realized the time. It was after 9 P.M. "I'm sorry—did I catch you at home?"

"Just got home actually," he said.

I felt the heat of embarrassment rush up my cheeks. "It's a bit early to be home from a date," I tried to tease, but it fell flat.

"I was at work," he said. "Mrs. Pearson's grandson got pulled over for a DUI." He paused. "Were you fishing to find out if I'm seeing anyone? Because I've been waiting for you to call about that drink you promised me."

"Me, fishing? Not really. I just didn't want to interrupt." My cheeks burned hotter.

"Taylor, when I'm with a beautiful woman, I don't answer my phone. It's that simple."

"Oh, right."

"And that drink?"

"I do owe you that," I said with an embarrassed chuckle. "I've got this thing tomorrow night, but I'm free on Sunday."

"Good—I'll pick you up at eight."

"Okay . . . nothing fancy, right? Just drinks."

"Just drinks, Taylor," he said with a warm chuckle. "But you can wear something fancy if you want."

"Right—because I'm such a fancy girl," I muttered.

"Bye, Taylor."

"Thanks, Patrick!" I hung up and stared through my patio doors at the dark night sky. I should have called him a couple of weeks ago. The thing is, I thought maybe Ron Hennessey would've asked me out before this. Yes, I was kind of sweet on the sheriff.

Trust me, he wasn't as polished and handsome as Patrick, but there was something rough and action hero about him.

But he'd never called, and I couldn't keep pining over something that never happened. It's not that I didn't like Patrick. I mean, what's not to like? The man had a law degree from Berkeley and was movie-star handsome. He also was patient and kind with me. Any other lawyer would have given up on my antics, but not Patrick. It wouldn't hurt to have a drink with the man.

Then I remembered Chelsea. I dialed her next.

"Hi, Taylor, what's up?" I could hear that she was in a noisy place.

"Hi, Chels, where are you? Are you busy?"

"I'm at work," she said. "Just put the finishes on tomorrow's story. There was an incident with a gang member at the train station today."

"Oh no, was anyone hurt?"

"He threatened some kids, but a couple of good Samaritans stepped in and contained him. Turns out they were Marines on leave from Afghanistan. Great guys. It was a feel-good piece. How are you? I haven't heard from you lately. Is everything all right?"

It was the second time in the last hour that I'd felt embarrassed. "I'm sorry, Chelsea," I said. "I've been a bit self-absorbed. I'm still trying to get my business off the ground."

"I keep telling you to go into murder mystery tours," Chelsea teased. "Speaking of which, were you part of fishing that dead guy out of a vat of grape juice?"

"Yes," I said.

"Is that what you're calling for? Because if you're giving me a scoop, all is forgiven on not calling me lately. We are friends, you know."

"I'm the worst friend," I said. "And yes, I'll give you the scoop. Did you meet my friend Tim?"

"Hmmm, Tim . . . I don't know—is he cute?"

"He's older and owns Rocky Path Winery . . . blond hair?"

"He's the proprietor of the winery with the body in the vat?"

"Yes," I said.

"We didn't meet, but I'm happy to tour the place and get the scoop."

"The scoop is that he is innocent, but they put a warrant out on him for murder," I said. "He turned himself in a bit ago."

"Oh, juicy," Chelsea said with a laugh. "I'll be over there within the hour."

"Pack a bag," I said. "You can stay with me at the poolhouse."

"There's more than the man's arrest?"

"There's this weird healing guru in town, and I thought you might help me dig up more information about him."

"Did I mention you are my favorite friend?" Chelsea asked.

"I won't tell Holly you just said that."

"Oh, right, that was completely off the record. Do you want me to meet you at your place, or are you going to the jail?"

"I'll meet you downtown." I hung up and stood. I really should go see if there is anything I can do for Tim, or Mandy for that matter. She must be beside herself over this terrible turn of events.

Chapter 8

"**O**h my gosh, Taylor." Mandy rushed toward me the moment I entered the sheriff's station. "I'm so glad you are here." She smothered me in a Chanel hug. "Mateo called me at work to tell me about Tim. I've been trying to get in to see him ever since."

"I don't think you can visit like a hospital," I said. "Tim called me, and I sent Patrick Aimes out. He's a lawyer and a good one. He helped me in my last run-in with the law."

"A lawyer." Mandy pressed her fingers to her cheeks. "I didn't think of getting Tim a lawyer. Is he going to be in there all night? Are they going to make him wear an orange jumpsuit? You know how he feels about other people's clothing and such."

"They will have already put him in the jumpsuit," I said from experience. "He will have to wait until he goes before the judge for a bail hearing. Then if he makes bail, he can get out."

"How long will that take?" Her eyes were wide and she looked horrified.

"It takes twenty-four to forty-eight hours," I said. "It could take longer, but we have Patrick, so I'm sure it will be only a day or two before Tim gets out. Are you staying at the house?"

"I was, but I haven't been out there since the murder. I certainly won't stay there alone," she said. "I've been staying with my sister. My boss was murdered not a hundred yards from the back door. You can't pay me to sleep in that house again."

"I'm sure you would be safe," I said. "Who's taking care of Maisie?" Maisie was Tim's beloved dachshund. She was a farm dog and usually left to run free, except at night when Tim called her in to spend the evening on the couch with him or in bed.

"Oh, Maisie—I forgot about her. I'll call Emily, the pet sitter who takes care of Maisie when Tim's in Seattle on business." She pulled out her phone and dialed.

"Wait—does this Emily have a key to the house?"

"Sure, she watches Maisie on a moment's notice," Mandy says. "Why?"

"We need to see if she was at the winery the night the guy was murdered," I said.

"No, she wouldn't have been," Mandy said. "I left that night, and Tim was still there. There would have been no reason for Emily to be there."

"If it were a stranger, though, wouldn't Maisie have alerted Tim that someone was on the property?"

"Sometimes," Mandy said and pursed her lips in thought. "I'm not sure she would bark at a stranger—we have visitors most every day at the winery."

"So Maisie may not have barked had she witnessed a stranger at the winery."

"She might have gone out to investigate without barking. Sometimes Maisie will go to the door and ask out. We'll open the patio door, and off she'll go. Tim doesn't generally worry about her since there are so many acres between us and cars and such."

"Did you see anyone at the winery when you left that night?"

"Gosh, not that I can remember," Mandy said. "I was pretty peeved at Tim. He said some bad things about Dr. Brinkman, and the thing is, he has never once attended a seminar to see just how smart and gifted Dr. Brinkman is. Poor Tim—he could really use Dr. Brinkman's spiritual guidance."

"Can I help you, ladies?" A deputy stood behind the front desk and studied us. He was tall, with dark hair and blue eyes. His name tag said "Bloomberg," and I remembered he had been at the crime scene, questioning my group.

"We're here to check on our friend," I said.

Just then Sheriff Hennessey walked by the front desk. "I've got this," he said to Deputy Bloomberg. "Taylor, what are you doing here?"

"Tim asked me to call Patrick," I said. "I came down to see if there was anything I could do."

"There is nothing to do," Sheriff Hennessey said. "Go home. It will be at least twenty-four hours before a bail hearing."

"Did you happen to check on Maisie?" I asked.

"Who?"

"Tim's dog, Maisie. She might have evidence as to what happened that night."

"A dog could have evidence?" He sounded incredulous.

"Well, she might have come in contact with the killer and have—I don't know—a hair or something in her fur."

"You've been watching too many police shows," Ron said. "To begin with, there is no way to prove that any evidence we may find on Maisie came from the night in question. Even if we did find something, it will be months before it can get analyzed. I'm sorry, Taylor—you're reaching. Maisie isn't a smoking gun."

"Maybe not, but she should have barked when the FDA inspector entered the barns."

"Not if Tim went out to meet him," Ron said.

"Well, what about Mr. Hoag's car? Did you find it? I mean how did he get out to the winery without a vehicle?"

"We're looking into that." Ron put his hands on his hips. "Taylor, when are you going to trust me to do my job?"

"When you don't arrest my friends for crimes they didn't commit."

"Taylor? Why are you here?" Patrick asked as he walked into the lobby area from behind the door. The man was gorgeous in an open-necked dress shirt and slacks.

"I'm checking on Tim," I said. "Did you see him? How is he?"

"Yes," Mandy said. "How is my Tim? Is he doing okay?"

"Who are you?" Patrick asked.

"Mandy Richards," she said and stuck out her hand. "Tim's girlfriend."

"Are you the one who was living with him during the night in question?"

"'The night in question'?" she asked and looked at me to interpret.

"The day the guy died."

"Oh, yes," she brightened. "Tim and I had a bit of an argument, and I went to spend the night with my sister."

"That's pretty convenient," Patrick said.

"My sister lives nearby," Mandy said. "She knows I love Tim, but sometimes he gets a bit sour. When he's in a bad mood, I prefer to spend time with nicer people."

"When did you leave that night?" Patrick asked.

I noticed that Ron leaned on the edge of the reception counter and watched the exchange.

"I'm not sure," Mandy said. "Nine-ish maybe. We were supposed to go out for dinner—Tim loves fancy dinners. We had reservations, but he was being mean about my new opportunity, so I left."

"What new opportunity?" Patrick asked.

"I'm going to be a spokesperson for Dr. Brinkman. He's a healer and a visionary. He's been talking to God and says the world is in desperate need of change. I'm going to help him with his cause."

"Was this Dr. Brinkman there that night?" Patrick asked.

"Oh, goodness me, no," Mandy said. "No, no, no. He wouldn't bother to come to where I live. He's above making money and all that, you know."

"I see," Patrick said.

"Hi, people," Chelsea said as she walked through the door. "What'd I miss?"

"We're not making an official statement until morning," Sheriff Hennessy said.

"Patrick?" Chelsea asked and took out her phone and hit her Dictaphone app to record.

"My client is innocent," Patrick said. "It's best if this doesn't hit the papers. It may cause people to form an opinion before they should."

"Well, we're not about giving people opinions," Chelsea said. "The news is about the truth. That truth is that your client,

Tim Slade, has been arrested for the murder of Jeffery Hoag, who was found dead in one of Mr. Slade's wine vats."

"It's still early," Patrick said. "I think the police are fishing."

"It's more than fishing," Sheriff Hennessey said and crossed his arms. "It takes a lot of evidence to make an arrest."

"Rush to judgment," Patrick said. The two men stared at each other.

"Okay," I said. "What is the motive for Tim to have done this? Why would he then stir the vat with the dead man in it in front of an audience?"

"Those are details for the courts," Sheriff Hennessey said. "Why don't you all go home now. There is nothing you can do for Tim here."

"Why are you waiting so long to make a statement?" Chelsea asked. "People want details."

"We need time to process evidence to ensure we don't make any mistakes or false accusations," Ron said. "You have to wait."

"Fine, I have other sources you know," she said and stopped recording. She walked out the door with the phone to her ear. I don't know who she called, but I knew she wouldn't go far as we still had the whole Dr. Brinkman thing to talk about.

"Oh, Taylor, thank you for calling Patrick for Tim." Mandy hugged me again. "I'll get Emily to check in on Maisie. I guess there is nothing to do but wait." She pulled a tissue out of her handbag and dabbed at her eyes. "Poor Timmy. I don't know how he'll survive a night in that jail cell."

"I'm sure he'll manage," Sheriff Hennessey said.

"Come on, Mandy, let's get you home." I put my arm around the girl and stepped her outside.

Patrick stayed behind and spoke to Deputy Bloomberg at

the front desk. It looked like he was filling out paperwork of some sort.

"Thank you for coming," Mandy said again.

"Are you going to be all right?" I asked as we stood just outside the door.

"Yes," Mandy said with a sniff and raised her head. "I'm going to talk to Dr. Brinkman about this. He'll know what to do."

"Bye, Mandy." I watched as she walked off and got in her car. Chelsea came up beside me, and we watched her leave.

"What's her story?" Chelsea asked. "She seems a bit young to be caught up with Tim Slade."

"She was a part-time manager at the realtor office that the deceased owned, and also the hostess at a Japanese steak house. Tim picked her up on one of his foodie nights."

"She was working two jobs?" Chelsea tipped her head sideways and studied me. "She doesn't seem the type to work that hard."

"She's harmless," I said. "She's spending a lot of money on her guru. She claims Tim is helping. Tim claims she needs to work both jobs."

"Interesting," Chelsea said. "I wonder who's right? Say, do you have access to Tim's place? I'd love to look around and get a feel for the crime scene."

"I can take you out there after the press conference, but we can't stay long. I have a tour in the afternoon."

"Okay," Chelsea said. "What was the other thing you wanted to talk to me about?"

"Actually, Mandy's involved in that thing, too," I said. "Do you want to go get some coffee?" I glanced at my watch. "Oh, darn it's nearly ten thirty. The Beanery closes at eleven."

"How about I meet you back at your place and we can have a nightcap?"

"Sounds good."

*   *   *

"Here you go," I said to Chelsea. "Aunt Jemma's finest pinot noir."

"Yum," Chelsea said. She was curled up on my couch in the poolhouse. Millie sat in her lap and begged for pets. Clemmie stalked around on the back of the sofa also looking for attention. "So why did you really call me out here?"

"There's this guru in town giving seminars," I said.

"A guru? There are a lot of those that go through California, you know. They pop up like mushrooms, depending on the time of year."

"Hmm, right," I said and sat down in the overstuffed chair beside the couch. "This one seems to be different."

"How so?"

"Holly and I left the Chamber of Commerce workshop yesterday, and there was this crowd on the corner. It was as if someone famous were visiting. People were three or four layers deep. That's a lot of people for little Sonoma in the middle of a Friday afternoon."

"Maybe he pays people to be his paparazzi," Chelsea said.

"Really?"

"It's how some of them make their cons look legit."

"Huh, I guess that makes sense. We certainly couldn't resist the crowd. Anyway, this guy turns to us and says that we should attend one of Dr. Brinkman's seminars to see what all the fuss was really about."

"Is it a con?" Chelsea asked.

"I'm not sure," I said and took my ticket out of my pocket. "Are you going to go?"

"Maybe . . . okay, yes," I said. "I'm curious. I tried to do some research on him. All of his online reviews are glowing. Lots of testimonials—even on review sites that aren't connected to his site."

"Those reviews can be bought, you know," Chelsea said. "It's like Yelp—if a restaurant pays them enough money, they bury the bad reviews or take them down all together."

"But that defeats the purpose of the review system," I said and frowned.

"Ask any restaurant or hotel owner. Yelp is like the local mafia. As long as they pay, the good reviews go to the top of the site."

"You should write a story on that," I said and sipped my wine.

She laughed. "It's been done. Most people don't believe it or they think that we're having a slow news day."

"The internet is a very strange thing," I said. "Maybe I should start a winery review site. That way I can ask the locals to advertise on the site."

Chelsea smiled. "I think that's been tried. Maybe you should stick to tours."

"Yeah, I'm not that big into internet stuff anyway."

"Rebel," she teased me. "What do you want to know about the guru? Do you think there's more to the story? I mean, why else get me involved?"

"I don't like how Mandy is looking to this guy for advice," I said. "I mean, everyone I've talked to seems to think he's on the up and up, but it feels like . . ."

"There must be more to the story?"

"Exactly."

"Huh, what if it's a cult?" Chelsea asked. "Did he ask her to give up all of her possessions? Come and live with him?"

"I don't think so. She keeps talking about money and destiny and fame." I shook my head. "Not that she couldn't get those things, but they aren't generally handed out by a positive-living spokesperson."

"What's the name of this guru again?"

"Dr. Brinkman," I said.

"First name?"

"Richard. I believe he's from San Diego. I checked out his website 'Reach your true potential.' It looks like it was put up two years ago. I have no idea where he got the title of doctor. There doesn't seem to be any record of a Richard Brinkman with a medical license."

"Maybe it's a PhD," she said thoughtfully. "I'll do some digging and get back to you."

"In the meantime, Holly and I are going to attend his lecture and see what it is about him that has people clamoring to get his autograph."

Chapter 9

The next morning, I met Patrick for coffee at The Beanery. "Thanks for meeting with me," I said. "I got you a latte with an extra shot."

"I hope this doesn't mean you aren't meeting me for drinks," he said and took the latte from me. I'd gotten our drinks in to-go cups because I didn't want to stay at The Beanery.

"No, we're still on for drinks," I said. "I wanted to know if you could get me in to see Tim."

"Why?"

"Because I want to see if he needs me to do anything for him while he's out. Mandy told me she got a pet sitter for his dog, but he might want me to water his plants or stir his vats or something."

"You don't have to go see him for that," Patrick said and opened the door for me. "I can find out and relay the information to you."

It was a sunny and cool fall day. The streets of Sonoma were just waking up, and business owners were opening their shops and putting out their signs.

"I'd rather talk to him myself," I said.

He gave me a sideways look. "You really like Tim."

"He's like a brother to me," I said with a shrug. "An older brother with too much money and a smart-alecky mouth."

"I'll see what I can do, but remember jail isn't like the hospital. You can't just go in during visiting hours. Especially with his bail hearing set so quickly."

"Thanks for your help," I said and kissed him on the side of his cheek. "Text me when I can come, and I'll be there."

I crossed the street to my car. The press conference was in an hour, and I wanted to be there when it happened. In the meantime, I drove over to La Galleria. Holly was working the day shift so that she could attend tonight's seminar. The contemporary art gallery was open during the day for tourists but did most of its business at night, when it offered art showings and exhibits.

"Good morning," I said to Holly as I walked in. "I brought you coffee—mocha with two shots, and an extra pump of raspberry syrup and whipped cream on top."

"You are a life saver," Holly said as she took the cup from my hands. "What brings you here so early in the morning?"

"They arrested Tim for the murder of Jeffery Hoag last night."

"Oh no, that's terrible."

"I called Chelsea like you suggested, about the guru. She came when she heard about Tim's arrest and then I told her about Dr. Brinkman."

"What did she say?" Holly asked as she sipped her coffee and then set it down on the shelf under the cashier counter.

"She'll look into it."

"That's good, right?"

"Yes," I said and took a swallow of my own coffee. "She also asked that we not join any cult or allow ourselves to get brainwashed until she can figure out what his deal is."

Holly laughed. "Why would we join a cult? We both have jobs and families and friends we care about."

"Don't laugh," I said. "You saw Mandy. There might be something in the air with this guy."

"Like hypnosis?" Holly's eyes went wide.

"Maybe," I said a trifle too eagerly. "I've always wondered if hypnosis works. I guess we may be about to find out."

"Maybe I'll wear ear plugs," Holly said. "That way if you start to look glazed over and willing to do whatever Dr. Brinkman says, at least one of us will still be in her right mind."

I laughed. "There's probably nothing going on with the man other than he's good at convincing desperate people to do his bidding."

"Whew—then we're in the clear," Holly said. "Neither one of us is desperate."

"Well, I might be a little if my business doesn't pick up," I said. "Who's your latest artist?" I noted the colorful abstracts made with paint, gesso fiber, and twine. La Galleria specialized in Northern California art, which was a bit more abstract and colorful than your average living room art.

"This is Orson Summar," she said. "He has a real flair for color and light."

I went to look at a few of the abstracts. "How's he selling?"

"He's doing okay," she said. "Let me tell you, I think in a few years he'll be a big name. Now is the time to get one of his pieces. I'm betting his prices double or triple."

"You bought one?" I asked, looking at her. Holly always said she wouldn't buy from the gallery because that meant she was playing favorites with the artists.

"Shh," she said and glanced around the empty room. "Maybe I talked Jeremy into picking up a couple pieces for his new resort. It's a good investment."

"You are a good salesperson," I said with a smile.

"Thanks. I try."

I glanced at the time on my phone. "Oh, I've got to run. They're holding a press conference on Tim's arrest, and I want to be there to see if they'll spill any of the details as to why they arrested him."

"Good luck," she said. "See you at the seminar at eight tonight?"

"I'll be there," I promised.

The sheriff's office wasn't too far away, and I decided to walk there. There was something lovely about a clear California morning, especially in the fall. I waved to a few of the shop people, who all waved back.

"Sorry to hear about Tim," Mr. Feldman called from the newsstand.

"He's innocent, you know," I said.

"I'm sure that's what they all say," Mr. Feldman said.

I shook my head and walked into the sheriff's station. Inside the lobby was a small handful of local reporters—one from each TV channel—Chelsea, and two other print journalists. Not exactly a big crowd. "Hey, Chels," I said and stood beside her. "Am I too late for the announcement?"

"No," Chelsea said. She glanced around at the small

handful of reporters. "It seems that the death of a small town realtor isn't a big ratings draw."

"Maybe it's because they don't think that Tim is the real culprit," I suggested. "I don't know what evidence they have on him, but it can't be much. I know Tim. He'd rather talk bad about someone then physically fight with them. Plus, his wine is really important to him. There is no way he'd ruin a whole batch that way."

"Excuse me, do you know the defendant?" A man with a CBS microphone asked me.

"I'm sorry," Chelsea said, "but she's my exclusive." She stepped between me and the other reporter. Two others were watching with interest.

"What's your angle?" A woman with an NBC microphone asked Chelsea.

"Read tomorrow's *Chronicle* to find out," Chelsea said.

The door from the front pushed open, and the mayor came out and stood behind a podium that was placed to the right of the reception counter. "Ladies and gentlemen, we brought you here to let you know that we have made an arrest in the Rocky Paths Winery homicide. The suspect is thirty-nine-year-old Tim Slade of Sonoma County. Fred Ranch, Sonoma County prosecutor, will be giving more details in a moment. But first, on behalf of the Sonoma County sheriff's office, we'd like to extend our condolences to the family of the man who lost his life. We have worked diligently and quickly to bring the person responsible for this crime to prosecution. Ladies and gentlemen, Fred Ranch."

The county prosecutor stepped up. He was an older man with a close-cut white beard and a bald head. He wore a dark gray suit and white shirt and a gray and red striped tie. "We have reason to believe that the cause of death was due to a blow on the head with a blunt force instrument. Our suspect is being charged with murder in the first degree. He's being held in the Sonoma County Jail until such time as a bail hearing can be met. If the public has any information on this case, we ask that you come forward or call the crime stoppers hotline."

"What is the evidence against the suspect?" Chelsea asked.

"There was DNA on the victim that matched the DNA of the suspect," the prosecutor said.

"I understand the suspect performed CPR on the victim," Chelsea said. "Couldn't the DNA have been shared during that life-saving action?"

"The merits of the DNA will be debated during the trial," the prosecutor said.

"Aren't you rushing to arrest a suspect?" Chelsea pushed.

I felt pride that she wasn't letting them get away with being smug about arresting someone quickly.

"The first forty-eight hours are the most important after any crime. Our Sheriff's office and forensic team have worked diligently to find and arrest the suspect."

"I heard he turned himself in," Chelsea said. "It's not like you went down and dragged a reluctant man in."

The prosecutor scowled at Chelsea. "We are confident we have the right man. Thank you for your attention." He turned on his heel and stormed off.

"Hmmm," Chelsea said. "That was interesting."

"It didn't sound like they had concrete evidence," I said.

"They had enough to charge Tim with murder," Chelsea said. "They aren't telling us what else they have."

"He didn't mention a murder weapon," I pointed out. "Maybe they didn't find one yet."

"Why don't you take me out to Tim's place," Chelsea said. "I'd love to get a good look at the scene."

"Are you going out to the winery?" The CBS lady asked.

"I'm sorry," I said. "Rocky Path is not open at this time."

The CBS lady shrugged and walked off. "Not much of a story here," she muttered.

"That's because Tim is wrongfully accused," I said. I grabbed Chelsea's arm. "Come on—let's go get some coffee."

"At Rocky Path's?"

"Well, I may need to check on Tim's dog," I said.

"Cool. I have a dog biscuit or two," Chelsea said. "Your car or mine?"

"Let's take mine. I don't think the reporters will follow me, but they might get snoopy and follow you."

"Got it. Let's go."

* * *

The trip out to Tim's place took about twenty minutes. Luckily, we weren't followed, though there were a couple of news vans hanging out on the street.

"Do you think they're waiting for Tim to get out on bail?" I asked as we drove slowly by the vans and turned onto the property. Mateo stood in the middle of the drive. He flagged me down, and I stopped and rolled down my window.

"Oh, Miss Taylor," he said, "what brings you out here?"

"Hi, Mateo," I said. "What are you doing in the middle of the drive?"

"Keeping the news reporters off the land," he said. "I put up a sign that says the winery is closed, but they still try to come snooping around. So I've been keeping close to the driveway and stopping anyone who comes down."

"I remember when the press was all over Aunt Jemma's place," I said. "José put a chain across the drive. You might want to try that."

"Mr. Tim likes to have the place accessible to the public, but I think it's best to wait until he gets back before we let anyone on the property."

"I agree," I said. "Listen, did you ever find the victim's car?"

"I'm sorry?"

"The victim—he had to get out to the winery somehow. I assume in a car or truck. Did you ever find it?"

"No," Mateo said with a deep frown. "I've covered most of the vineyard the last two days, mulching the vines and such. If there were a car somewhere on the property, I would have seen it."

"I think the killer took the car," I said. "It's how they left."

"Who would have come on the property to kill a man?" Mateo asked. "It doesn't make any sense."

"It has to be someone who works here on a regular basis," Chelsea said. "Please be careful. There's still a killer on the loose."

"Yes, ma'am, and you as well."

"How's Maisie holding up?" I asked.

"She's moping around. She really misses Tim."

"I brought her a toy. Is it okay if we go up to the house?"

"Sure," Mateo said. "You know where he keeps the spare key?"

"I do. We won't be long," I said. "I know you have a lot of work to get done before the weather turns. Speaking of turns, are you turning the juice vats?"

"Twice a day like clockwork," Mateo said. "Mr. Tim is very particular about his wines."

"I hope you're protecting them," I said.

"Yes, we've had a security company come in. We have cameras everywhere and motion sensors now. If anyone—even me—gets near the vats, it'll be recorded. Mr. Tim wanted to put up a fenced enclosure, but they can't come out and put it up for at least a week."

"I know a guy who might be able to do it sooner," Chelsea said. "Do you want his number?"

"I'm sorry, Miss Taylor, but do I know this woman?"

"Oh, Mateo," I said, "I'm sorry not to have introduced you. This is my friend Chelsea McGarland. She met Tim last month when I was going through all my trouble."

"Hello, Mateo," Chelsea said with a small wave. "Do you want the name of the fence guy?"

"I'll take it," he said. "As foreman, I've been tasked with getting this started."

"Cool." She wrote on a business card and handed it to him through the window.

"We'll just go in and check on Maisie," I said. "We won't stay long."

"Okay," Mateo said and waved us through.

I slowly moved the car up the hill, beyond the curve that turned wine tasters around the main house to the tasting barn. Instead, I moved straight up to the large mid-century ranch home. We parked in front of the garage and got out.

"Nice digs," Chelsea said.

I grabbed the spare key from the third rock on the left of the garden edge and opened the front door. Maisie barked and came out to greet us. "Hey, girl," I said and bent down to scratch her behind the ears. "I've got a treat for you. Are you lonely?"

"So where was the dead guy?" Chelsea asked.

Maisie went over to her for petting. Chelsea obliged by scratching her behind the ears.

"Come through the house," I said.

We walked through the great room to the patio doors in the back. The entire back side of the house was a wall of windows. We stepped outside onto a brick patio. Maisie ran out with us and squatted in the grass just off the patio. From the patio, you could see the back buildings and the wine barn just down the hill from the house. Beside it was the lean-to with the vats. One hundred feet beyond that was the tasting room, with the parking lot and bocce ball court beyond. Redwoods planted around the patio were old and very tall and shaded the patio. The bottom branches were trimmed so that you could see through them to the buildings behind.

"Is that where they found the victim?" Chelsea asked as she pointed to the vat shed. "It's not that far from the house."

"Yes," I said and explained what had happened the day I brought my tour group here.

"Can we get closer?" Chelsea asked as she moved to the edge of the redwoods.

"I don't think so," I said. "You heard Mateo. He has the place alarmed."

Chelsea lifted her phone and took pictures of the bar area. "And the dead guy was floating in one of the vats?"

"Yes," I said. "There was a scaffolding that was the height of the lid, so you could climb up and look into the vat. I think that he was up there and then got hit and pushed into the wine vat."

"They did say he died of blunt force trauma. What do you think he was hit with?"

"I don't know. It could have been something long, but even then it would be difficult to hit him hard enough to kill him from down below. Maybe the killer was on the scaffolding with him?"

"Maybe he slipped and hit his head, fell into the vat, and drowned," Chelsea suggested.

"It's kind of hard to drown in a wine vat. I think that it's only about eight feet tall. A guy the height of the victim could reach up and hang from the edge. No, he had to have been killed before he entered the vat."

"We'll have to wait for the medical examiner's report," Chelsea said and took a few notes.

"What are you writing?"

"I'm making a diagram of the area," she said. "I'm trying to figure out the sequence of events. For instance, how did the dead man arrive? We really don't know if he drove a car or if someone dropped him off."

"I suppose he could have taken a car service or a taxi, but then it's not easy to get one to come back out this way." I pointed toward the long drive. "We are out in the country."

"So most likely he drove here."

"Yes," I said, "but there's no sign of his car. That troubles me."

"Unless the killer drove off in the car," Chelsea said. "Also, we don't know that the dead man arrived alone. We have no idea why he came out here."

"I suspect to talk to Tim about the new zoning. They had a pretty open fight at the last meeting of the appellation. Maybe

Mr. Hoag had a partner and they fought. He was struck and fell into the vat. The partner then took the car and left."

"If he came here to confront Tim, why come at night?" I asked and drummed my fingers on my chin. "Why not during the day?"

"Are you sure it was at night?"

"They think the time of death was after the tasting barn was closed for the night."

"There could have been another reason for him to come to the winery, besides talking to Tim."

"I guess he could have come looking for Mandy. She worked for him part time. Why was he here after the place was closed? Was he going to fire her?"

"Maybe he was dropping off important papers for her to file."

"He could just email those," I said. "Wait—Tim said he stirs the vats at ten A.M. and ten P.M. We found the body at ten *A.M.*"

"That means that the murder happened after the vats were stirred at ten P.M."

I made a face. "I supposed he could have come out at eight or nine A.M. to talk to Mandy and been murdered in time for us to find him at ten . . ."

"But didn't they say he was dead awhile?"

"So seven A.M.? Plus, we don't know what effects the fermentation of the grapes has on the body."

Chelsea bit her bottom lip and made a note. "I'm going to talk to my friends at the coroner's office and see if I can't find out what the estimated time of death was."

"Thinking about it a bit more, remember biology class? Isn't alcohol a preservative?" I asked. "It could slow down the effects of the death process."

"But we know he was killed between ten P.M. and ten A.M.," Chelsea said.

"We're assuming we know. What if no one stirred that vat at ten P.M.?" I pointed out.

"Mr. Tim is religious about his wine," Mateo said as he stepped onto the patio. "He would not have left a vat unturned."

"Hi, Mateo," I said. "We were talking about who might have killed that man. I'm hoping to help Tim with a good alibi."

"Good luck with that," Mateo said. "As far as I know, Mr. Tim doesn't have one."

Chapter 10

"Thanks for taking me out to the scene of the crime," Chelsea said, "but I think Mateo was on to us."

"He's a smart man," I said. "There was no way he would have let us in if he thought for one minute that he couldn't trust me. Plus, we didn't go near the scene."

"I have pictures," Chelsea said. "I'm going to go to digital maps and mock up a three-dimensional rendering. Maybe we can figure out where Jeffery's car is."

"Sounds pretty high tech," I said. "But right now we have to meet Holly. We have a lecture to go to."

"The tickets to this thing are incredibly hard to get," Chelsea said. "I did some research. This guy came out of nowhere about two years ago and has taken the West Coast by storm. I mean, all of his lectures have sold out. The only reason I got a ticket was because I flashed my press pass and said I was going to write a piece on him."

"They must be confident that you won't say anything bad about him," I said.

"I'm just sorry we won't be sitting together."

"Well, Holly and I were given two second-row tickets. It was crazy."

"More like suspicious, if you ask me," Holly said as she walked up to the car. We were standing outside of Chelsea's car parked in an overflowing parking lot. The line to the lecture was around the corner.

"Holly thinks he must be using hypnosis or something to get people to follow him like this," I said as we walked up to stand in line.

"Oh, girls, I'm so glad you are here." Mandy came around the line. "Come on—I can get you in faster." She grabbed my hand and Holly's.

"Wait—Chelsea is with us," I said.

"Chelsea?"

"Our friend," I said. "Chelsea, Mandy. Mandy, Chelsea . . . she had to get a ticket in the back row."

"Oh, that won't do," Mandy said. "Come with us. I can get you up close as well." She smiled at Chelsea. "Any friend of Taylor's is a friend of mine."

"Cool," Chelsea said and followed behind as Mandy squeezed us past the bodyguards at the door.

Inside, the auditorium was cool and dim. There were binaural beats and soothing music. I thought I could detect the scent of essential oils.

"Is that bergamot?" I asked.

"Oh, you are good," Mandy said with a smile as she held my hand and drew us down the long aisle to the base of the stage. "Yes, bergamot is quite calming. Essential oils are a great way to clear the mind and relax the body. Hold on a minute." She let go of us long enough to wave down an attendant dressed in long, flowing white robes. "Sunshine, these are my friends, Taylor, Holly. and . . . what is your name again, honey?"

"Chelsea," she said.

"Yes, Chelsea," Mandy said. "Now, ladies, I have to go take care of some things backstage. Sunshine will take good care of you."

Sunshine was blond and young, with big blue eyes and black-winged eyeliner. "Ladies, please help yourself to a cleansing drink." She lifted the tray of drinks in her hands.

We each took one of the small plastic cups. Chelsea sniffed it. "What is it?"

"Dr. Brinkman's special recipe. It'll relax you and help you get in the best state of mind for the lecture." Sunshine smiled. "It tastes yummy too. Now, let me take you to our special box for friends of the family."

"You don't need to see our tickets?" Holly asked.

"Oh, goodness, no. Mandy said to take care of you. That means you get the special box. Follow me."

"I'm not sure we should drink anything," Chelsea whispered to me.

"I kind of agree," I whispered back.

"It's really good," Holly said and took another swig from her small plastic cup. "What? It's calming."

We followed Sunshine up a flight of stairs to a mezzanine level. She pulled back a curtain and revealed a small theater box with four chairs.

"Right through here, ladies," Sunshine said. "I'll be back to bring you a few snacks to refresh you while the audience takes its place."

We stepped into the box and took our seats in plush velvet chairs. Holly and I took the front seats, and Chelsea took one behind us. She pulled a small container out of her purse and dumped half her drink in the container and screwed the lid on.

"What are you doing?" Holly asked.

"I'm going to take this to a friend at the lab and see what the heck is in it."

"Do you think they drug the audience?" I asked. "I mean it could explain the monster following this Dr. Brinkman has."

"Well, I drank mine, and I don't feel any different," Holly said. "Plus, it's not like they force you to drink anything. I think it's just a nice thing that they offer refreshments. Especially with the price of the tickets."

The theater was small, but recently renovated. Our box was one of four—two on either side of the stage. The boxes were halfway between the main floor and the balcony.

"Well, the view here is certainly better than the one for my original ticket," Chelsea said. "I've got to give them props for that."

"What about our seats?" Holly asked. "Will they stay empty?"

The velvet curtains behind us opened, and Sunshine floated in with a tray full of tiny cakes and small sandwich rounds in one hand. In the other, she had a pitcher full of what looked like water with cucumbers floating in the top.

"Ladies, I hope this will keep you refreshed until Dr. Brinkman comes on stage." She placed the goodies on the table and eyed my untouched glass. "I see you haven't tried the specialty drink. Was it not to your liking?"

"Oh, I'm not thirsty," I said.

"Well, you let me know if you would prefer a new glass for the water." She smiled serenely, nodded, and left.

"Did that seem a little suspicious to you?" I asked.

"I think you are being silly," Holly said. "I drank it, and I'm feeling just fine." She waved her hand. "I'm hungry, though. These sandwiches look yummy."

I glanced at Chelsea, and she shrugged. "It does look tasty," she said and picked up a napkin and took a sandwich.

"What's in them?" I asked.

"Some sort of cream cheese and I would guess sun-dried tomatoes," Holly said. "Really good."

"Mine is cucumber," Chelsea said between bites. "They are good. You should try one."

"I'm fine, thanks." I said.

The lights dimmed twice—a sign that the show was about to start. If you could call a lecture a show. It did seem very theatrical. The crowd hushed as the lights went down and Mandy walked out to the middle of the stage. The curtains opened behind her, revealing a large screen, and pictures of flowers moved slowly behind her.

"Welcome, ladies and gentlemen," Mandy said. "On behalf of Dr. Brinkman and the rest of our staff, I want to thank you for coming. For the next two hours, you will be immersed in the mystic way of positivity and the law of attraction."

The crowd applauded.

"Thank you. In today's world we have so many conveniences, but the more time we get back with technology, the more time we spend filling it with more stress, more negative thoughts, and more worries. Well, that can stop right now. We are here today to take a few hours to learn how to change our lives. To discover how to unplug from technology and bring our focus back to our original way of being as children of the stars."

The pictures behind her were gorgeous and mesmerizing.

"Wow," Holly said and leaned forward. "Cool."

"Shush," Chelsea said.

"Ladies and gentleman, I'm here to introduce you today to Dr. Brinkman. He is a world-renowned teacher of positivity and attracting the best life for you. Please welcome Dr. Brinkman."

The audience erupted in applause. I watched carefully as a thin man with a white turban walked across the stage. He was tan and healthy looking. and wore a beige suit. He opened by telling a story in a gentle and lulling tone. He spoke with a cadence that had the entire auditorium leaning forward, as if catching his next word would solve all their personal problems.

A quick glance over at Holly. and I could see her pupils were dilated and she seemed to be hypnotized by the man. I glanced at Chelsea. She was taking notes. I sighed. It was apparent I wasn't the right personality for the positivity stories. I thought I needed to try harder.

My phone buzzed. I got up and stepped out into the hallway to see who was calling me. It was Tim.

"Tim, thank goodness—are you okay?" I asked as I walked toward the door to the lobby. I was surprised that no one sent me any looks for being on the phone during the lecture. They all seemed to be hypnotized by the good doctor.

"Taylor, I'm out on bail," Tim said. "Mateo said you came by and brought a reporter."

"Chelsea," I said. "I think you met her last month when I was under investigation."

"Well, maybe," he said. "You didn't take her down to the scene."

"No, Mateo said it was all alarmed. I didn't need to anyway. We got a good look from your patio. She's going to mock up a three-dimensional map of the scene. We're going to see if we can figure out how Jeffery got on your property without a car."

"Yeah, I'm wishing I had put in the new camera system sooner."

"It's crazy to think that you could possibly put cameras everywhere on a vineyard. You might not be the largest, but you certainly have a lot of area to cover."

A man in a white robe glared at me from across the lobby. I shrugged and stepped outside.

"Maybe it would be better if I'd put cameras in my house to give myself an alibi."

"That might not be such a bad idea," I said thoughtfully. It was a cool evening, and the streetlights glowed, blocking out the stars. "What did Patrick say? Did he help you get out?"

"He did some fancy paperwork and called in a favor so that I could post bail. Then he said to go home and get some rest. The problem is, I have the press hanging outside the gates."

"That should die down soon," I said, "once the sensational-ism wears off. Just don't do what I did and find another body. Then they never go away."

"I'm going to shower off the orange jumpsuit smell. Can you come over, though? I need the company, and Mandy's not answering her phone."

"Oh, it's because she's hosting Dr. Brinkman's talk tonight."

"Hosting? You mean her latest guru is actually putting her in charge of something? I didn't think she had it in her."

"She's quite good at it," I said.

"How do you know?"

"I'm at the talk. Well, I was, but then you called, so I stepped out to talk to you."

"Why are you at the talk? I never took you for the type to need all that positive self-help crap."

"I got a free ticket," I said with a shrug.

"Well, at least you didn't waste your money. So, what's he like?"

"I don't really know. I'm missing it, but it's kind of weird. They hand out calming drinks before the lecture. We saved a sample to find out what the heck is in it. I mean, you should see these people. They are all in some state of trance about this guy."

"It's probably just herbal tea," Tim said. "Mandy's big on the junk. I think that's where this guy makes his real fortune. He sells the stuff at seventy-five percent markup."

"Huh, and here I thought it was the tee shirts."

"Tee shirts?"

"Joking," I said. "At least I think I'm joking. I haven't seen any merchandise for sale yet. Listen, I've got to go before Holly gets too sucked into this guy's shtick. She seemed pretty into it when I left."

"Did she drink the Kool-aid?"

"Come to think of it, she did. I'm going to go rescue her now."

"Good luck with that."

I snuck back into the lecture hall and was surprised to catch a glimpse of Bridget Miller. I watched as she talked to a man in a white outfit. They headed backstage.

It seems she'd one-upped me again. I might have gotten boxed seats, but she'd gotten a backstage pass. I sighed and sat down to catch the last half of the presentation. Then Mandy came on stage and closed the lecture. "He's such an inspiring speaker," Holly said as the lights came up.

"What did you think, Chelsea?" I asked, knowing that she hadn't had any of the tea.

"I'd say it's a lot of the same things that other positivity coaches are saying." Chelsea frowned. "Still, I have a gut feeling that this guy is better than the rest."

I put my arms through Holly's and Chelsea's and walked them out into the fresh air. "Maybe it's not just the drink. Maybe it has to do with the scent in the air as well. I mean, everyone in there seemed glued to every word this man said."

"Except you," Holly said and drew her eyebrows together. "What happened? Why can't you see it?"

I shrugged. "I didn't drink the tea."

"Neither did Chelsea, and she still got it."

"Tim called while Dr. Brinkman was speaking, and I left to take it. Maybe I got more fresh air than you all did."

"Well, we can't test the air," Chelsea said. "But we can test the tea." She pulled the vial out of her pocket.

"I say we forget about the tea for now and go back to Aunt Jemma's and have some wine and girl time."

"What about Mandy?" Holly asked.

"Oh, right," I said and let the girls go. "How about you two go to the car, and I run and get Mandy and invite her as well. Maybe she can tell us more about Dr. Brinkman."

"Great!" Holly's eyes sparkled. "I'm excited to learn more."

Frowning at her weird enthusiasm, I turned and fought my way through the exiting crowd to go backstage. When I entered the auditorium, the stagehands were sweeping up and removing the microphones and the chair that Dr. Brinkman had been sitting in as he spoke. I went up the stage steps and behind the curtain, in search of Mandy. There were two women talking who seemed to know a bit about what was going on.

"Excuse me, do you know where I can find Mandy?" I asked.

The first woman blinked at me as if I hadn't spoken English. "Who?" The second woman asked.

"Mandy, the woman who introduced Dr. Brinkman tonight?"

"Oh," the second woman said with a touch of disdain. "She's probably with him right now. Down the hall, second door on the right."

"Thanks." I made my way through the cleanup crew. The hallway was quieter than the stage area. The first door on the right was open. The room appeared to be a dressing area and was empty. The second door was open a crack. I pushed the door farther open. "Mandy?"

I was shocked to find her in a passionate embrace with Dr. Brinkman. "Oh, excuse me." I quickly backed out, closing the door behind me. I thought I heard her giggle behind the closed door. I turned and hurried out of the hall and out the door.

One thing was suddenly crystal clear. Mandy was having an affair with Dr. Brinkman. Before I could think about that shocking news, I ran into Bridget and the man with brown hair who had given me the tickets. "Well, well, Taylor O'Brian, what brings you here?" Bridget asked with false niceness in her voice. "I hope you aren't thinking about adding Dr. Brinkman's lectures to your tour group." She sent me a small smile. "Quirky tours just inked the rights to Dr. Brinkman's lectures and the compound. Isn't that wonderful?"

"Brilliant," I muttered under my breath. I hadn't even thought about the guru as a part of the tours. I guess it is both quirky and expected by California tourists. I sighed. This having a rival was going to be tough. I needed to start to think outside the box, or I was about to lose my fledgling business.

Chapter 11

"What's the matter?" Holly asked. She was curled up on the outdoor settee in front of Aunt Jemma's outdoor fireplace. "You look upset."

"I ran into Bridget. She signed a contract for Quirky Tours to get tickets to Dr. Brinkman."

"Oh dear," Holly said. "I'm sorry." She got up and gave me a quick hug.

"I just hope they don't flock to her tours like they are to the lectures."

"I'm sure there's room enough for both businesses to thrive," Holly said and walked me to the sitting area. Aunt Jemma had a wine bottle open and breathing, with wince glasses on the little deck table.

"Did you get Mandy?" Chelsea asked as she walked out of the house and joined us on the front patio of Aunt Jemma's house.

"No," I said and shook my head. "I walked in on her kissing Dr. Brinkman. It was embarrassing because it was so much more than a kiss between friends."

"She was kissing him?" Holly asked. "Are you sure? I thought she was Tim's girlfriend."

"*Was* is the key word here, I think." I poured the wine and handed out glasses of Aunt Jemma's zinfandel. "I know what I saw. When I apologized and closed the door, I heard her giggle as if it was funny to get caught."

"She must not have known it was you," Chelsea said and sipped her wine, clearly relaxed. It was a crisp fall night, but we had a warm fire going in the fireplace that sat at the edge of the patio. The rest of it was surrounded by Mediterranean cedars so that only the smell of the grape vines and a slight scent of the ocean fog mixed with the smell of the wood burning.

The stars shone overhead brighter than they did in town. I leaned my head against the back of the wicker chair and put my feet up on the footstool. "I guess she couldn't have known it was me. She was enveloped by Dr. Brinkman. I wonder if she thought I was a stagehand." I sat up. "I think the crew knew about the affair. They knew exactly where she would be."

"The next question is does Tim know about the affair?" Holly asked.

"Would he care?" Chelsea asked. She sat up. "It could be a motive for murder."

"Mandy's affair? How?" I asked.

"Tim said Mandy was gone the night of the murder," Chelsea pointed out.

"Yes," I drew my eyebrows together. "I think he said they had a fight, and she went to stay with her sister."

"That's convenient. She has to know something, or maybe Tim fought with her to get her off the property. You know, Sonoma County is a small area. Everyone knows everyone else. Maybe Tim didn't kill Jeffery for the zoning. Maybe Jeffery, being Mandy's boss, came to tell Tim about Mandy's affair, and

Tim got enraged and hit the guy in the head, then dumped the body."

"In his cherished blend of grapes?" I asked. "He's been working on getting the perfect blend of old and new zins for years. His new zins finally had a good enough year to give him the ratio of old to new to make a custom blend. No, if Tim were going to kill someone, he would have buried them out back in the vineyard. He wouldn't let anyone near his precious batch."

"It still seems like a strange coincidence that she wasn't here that night. Either Tim wanted her gone, or she wanted to be gone."

"Or, as you said, Sonoma is a small town. Maybe the killer knew Tim and Mandy had a fight, and Tim was alone. So they killed Jeffery to frame Tim and put the body in the special grapes as a message."

"That's a lot of work," Chelsea said thoughtfully, "but it's remotely plausible. Does Tim have any enemies?"

"Tim certainly tries hard enough," I said with a wave of my wine glass. "Don't get me wrong; I like the guy, but his sense of humor is dark. Most people take it badly. I'm one of the few friends he has."

"And me, of course," Aunt Jemma said. She walked out in a long, flowing orange and blue swirled caftan. Her hair was pulled back and she had a glass of wine in her hand. "Hello, ladies Sorry I'm late. What have I missed?"

Holly filled her in on everything.

"You don't need a guru to attract business," Chelsea said as she poured a glass of wine and sat down. "You have notoriety."

"For what?"

"For solving a murder," Aunt Jemma said. "People love detectives. You should play that up."

"Speaking of detective work, Mandy is having an affair with Dr. Brinkman," Holly said. "Taylor caught them kissing in his dressing room."

"Well, that's interesting," Aunt Jemma said. "Does Tim know?"

"We don't know," Chelsea said. "Someone should find out."

"Why are you all looking at me?" I asked and sat up straight.

"You're the one who saw them kissing," Holly pointed out.

"And you are closest to Tim," Chelsea said.

"No, he's closer to Aunt Jemma—isn't that right, Aunt Jemma?"

She took a sip from her wine. "I think he isn't particularly close to anyone, but I have known him longer. Do you want me to tell him? I mean it seems a little like telling tales out of school. Since I didn't witness the feat."

I bit my bottom lip in worry. "I suppose I should be the one to tell him."

"Mandy should actually be the one to tell him," Chelsea pointed out. "She's the one who is being dishonest."

"How was the lecture tonight—I mean besides the insight into Mandy's relationship?" Aunt Jemma asked. "Was Dr. Brinkman all that and a bag of chips? Is there even anything to worry over Quirky Tours' new contract?"

"Everyone there seemed to be mesmerized," I said.

"How would you know? You walked out a third of the way through," Holly said and pouted. "You missed all the magic. The man is magic, you know. I have this strong urge that I need to go back and hear him again. In fact, I just bought another ticket on my phone. Do you know he has an app that you can download for free and then schedule a seat at any of his talks? This time I got a seat up front." She closed her eyes. "I just want to bask in the glow of his words. He makes me feel all warm and safe." She opened her eyes. "Do you know what I mean?"

I reached over and put my hand on her forehead. "She doesn't feel feverish," I said.

"I'll take her phone," Chelsea said. She grabbed the phone. Holly tried to grab it back.

"Ladies, what is going on?" Aunt Jemma asked.

"I think there's something in the drink they give you when you enter the auditorium," I said. I turned to Chelsea. "You're having that tested, right?"

"I shipped the sample off to the lab right after we left the auditorium. I did it right away because I was starting to feel like it might be a bad idea."

"There was something in the air as well," I said to Aunt Jemma. "Mandy said it was essential oils, but I think it's some kind of mind control."

"Hmm," Aunt Jemma said. "Seems like a lot of work for a guru. Most of them are charismatic speakers. They give some truths in their talks that make people want to follow them. Does he have a self-help book out?"

I picked up my phone and checked the search feature. "He has three books out. They are all *New York Times* bestsellers." I looked up at my aunt. "That can't all be due to tea and essential oils."

"The tea and essential oil might simply be part of the theater of his work. People love theater. They love ambiance—like in our séance. It really is all about the feeling it provokes."

"Well, this guy certainly provoked a feeling in Mandy," Chelsea said.

Holly grabbed her phone back from Chelsea. "I think he's brilliant. I want to hear more."

"How much did you pay for your next ticket?"

"Only five hundred dollars," she said. "I got a deal. If you join the group, you get two more lectures, top pick of seats, plus ten percent off all the products from his store. You know—books, tea, essential oils to recreate the atmosphere in your own meditation room."

"Gee, the guy is making money hand over fist," Chelsea said. "No wonder he was able to give away a couple of two-hundred dollar tickets. He's already profited one hundred dollars in return. Not a bad investment, if you ask me."

"Okay, so this guy seems a little shady. What's the plan?" Aunt Jemma said.

"Keep Holly away from the app until whatever she drank wears off." Chelsea pulled the phone out of Holly's hands again.

"Hey—"

"It's for your own good, honey," Chelsea said.

"Listen to her," Aunt Jemma said. "You're saving for that trip to France, right? Trust me, you really don't want to follow this Dr. Brinkman more than you want to go to France."

"I have wanted to go to France my entire life," Holly said and leaned back in her chair. "I want to go where all of the great artists painted. I want to walk the streets of Paris and see artists at work."

"You can't get that if you're paying five hundred dollars or more for tickets to see Dr. Brinkman," Chelsea said.

"But you were there—you heard him," Holly argued. "He said if you follow his program to the letter, then all of your dreams will come true. That means if I spend a little money on his system now, I will have my trip to France before I know it."

"Keep her phone," Aunt Jemma said.

Holly pouted and crossed her arms over her chest. "Didn't anyone else understand how good Dr. Brinkman is?"

"Trust me, he's most likely a con man." Aunt Jemma patted Holly's knee. "Nothing is ever as good as they tell you it will be. We're looking out for your own good." She turned to me. "What else are you going to do?"

"Hmm," I said. "Chelsea, can you look further into Dr. Brinkman? I have a feeling that his affair with Mandy is more than a coincidence."

"I'm on it," she said and toasted me with her wine glass. "I did some preliminary work and didn't find much. I think it's time I started doing some serious digging. Thank goodness for public records. Without them I would have to pay someone to hack into databases." She grinned. "I'd rather do the research on my own."

"Good," I said. "Now we need to help Tim out."

"Are you going to tell him about Mandy?" Chelsea asked.

"I'm going to get Mandy to tell him about Mandy," I said with as much confidence as I could muster.

"Good luck with that," Holly said.

"We also need to figure out who killed Mr. Hoag and why they are trying to frame Tim," I pointed out.

"We could let the sheriff handle that," Aunt Jemma suggested. "He is pretty good when it comes to these things."

"Aunt Jemma!" I was aghast. "He just arrested Tim. There is no way he's going to investigate anyone else."

"You should tell Sheriff Hennessey about Mandy's affair," Aunt Jemma said.

"How will that help Tim's murder case?"

"Maybe Mandy wasn't altogether honest with the police

about where she was the night of the murder," Aunt Jemma suggested.

"And?"

"If she lied about where she was, what else could she be lying about?"

I shook my head. "Mandy doesn't seem smart enough to get away with murder."

"That was a bit of a low blow," Holly said. "Dr. Brinkman said we are all smart enough to accomplish our goals."

"When is that tea going to wear off?" I asked.

"Hey." Holly frowned at me. I reached over and gave her a big hug.

"I'm sorry," I said. "That was mean. I must be feeling cross. I just don't understand the Dr. Brinkman thing, and I really don't understand who would try to frame Tim. I'm a bit frustrated that I can't seem to help."

"Why don't we all get some rest," Aunt Jemma said and stood. "Holly, come with me, honey. I'll get you set up for a good night's sleep. You'll find that your mind will be much clearer in the morning."

I stood. "I've got a tour group that leaves at ten A.M. Chelsea, you can stay the night as well."

"I've got two guest rooms," Aunt Jemma said. "I'd feel better if you girls all were safe under my care." She put her arms around us. "I don't know what happened at that lecture, but I think you shouldn't be alone tonight. Let's make a slumber party of it."

"I've got extra pajamas," I said.

"I've still got my overnight bag in the car," Chelsea said, "but I do have to be off in the morning. I've got a deadline and some research to do."

Millie hopped up from her place by the fire and followed us inside. Clemmie purred and rubbed against my ankles. I picked up my sweet kitty. "We're all going to have a slumber party," I said to the cat and cuddled her. "Aunt Jemma, you don't mind if Clemmie is part of the party, do you?" I teased. My aunt didn't have the best relationship with my orange and white striped kitty. I suspected she secretly loved the cat. It was a mission of mine to make her admit it.

"I suppose if the cat must be part of the party, it's all right. But you must try to keep her off my counters."

"She'll be with me the entire time," I said and took Clemmie's paw. "Cross my heart." I crossed the paw over my heart. Clemmie mewed at me, and I winked at her.

Aunt Jemma huffed. But we all settled in for the night.

Chapter 12

It was Sunday morning, but there was no lazing around for us. Chelsea left bright and early. I sipped coffee and stood outside, waving goodbye as Millie chased Chelsea's car down the drive. Inside, Holly was nursing a headache.

"I swear it feels like a hangover," she moaned as Aunt Jemma passed her a glass of lemon water.

"This will help your hangover," Aunt Jemma said. She turned and frowned when she caught Clemmie sneaking across the breakfast bar countertop. "Get down!"

I put down my coffee cup and snagged Clemmie, giving her a squeeze. "I'll take her over to the poolhouse."

"She's more than welcome here," Aunt Jemma said. "Just not on my countertops."

"And not on your car."

"I don't want her to get hurt."

"She's a cat," I said. "Come on, Clemmie, we won't let big bad Aunt Jemma ruin your day." Clemmie mewed her agreement. I opened the sliding glass door and slipped Clemmie into the poolhouse and closed the door behind me. I stared at my reflection for a moment. Today's tour was a spooky hike through wine country. So I was dressed in a tee shirt under a long-sleeved plaid shirt, beige shorts, and thick socks and hiking boots. My wavy hair was pulled back to keep it under control.

I had slept like a rock last night. Even though I'd chosen to stay with the girls and sleep on Aunt Jemma's couch. Whatever was in the air at the lecture had gotten to me as well. I certainly hoped that Chelsea would find out what was in the tea.

"Do you want a lift into town?" I asked Holly as I stepped back into the big house. I was heading out to Sonoma to meet my tour group for the day.

Holly had packed her large tote bag and was scratching Millie behind the ears. "I think I'll be fine to drive. If I can have my phone back . . ."

I smiled and pulled the phone out of my pocket. "Promise me you will call me and wait twenty-four hours before you sign up for any more of Dr. Brinkman's work."

She took the phone out of my hand. "I promise. I'm just glad you were able to refund my money so fast."

"Chelsea said you didn't hit the 'Send' button."

"Thank goodness for that. I really am saving up for a weeklong trip to France."

"I know," I said. "Maybe you can get your boyfriend to take you."

She shook her head as we walked toward the door. "Jeremy's focused on the restaurant right now. Which is fine, since I'm only halfway toward my savings goal."

"Have a good day, ladies," Aunt Jemma said. "I'm off to my Pilates class." She brushed by, wearing yoga pants and a long tunic swirled with a paisley print. Her gray hair was up in a small ponytail, and she wore a headband like I'd seen in an old Jane Fonda video.

"Your aunt is the coolest," Holly said.

"She is that," I said and got into my old VW van. The van was part of the California lore, and although it was beat up from the outside, it was super reliable. The inside could easily hold a tour of seven people, plus me in the driver's seat. Some days I took Millie with me. Today was one of those days.

Ever since a good friend had gotten into a car accident that killed her unrestrained puppy, I made certain that any animal riding in my car was safely restrained. That meant Clemmie always rode in a cat carrier, and Millie—who came with me more often—was hooked into a seatbelt connected to her halter. That way, should anything happen, she would be safe.

"Are you ready for a spooky hike?" I asked Millie. She sat in the seat behind me and to my right. She looked at me with a happy puppy smile on her face. "Off we go."

Today's tour group was interested in the haunted areas for Sonoma wine country. I loved to mix hiking and themes with my tours. This one had been fun to research. Patrick Albert, the group organizer, had asked me to put together a spooky tour for October's Halloween season. So I planned a hike through Sonoma County's most paranormal trail. Lucky for me, it was close to home.

The Jack London State Park Mountain Trail was listed as one of the spookiest trails in the area. It featured tall redwood trees casting shadows, creepy ferns, gnarled oaks, thick madrones, and spooky legends of witchcraft and pagan rituals. The oaks were losing their leaves, adding to the spooky feel of the dark hollows.

We met the group at the shopping center just off First Street, across from the Sonoma Valley Visitor's bureau. I liked to meet people there so they had time to go to the Visitor's Bureau and gather flyers. That way they could plan their next trip or point out to me different places they might want to see on our way. I usually set aside time for one or two detours.

I pulled the van up to a parking spot and got out. What caught my eye was the big pink tour bus parked right in front of the Visitors Center. It had "Quirky Tours" written on the side in a scrolling font. Bridget Miller gave me a wave. I waved back slowly. There was a line of fifteen people beside her bus.

"Oh, I forgot to say thank you!" Bridget called out to me.

Confused, I walked across the street toward her. "Why the thanks?"

Her smile widened. "Since the news broke about your last tour, my requests have doubled. So I thought I'd say thanks. At Quirky Tours, everyone's safety is our top priority."

"No one was hurt on my tour," I pointed out.

"Physically," she said. "People come to Sonoma for fun, not to get involved in the court system." She pointed at her line. "The proof is in the pudding."

"Where are you going today?" I asked. Maybe I could mention how different our groups were.

"We are off on a haunted tour," she said. "It is that time of year, and Sonoma has some great history."

For a brief second, my smile slipped. How did she know? Was it a coincidence that we were doing the same tour? "Yes, haunted tours are pretty typical this time of year. Where are you going?"

"I got permission to take them through the old Henderson Sanatorium."

"I thought that place was abandoned."

"It was recently purchased by a friend of mine," she said

with a shrug. "They say it is so haunted that people can hear and see ghosts in the daytime. Which is why we're going. My tour wants a real scare."

"I thought safety was your highest priority," I said flatly. "That old building can't be safe."

"It's been fully inspected," she said and lifted up the paper on her clipboard. "I have the report right here. Do you want to see it?"

"No," I said. "Well, I've got a tour. Have fun with your old building."

"Where is your tour going?"

"We're hiking," I said. "Fresh air and no chance of anything falling down around us."

"Sounds . . . well, I was going to say 'safe,' but didn't someone die on one of your hikes?"

I sent her a short smile. "Bye, Bridget."

"Tootles." She waved me off and turned to the driver of her bus.

I tried not to sigh too loudly as I walked toward my van. I had to gather up my group before they got distracted by the big pink bus.

A young man with a hipster beard and black square glasses was hanging out, by a car, with a woman about my age dressed in hiking gear and another young man who looked like he spent a lot of time on a computer. The "Think Geek" tee shirt and ratty old jeans gave him away. His blond hair was brushed to the side and shaggy.

"Hi, are you Patrick?" I asked.

"Yeah, Patrick Albert," the hipster guy said. "This is T.J. Thomas and Sally Field."

"Like *the* Sally Field?" I asked as I shook hands.

She shook her head. "No relation—my mom was just a big fan. I swear she married my father just so that she could name her daughter Sally."

"Cool," I said. "Are there other members of the group? I have reserved for six."

"Yeah, they're over at the Visitor's Center on the other side of the big pink bus," Patrick said. "That thing is a little too gimmicky." He looked at my VW van. "That's our ride, right?"

"Yes."

"Good." He took out his phone and texted. "I'll let the others know you're here."

"Where are we headed?" Sally asked.

"I've got us going up to the Jack London State Park Mountain Trail," I said. "It's got some spooky hollows, and there are tales of witches and spells and apparitions."

"During the day?" Sally asked, her eyes growing wide.

"Well, there are spots that grow quite dark beneath the redwoods. The light is lower now that it's autumn, so shadows get tossed around."

"Oh, is there, like, a creepy cabin in the woods?" T.J. asked.

"We'll have to see," I hedged.

The rest of the group consisted of two women about my age and an older man. I loaded them and their equipment into the van. Millie was happy to sit with Sally and Patrick. The older man named Ben sat in the passenger-side front seat. He had a brochure out with a map of the area and paranormal tours.

"So," he said as I headed out of town, "that other tour lady—the one with the pink bus—said that they were going to tour a haunted sanatorium. Is that on our tour?"

"No," I said. "It's a derelict building. I'm not confident it's safe enough for a tour."

"I understand that you actually lost a person on one of your wine country hiking tours."

"Excuse me?"

"The yoga teacher," he said. "I heard that went bad. What's the possibility of that happening to us?"

"I assure you that you are perfectly safe with Millie and me," I said.

"We heard that on your last tour you found a dead body floating in a vat of grapes. Is that true?" Sally asked as she leaned forward.

"Well," I said, "it was a crime scene. But no one on my tour was hurt."

Patrick laughed. "Don't worry," he said. "We picked you because of your reputation for finding the dead."

"What?"

"Your reputation for stumbling over dead people," Ben said. "We want in on that action. We're pretty sure you can't get that on a big pink bus."

"Seriously? That's kind of—"

"Gruesome?" Sally asked. "Yeah, we know, but we're really into the paranormal, and what's more paranormal than dead people?"

"Let's hope we only see ghosts on this tour," I said with the best smile I could muster. "Right, Millie?"

The dog barked with joy.

"We can see ghosts after we taste wine," Amber, one of the girls in the back, said. Her black hair was a curtain of silk. Her almond-shaped eyes were expertly lined, and her pale skin was luminous. She was dressed in yoga pants, a tee shirt, and hiking boots.

"I'm looking forward to visiting some wine-tasting places too," Annette said. She was blond with blue eyes, and dressed in shorts, a pale blue blouse, and hiking boots.

"Whiskey's more my thing," T.J. said from the back. "Do you have any whiskey-tasting places in Sonoma?"

"Yes," I said, glad for the change in subject. "We do have a few distilleries. In fact, there is a winery and distillery on our route back. I can add it to our tour if it's okay with everyone in the group."

"Works for us!" they all agreed.

The trip up to the park was filled with easy laughter. The group was from San Francisco. They lived and worked in the South Bay and had wanted to try mixing their love of the paranormal with a day trip to Sonoma.

"What do you know about Jack London?" I asked the group.

"He wrote *Call of the Wild*," Sally said.

"He was a handsome adventurer, according to this brochure," Ben said.

"He was a very famous writer for his time, and he lived and worked the land at the state park we are about to visit," I said. "He died young."

"Yep, it says he was forty," Ben said. "That's harsh."

"Didn't his house burn down or something?" Amber asked. "I think my brother and his friends went to hike the trails and talked about a fire."

"Says here it burned down right before he was getting ready to move in," Ben said.

"Another tragic paranormal episode," Patrick said and rubbed his hands together with glee.

"It says they did some forensics on the site in 1995," Ben continued to read, "and ruled it as nothing more than a fire caused by linseed oil on rags."

"Linseed oil?" Patrick asked.

"It's highly flammable," I said, "and was often used as a paint binder, putty, or wood finisher."

"Now people eat it," Sally said.

"Seriously?" Patrick asked.

"Yes, it's good for you. It's made from flax seed."

"That's crazy," Patrick said.

We arrived and I parked on the edge of the parking lot. "Let's try to stick together," I said as they hopped out of the van. Sally took Millie on her leash. "I've got water and snacks. When we hit the halfway point, we'll stop and take a rest. Afterward, I've got a small picnic, and then we'll go visit the local wineries to taste their wares."

The air was cool, but dry. The tree limbs rustled around us as we started off on one of the many hiking trails in the park. I loved being outside. Sonoma Valley was a pretty place of rolling yellow hills with tall grasses and patches of woods that included redwood trees and madrones. We crunched past the welcome center, where we stopped to grab some more brochures and ensure everyone had what they needed for the hike.

"Whatever you take in, you haul back out," I said and pointed to the sign that agreed with me. "We want to help keep the park clean."

"Good thing I'm not taking anything in," T.J. said with a grin.

"Oh, dogs are only allowed in the ranch area and on the trail to Wolf House ruins," Sally said and handed me Millie's leash. "That might put a crimp in our hike."

"No problem at all," I said. "Millie will be staying here with my friend Joyce." I waved as Joyce walked across the parking lot. She squatted down and gave Millie's ears a good rub.

"How's my little puppy dog?" Joyce asked.

"She's good," I said and handed Joyce the leash. "Thanks for watching her."

"Oh, it's always a pleasure. Besides, my Sadie loves Millie."

Sadie was a big old chocolate Labrador that Joyce had in the ranch area of the park. Joyce worked as a park attendant and would bring Sadie with her to greet people. Sadie was kept in a small penned area whenever Joyce was off the ranch.

"Why aren't dogs allowed on the trails?" Amber asked.

"It's not good for them or the environment," Joyce said. "We've got poison oak and rattle snakes. Plus, the scent of a dog in the area can ruin your chances of seeing local wildlife."

"We're not here to see wildlife," Patrick said and rubbed his hands together. "We're here for the paranormal activity."

"Ah," Joyce said, smiling. Her raven hair floated around her face. "You're here for the spooky hike. I hear that your soul can get pretty twisted in the darker hollows. I'd be extra careful if I were you."

"I've got my camera," Patrick said with a grin. "I'm going to document any paranormal activity we see along the way. Come on, everyone. Let's get started."

They all turned to the trailhead. I turned to Joyce. "Thanks again for watching Millie. I didn't want to leave her home alone. Aunt Jemma had several things going on today."

"Your aunt is pretty active," Joyce said. "I hope I'm active at her age."

"You will be," I said.

"Which way are you taking them?"

"We're going up to the Grandmother tree and then back down. So we'll be back in two hours or so."

"I would have thought you would take them on the longer trail."

"Are you kidding me?" I asked and pointed to Amber. "Her boots are new. There's no way they're prepared for a seven-hour hike."

"Let me know if you spot any ghosts," Joyce said with a quick grin. "I can spin that story until we have people begging for season passes."

"I'll do my best to find a ghost for you," I said and tugged on a ball cap to keep the sun off my skin.

"A documented spirit," she said as I walked off.

"I've got a man with a camera. If anything happens it will be documented."

Chapter 13

The hike to the Grandmother tree was fairly uneventful. The group had started off laughing and chatting and looking for ghosts. But all we saw were gorgeous views and signs warning about the occasional mountain lion in the area. At the first sign, I was glad I'd left Millie at the ranch area with Joyce. The last thing I wanted was my puppy attacked on a hike.

I always started off at the front of the group, but once we got going, I would fall back to ensure that the stragglers and those who were slower hikers did not get lost.

"This has been a bit of a bust for paranormal activity," Patrick said as he slowed down to walk with me at the rear of the trail.

"It's still a nice hike," I said. "Maybe next time we'll come closer to the evening and see if we can't rattle a few bones."

"What made you say this was paranormal, anyway?"

"It was listed on a website as one of Sonoma Valley's top ten paranormal hikes," I said. "Surely that counts for something."

"I think you have seen more death than on this trail," T.J. said.

"Hey, the Grandmother tree is nearly two thousand years old. Think of all the things that tree has seen," I pointed out.

They sighed and turned back to the view while I unpacked the waters, small bottles of wine, cheeses, apples, carrots, hummus, and crackers. It was a nice picnic. While the paranormal angle of the trip might have been a bust, at least the hike was beautiful.

"I heard that new guru, Dr. Brinkman, was speaking in Sonoma," Amber said to Sally. "We should stay up here for the night and see if we can't get tickets."

"You've heard of Dr. Brinkman?" I asked and sat down beside the women. I poured wine into their plastic glasses.

"Yes, he was on *Late Night with Dwayne*. It's one of my favorite San Francisco late-night talk shows." Amber dipped a carrot in the hummus and took a bite. "Dr. Brinkman gave a five-minute talk, and everyone felt so inspired. It's what got me to come on this tour."

"Really?" I asked, confused.

"Really," Amber said. "I have been pretty depressed and staying at home, locking myself away in my apartment."

"You don't have to work?" I sipped a nice Syrah.

"We can work remotely," Sally informed me. "It's pretty easy to just stay home in your pajamas for days in a row."

"That was me," Amber said, bouncing her blond ponytail. "Then I heard Dr. Brinkman speak. He made so much sense. I simply got up and walked outside and took a deep breath. It was great. I'd forgotten how warm the sun felt on your face on an autumn afternoon. It smelled of the beach and fall leaves."

"Did you go out in your pajamas?" Sally asked. She had polished off her glass of wine and pushed her glass to me to pour her some more.

"Yes," Amber said with a twinkle in her eye, "but it didn't matter. There was no one on the street. Everyone was at work."

"Wait," I said, even more confused. "I thought you said that you were watching late-night television."

"No, I said I was watching a late-night talk show. I watch them on demand when I get bored with work."

"So you stepped outside in the middle of the afternoon in your pajamas to take a deep breath . . ."

"Yes," Amber said. "Then I went inside and took a shower, put on my bike shorts and a tee shirt, and went for a long ride. I've been out hiking and biking and kayaking every day since. Dr. Brinkman changed my life in that short five-minute talk."

"That's incredible," Sally said and polished off her second glass of wine, then grabbed a bottle of water.

"Almost unbelievable," I muttered.

"I'm not the only one," Amber said. "Ben was the same way, only he went to one of Dr. Brinkman's lectures, and look at him now." She pointed to the older man, who laughed and joked with T.J. and Patrick. "I heard he had agoraphobia very badly and hadn't been out of his house in nearly three years."

"That's terrible," I said.

"But better now," Amber said. "Hey, Ben, come over here and tell our tour guide about your experience with Dr. Brinkman."

"What do you want to know?" Ben asked. He grabbed a handful of carrots and dipped them one by one in the hummus.

"I went to one of Dr. Brinkman's lectures last night," I said. "I'd heard a lot about what he does for people. Did you get offered something to drink while you were there?"

"The tea?" he asked. "Yes, but I didn't drink it. I was quite uncomfortable. I hadn't been out of my house in a few years. I was there because my sister came with a ticket and performed an intervention. I was skeptical. In fact, I told my sister I had a Lyft car coming to get me after five minutes."

"So did you go back home?"

"No," he said with a shake of his head. His blue eyes turned sincere. "There was something about the way the man talked. He made so much sense. He pulled me right out of all of my fear and made me long to go out and live."

"Then what happened?"

Bed shrugged. "I went out and lived. Seriously, I cashed in my stocks and spend most of my days traveling now, seeing the sights. Living!" He pounded his chest and laughed. "I've been less than two hours away from a two-thousand-year-old tree on Jack London's property, and I'd never been here. That's just crazy—crazier than listening to some old man talk. I had no idea how much it was going to change my life."

"But I didn't have a life-changing experience," I said. "So what was I missing?"

"Maybe you didn't need one," Ben said and grabbed a handful of nuts. "It's possible that you are doing what you always should have been doing." He flashed a grin at me. "You're taking us out into the countryside and showing us parts of our backyard we've never seen before. I'd say that's a pretty good talent."

"Thanks," I said. "Let's pack up. We have more hiking to do."

"You mean more ghost hunting," Patrick said.

"I think the only ghosts we'll see are the ones that hang around once you've had a bit too much wine," T.J. teased.

"Wait—was that a dark shadow?" I asked and pointed to an oak with low-hanging branches. "I think that was a hanging tree."

"Seriously?" T.J. went toward the tree.

"You've got to work on your storytelling," Sally teased me. "I've got the brochure. As far as the official story goes, there wasn't a hanging tree."

"Well, now we don't know for sure," I said. "Someone could have been hanged there. It's about the right height."

"You are morbid," Sally said.

"Maybe just a little." I packed up all the food and what was left of the waters and stowed it all away in my backpack. Then we hiked by Fern Lake and took in the old vineyard. I listened to my group laugh and joke. What a different group they were from my last group of hikers. But then again, I'd never had anyone ask for a paranormal tour.

"So you really didn't learn anything from listening to Dr. Brinkman speak?" Amber asked me as we approached the ranch and the parking lot where we started out.

"No, nothing," I said with a frown. "But then again, I may have been distracted. I got a call from a dear friend. He needed to talk to me. He'd just gotten out of jail on bond."

"Oh no, what happened?"

I winced. "I kind of found a dead man on his property."

"Wait, are you talking about the dead man found floating in the vat of grapes? *You* found that body?"

"I didn't *find* it exactly," I said. "I was there when it was found."

"How gruesome," Sally said. "Maybe you need Dr. Brinkman more than you know."

"I thought he was a self-help guru," I said.

"He's many things to many people," Amber said. "He's a very smart man, and he has these powers to get to the truth."

"He does?"

"Yes," she said. "You know you should go with us tonight to see Dr. Brinkman again. I bet if you talk to him about your friend, he can figure out who the killer is."

"He can?"

"Sure," Amber said. "The man is a psychic genius. If anyone is hiding anything, he'll be able to tell right away. In fact, it wouldn't surprise me at all if Dr. Brinkman pointed you straight toward the killer."

"I think Dr. Brinkman might be too busy to hunt out a killer," I said. "But thanks for thinking about it."

"You should ask him," Sally said.

"He is close to a friend of mine. Perhaps I will go see him again tonight."

"We'll save you a seat," Amber said.

"But I don't have a ticket, and I know they are hard to get."

"Don't worry," Amber said with a wave of her hand. "I know one of the inside people. We'll get you squeezed in."

"What time do you need me to be at the auditorium?"

"How about by eight thirty?" Amber said. "That way they will have started seating the crowd, and we can get you in without too much difficulty."

"I'll be there," I agreed.

"Hey," Patrick shouted and waved at us. "I think I just captured a ghost. Come check out this photo."

The girls left me, and I shook my head. The only spirits in the area were the ones in the wine we'd just tasted. I glanced at my watch. Three wine-tasting stops after the hike, and I still had time left to see Holly before I went home to shower and get ready, then meet them at the auditorium.

What was the draw to Dr. Brinkman? Why was I so immune?

* * *

After dropping off the tour group back at the shopping center, I stopped by the art studio to see how Holly was doing. I was a bit dusty and disheveled, so I went around to the back of the studio and knocked on the locked door. I buzzed the doorbell, but no one answered. There wasn't anything left to do but go in through the front. I came around the corner to see Holly walking out the front door.

"Holly," I said and waved. "I was looking for you."

"Oh, Taylor," she said and glanced at her watch. "What are you doing here?"

"I was on my way home from my tour today and wanted to stop in and check on you. How are you?"

"I'm fine," she said with a shrug. "Good, really. How was your tour?"

"Not bad," I said. "We didn't see anything paranormal. One of the guys thought he caught a ghost, but it turned out to be the shadow of a bird. But the company was good and with the hike and the stops at the wineries and distillery, they all left in good spirits."

"Cool," Holly said.

"I ran into Bridget and her Quirky Tours bus. She was in front of the Visitor Center. Can you believe she was running a haunted tour as well? Her bus was full."

"Really?" Holly seemed distracted.

"Yes," I said and frowned. "Do you have some place to go?"

"No . . . maybe . . . look, if you must know, I have a ticket for Dr. Brinkman's next show. I promise not to drink the tea this time. I was wondering if I would feel the same about him if I didn't have tea."

"You might. I mean, he was using essential oils as well as tea."

"But the scents didn't affect you last night," she pointed out. "So I was wondering if his talk would do the same for me if I didn't drink anything."

"I guess we could try," I said.

"'We'?"

"Yes, the ladies on my tour today wanted me to come see Dr. Brinkman again. They are convinced he has magical powers and will not only help me find my true calling but will even be able to find Jeffery Hoag's real killer."

"Huh," Holly said thoughtfully.

"I doubt it, though." I put my hand on her forearm to connect with her via touch. "But I do want to go back and confront Mandy. She needs to come clean to Tim and let him know what she's doing with her new boss."

"I agree," Holly said. "I still think the man is gifted, but I certainly wouldn't sleep with him."

"That's my girl. Now, I've got to run home and get cleaned up. The girls can get me a ticket, but I need to come after eight thirty P.M. to ensure I don't get attacked by a mob of ticket-hungry citizens."

Holly giggled. "That's a funny picture."

"It's not funny," I said and indicated the two long lines already forming outside the auditorium. One was for those with tickets, and the second, even longer, was the line for people waiting for tickets. "That group in that line looks like they would hurt anyone who got between them and Dr. Brinkman. Seriously, what is with the guy? I'd understand if he were tall, dark, and handsome, but seriously, he's skinny and lanky."

"I think he's so sincere," Holly said.

"You're going to go stand in that line soon, aren't you?"

"Only if you can't cut me in line," Holly said with a smile.

"I can't give you cuts. I won't be back here for at least an hour."

"Then I have to go before the line gets any bigger. I'll see you inside."

"Right." I turned on my heel, and Millie and I went back to the van. I suppose if I were going to get arrested for cutting in line, then I'd better at least look good. "Come on, Millie," I said to my pup. "Let's go home before I get sucked into doing something even stupider than seeing Dr. Brinkman for a second time. How's that sound to you?"

She smiled up at me and tugged on her leash. I was pretty sure she heard the word 'home' and that was enough for her to maneuver me back in the van.

As for me, I made a quick phone call before we started down the road. Maybe it was time for Tim to come see what Mandy was mixed up in. If nothing else, Dr. Brinkman might be able to determine who really killed Jeffery Hoag.

Chapter 14

"Who's the older woman you brought with you?" Sally asked when she met me at the auditorium door. People were streaming in beside us, keeping a careful eye that we didn't try to slip in without a ticket.

"I'm Taylor's Aunt Jemma," she said and stuck her hand out to shake Sally's hand. "I understand you were part of her tour group today."

"Yes," Sally said. "I was. I'm afraid I was only able to get one seat. It's a sold-out show." She glanced around. "I'm not certain I can even let you in without getting the police called."

"Don't worry," Aunt Jemma said. "I have my ways." She pulled lipstick out of her purse and outlined her lips with a poppy-red color. "Come on then, ladies, let's go inside. I'm sure the show is starting."

She pulled the doorknob out of Sally's hand and walked into the building with her chin up as if she owned the place. Knowing Aunt Jemma, she might. Sally looked at me. I shrugged and we both followed my colorful aunt into the depths of the foyer.

"Tickets please," the usher said.

"Here's mine and one more," Sally said and showed the tickets.

"You go," I said to Aunt Jemma. "I've seen the talk."

"But you were going to ask him about solving the murder," Sally said.

"I can ask later," I said with a wave of my hand. "I'm going to stay and see if I can't talk to Mandy afterward."

"But—"

"It's all right, dear," Aunt Jemma said and put her arm though Sally's. "Let Aunt Jemma experience the wonder that is the guru with you. That's a nice girl. Taylor, you have the nicest friends." She walked Sally into the auditorium, and the doors closed behind them. I stared at the door a moment.

"I'm sorry, but if you don't have at ticket, you have to leave," the usher said. He gestured toward the glass doors in front. "Better luck next time."

I blew out a deep breath and took two steps.

"Taylor?"

I turned to see Mandy sticking her head out through the doors. "Mandy, don't you have to get inside and introduce Dr. Brinkman?"

"Come on," she said and grabbed my arm. "She's with me." She ushered me into the auditorium. "Your Aunt Jemma came and got me and told me you were outside without a ticket."

Aunt Jemma waved at us as we passed by. I sent her a small wave back. My aunt made herself comfortable sitting between Sally and Amber and said something to the girls that made them laugh. It was nice to have an extroverted aunt who could get along with anyone.

When I told her I was coming back to listen to Dr. Brinkman again tonight, Aunt Jemma had insisted on coming with me. She was certain there would be a place for both of us, and surprisingly, she was right.

"Come on—I have an extra seat behind the curtain," Mandy said. "It's not as fancy as last night's."

"It's okay," I said. "I was just interested in hearing Dr. Brinkman again."

"Of course," Mandy said. "He touches people's hearts, and then it becomes a sort of addiction."

"Aren't you going to introduce him?" I asked as she showed me to a stool and then stood beside me.

"Oh, not tonight. Tonight it's Delilah's turn."

"Delilah?"

"Yes, Delilah Howell, she's training under Dr. Brinkman, just like I am. I think she's going to be taking over the East Coast tours."

The curtains opened, and I noticed the strong scent of essential oils wafted onto the side of the stage from the auditorium. People clapped wildly as a young woman with blond hair pulled up into a soft bun strode across the stage. She welcomed the crowd, thanked them for coming, and started the introduction.

I glanced over at Mandy to see her mouthing the words. The introduction was exactly the same, so I knew it was prewritten. It seemed odd to me that the girls could be interchanged so easily. I guess it didn't matter who introduced a guru as long as you got to hear the guru speak.

Delilah waved her hand, and Dr. Brinkman entered stage left. The crowd was on its feet. The large screen behind him showed pictures of flowers and happy landscapes. I leaned forward.

Tonight I was intent on listening to his every word. Maybe, just maybe, I could figure out what the big deal was.

Dr. Brinkman's voice was soft, but commanding. He spoke of self-love and universal themes of encouragement. He went on about proper breathing and listening to your own body. I was perplexed. There didn't seem to be anything that I hadn't heard before. A glance at Mandy told me she was a little confused. Her hands were clasped together near her heart, and her eyebrows drawn together. What was wrong?

"Are you okay?" I whispered.

"Yes, of course," she said, but she glanced around. "Excuse me a moment." She pushed through the crowd of backstage watchers and workers.

I watched her stop and talk to a stagehand. Soon she was back at my side. Her expression was calmer, her gaze on the guru. I turned to concentrate on the speaker. After the talk, I clapped politely and stood. Maybe if I could catch Holly and Aunt Jemma, we could reconvene and go over what it was that I was missing. Surely something had to keep these people clamoring for more.

"Thanks for sneaking me in," I said to Mandy.

"Wait—don't go yet. I want you to meet Dr. Brinkman." She grabbed my arm and pulled me toward the back.

"I don't know," I said and dragged my feet. I mean, wasn't it being disloyal to Tim if I said nothing about Mandy and this guru? Besides, I didn't feel I understood the hype behind the guy enough to need to meet him.

"Don't worry. Once you meet him in person, you'll totally understand," Mandy said. We pushed through a wave of people and ran into Tim coming out of Mandy's dressing area.

"Tim!" Mandy and I said his name at the same time.

"What are you doing here?" Mandy asked.

I looked into the dressing room behind Tim and saw a man on the floor. "What's going on?"

"Call nine-one-one," Tim said. "This man is hurt." I noticed that Tim had blood on his hands. I grabbed him and pulled him just inside the door.

"Don't move." I pulled out my phone and dialed the emergency number.

"Nine-one-one, what is your emergency?"

"We have an injured man in the first dressing room in the Bel Aire Auditorium," I said.

"Yes, we are aware," the operator said. "You are the second caller. We have an ambulance and police on the way."

"Dr. Brinkman!" Mandy said and raced toward the downed man.

I looked over my shoulder to see Mandy kneeling at the man's side. She had rolled him over, and a knife was stuck to the hilt in his chest. Mandy screamed and scrambled back away from him. "Don't touch anything!" I said.

"What's going on?" The 911 operator asked from my phone.

"The victim has a knife sticking out of his chest," I said. "There's blood everywhere."

"Do not touch anything," the operator said. "The police are on their way."

"Yes, you said that," I said, my hand still on Tim's arm. He looked stricken and like he might try to run. I shook my head. "We aren't moving."

"Police!" Sheriff Hennessey shouted down the hall. "Nobody move!" The sound of shuffling stopped. I swear, all I could hear was my heart pounding in my ears. He came through the dressing room door with his gun drawn. "Nobody move," he repeated.

"We're not moving," Tim said.

I frowned at Tim. "Don't say anything."

Deputy Bloomberg entered the doorway. He held his gun on us too. My heart was racing. I trusted Sheriff Hennessey, but I didn't know this guy. It's scary when anyone points a gun at you, let alone a man you don't know. I raised my hands.

"He's dead," Sheriff Hennessey said. He looked at Mandy. "Is this Dr. Brinkman?"

"Yes," she said and hugged her knees to her chest. "He was a kind and gentle man. Who would do this?"

"Did you find him?" The sheriff looked straight at me.

"Mandy was bringing me back to meet him—"

"Stop," he held his hand up. "We'll get your statement later." He stood. "In the meantime, don't say a word to anyone." He looked at the Deputy Bloomberg. "Put your gun away. He's been dead awhile."

"But he was on stage not more than fifteen minutes ago," I said, confused.

"No, he wasn't," Mandy said with tears in her eyes. "You were listening to a stand-in. It's why I wanted you to meet the real Dr. Brinkman."

Sheriff Hennessey looked straight at Tim. "What are you doing here?"

"I thought you said not to talk." I elbowed Tim. Now was not the time to antagonize anyone.

"I did say that," the sheriff said and blew out a long breath. "Bring in the crime scene techs. I want this place gone over with a fine-tooth comb. I need everyone who was working backstage in the seats out front. Keep them quiet until we can interview them. The halls are filled with people—get them all in seats. We need to contain this quickly. No one in or out of the building besides Crime Scene and our own guys."

"Got it." Deputy Bloomberg put his gun away, turned on his heel, and headed out. I could hear him barking orders to others and the sound of the people in the hallway moving with purpose.

"I wasn't the first one to call this in," I said and stared at my phone. "Someone knew about it before we did."

"There will be a record of the call," Sheriff Hennessey said. "If you weren't the first, we'll find out who was."

"Do we stand here until the crime guys show up and take our picture or something?" Tim asked. "Can Taylor put her hands down?"

"Taylor, put your hands down," Sheriff Hennessey said. "You can hang up your phone." He pulled out his own phone and took three-hundred-and-sixty-degree pictures of the room, including the door and the doorframe. "You can go out into the hall."

I helped Mandy up. Tim put his arms around her and walked her out into the hall.

"Is there someplace private we can keep you?" the sheriff asked. "Tim and Mandy are covered in blood. We need to keep them separate from the crowd."

"Dr. Brinkman's office is behind you," I said.

"No, we need to keep that from being contaminated."

"There's the box seats you were in last night," Mandy said. "They are curtained off."

"See that they get there without touching anything or talking to anyone," the sheriff said to a third deputy in the hall. "If they talk to each other, separate them."

"Yes, sir," the deputy said.

Mandy led us down the empty hall to the boxed seats. I took a seat in the velvet-covered chair where I'd been the night before. I could see that there were two deputies on the stage, and the auditorium was a third full of people. They sat with various expressions. Some seemed stricken. Others appeared scared. A few seemed bored.

"No phones," the deputy said. "We'll be collecting them for now. You'll get them back once you are free to leave."

"The organizers have bottled water for everyone," another deputy said. "Sit tight. We'll bring you something shortly."

"How long is this going to take? I have kids at home," one lady piped up.

"We will be questioning everyone, one by one."

I noticed Aunt Jemma and Holly were in the crowd. They waved at me and I waved back. "Is everyone you know here?" Tim asked.

"Just Holly and Aunt Jemma," I said. "Holly is into Dr. Brinkman, and when I told Aunt Jemma I was coming to a second lecture, she forced her way in here. It's why I was backstage with Mandy during the speech."

"Stop talking." A deputy stuck his head through the curtain. "Or else I will separate you."

"How are you going to do that?" Tim asked. "The place is full."

Sheriff Hennessey stuck his head into the booth. "Take Tim Slade down to the station on suspicion of murder."

I stood. "Why? What did he do?"

"He was seen going into the room, and he has blood on his hands," Ron said. "Get him out of here."

"But—"

"We will talk soon," the sheriff said to me, his gorgeous gaze flinty.

I sat back down without another word. There was little I could do to help Tim. I had seen him in the room with the body. I was certain he hadn't killed Dr. Brinkman, but saying so now was not going to help. At least, that's what I told myself.

Chapter 15

It took hours of waiting while they cleared the scene and the medical examiner's office removed the body. The deputies slowly worked through the crowd, getting the story of how everyone had watched Dr. Brinkman give his speech on stage not fifteen minutes before his body was found. It was a mystery, because rumor had it that Dr. Brinkman had been dead at least two hours.

Which in my opinion would clearly rule Tim out. Although I didn't know for sure that he hadn't been in the auditorium for two hours, it had seemed to me as if he'd just found the body. The real question was, with so many people backstage, why hadn't someone else found the body?

And who had called 911 besides me?

Then there was the part about how Dr. Brinkman had been found dead in Mandy's dressing room. Sheriff Hennessey took me out to question me before Mandy. Unlike the rest of the crowd who was brought back behind the curtain and interviewed quietly, I was taken to the office near the box office. There, Ron had another deputy stationed, taking notes.

"Sit down, Taylor," he said.

I took the small chair that was empty.

"Why were you here tonight?" he asked.

"I was trying to figure out what all the fuss was about," I said. "I'd been given a free ticket last night, and Mandy put me and Chelsea and Holly up in the private box. But I didn't get what was so special about the talk."

"So you came back?" He crossed his arms over his broad chest and leaned back against the desk.

"The people at my tour today said that Dr. Brinkman was life changing."

"You don't think so."

"No," I said with a shake of my head. "But then I didn't drink the tea."

"You mean the Kool-Aid. The expression is 'drink the Kool-Aid.'"

"No, I mean tea. You see, they actually served tea before the lecture last night. I think there is something in it."

"Drugs?"

"Most likely an herb that leaves you in a euphoric state. Then there's the scent."

"Yes, I noticed it when I walked in," he said. "The team is analyzing it now."

"It's supposed to be essential oils. Good for calming the crowd."

"You think he was drugging the crowd. For what purpose?"

"That's what I came back to check," I said and leaned forward. "Last night, Holly said she was willing to pay five hundred dollars for another ticket to hear him talk about her life's purpose."

"That's a lot of money."

"Money Holly doesn't really have. That's what made me come back," I said. "I needed to know what would make Holly give up her lifelong dream of going to France."

"Makes sense," he said. "How did you end up with Mandy behind the scenes?"

"Two women from my tour group this afternoon had tickets to the lecture tonight. They offered me a seat, but when I told Aunt Jemma that I was going again tonight, she tagged along."

"She took your seat."

"Yes, but Mandy saw me and offered to take me backstage."

"You were backstage for the lecture."

"Yes."

"Did Dr. Brinkman seem okay to you? You must have seen him up close."

"You want to know how he could have been lecturing and dead at the same time."

"Something like that."

"Mandy said he had a double," I said. "I believe it. You see, I was at the side of the stage. I could hear him clearly, but I didn't get a good look at him. He entered from the other side of the stage and the lights were bright and there were a lot of people running around backstage doing things."

"Things like?"

"Changing curtains, hair and makeup on the woman who introduced the doctor. Backstage things, I guess you could say."

"Was Mandy with you the entire time?"

"Yes—er, not really," I said. "When he started talking, she looked confused. I suspect she knew it wasn't Dr. Brinkman. He must have been supposed to talk, but then he got switched at the last moment. She left my side, but not my sight. She went and talked to a stagehand and then came back and watched the rest of the speech with me. She wanted me to meet the doctor. That's the reason I went back to the dressing room. So if Dr. Brinkman was killed during the speech, I don't think Mandy did it."

"You think Mandy didn't expect it to be the double on stage."

"No, she seemed worried. But you know, whoever killed Dr. Brinkman had to know about the double. They also had to know that Dr. Brinkman would not be missed until after the show."

"Tell me about what you saw last night when you went behind the stage to meet with Mandy."

"I'm sorry?" I blinked at him. "Last night?"

"I know you saw Mandy and Dr. Brinkman in an embrace. You assumed they were having an affair, so you left."

"How did you know?"

"I interviewed your aunt," he said. "It gives Tim Slade a strong motive for murder. That, and the blood we found on his hands."

"Tim didn't kill Dr. Brinkman," I protested.

"How do you know?" Sheriff Hennessey asked. He straightened and towered over me. There was true concern in his eyes. "How?"

"I just know."

"That won't hold up in a court of law."

"Mandy didn't know Tim was in the building," I pointed out. "When we went back to see Dr. Brinkman, she was a startled as I was to see Tim."

"She didn't want him to meet her lover," Sheriff Hennessey speculated.

"I don't know what she wanted," I said and crossed my arms

over my chest. "She was simply surprised. Then we saw Tim's expression and knew something was wrong. As soon as I saw the blood and the body, I called nine-one-one. But someone had already called."

"We have a record of both calls," he said.

"Who was the other caller?" I asked, my curiosity strong.

"Someone from a theater phone. We haven't been able to trace who called."

"Was it a guy or a girl?"

"A guy. Where was Tim when you first saw him?"

"He was coming out of the dressing room," I said. "Do you think he called?"

"I doubt it. He had blood on his hands, and there was no blood on any of the phones."

"I think he got bloody because he was checking the pulse on Dr. Brinkman. I know that's what I would have done."

"What about Mandy?" he asked. "Was she with you the entire time?"

"She came inside the room behind me. She recognized Dr. Brinkman right away and went to him. It was Mandy who turned him over and saw the knife."

"Mandy turned him over? He wasn't a small man."

"She must be stronger than she looks," I said with a frown. "Or maybe he was tipped. You know how when someone is on their side, it's sometimes easy to turn them over?"

"Was he on his side?"

"Yes," I said. "I think . . . now I'm confused."

"It's harder to be a witness than people think. There is a lot of adrenaline pumping when you realize something has gone wrong."

"I can tell you, after she turned him over and I saw the knife, I told them both not to move."

"And did they listen?"

"They did," I said. "So if Tim were the killer, why would he just let me call the police and be caught at the crime scene? Why didn't he flee?"

"That's a good question and one I plan on asking him," the sheriff said.

"There were a lot of people backstage," I continued. "Anyone could have done it and run."

"We're talking to a lot of witnesses."

I stood. "Can I go now?"

"Yes," he said and put his hand on my arm. "Go home and get some rest, and please, stay out of the investigation. I don't want to see you get hurt."

"Me, either," I said.

"I still want to have that coffee date," he said in a low voice.

"Let's wait until after the investigation," I said. "I think it's for the best."

"I agree. I'll walk you out."

Holly and Aunt Jemma were waiting for me in the lobby. "Hey, you didn't have to wait for me," I said as I put my arms around them, "but I'm glad you did."

"We wanted to make sure you were all right," Aunt Jemma said. She glanced at Sheriff Hennessey. "It can't be easy being this involved. She's not a killer."

"I know that," he said and crossed his arms again. "She's not a suspect here. She's a witness."

"Good," Aunt Jemma said. "Well, then you are invited to the vineyard for drinks any time you have a free night." She winked at him. "It's nice to have a handsome man stop by for company on occasion."

"Aunt Jemma," I scolded.

"What?" she asked, her eyes round with pretend innocence. "I like looking at handsome men."

I rolled my eyes. "Come on. Let's go home."

We walked outside and into the cool evening. The scent of grapes and fog filled my senses. Aunt Jemma brought her car so I could leave the VW van at the vineyard. "Let's drive you home," Aunt Jemma said to Holly.

"Thanks," she said. "Normally, I'd walk because it's not that far, but there is a killer on the loose."

"I'll walk you up to your door," I said. "I don't want anything to happen."

"Thanks." Holly got into the back seat of Aunt Jemma's little Mini Cooper, and we drove the few blocks to Holly's apartment complex. "I'm glad Chelsea wasn't here."

"Can I ask you a question?" I turned to see her expression. "Was the lecture as good as last night? I mean do you still feel the need to sign up for more classes and spend all your money you were saving for your trip to France?"

"I think the information was great and very helpful. There's something about his voice . . ."

"See, I wondered. I didn't really listen yesterday, I guess. The sheriff thinks that Dr. Brinkman was already dead. Which means it wasn't him up on stage."

"What? That can't be."

"Think about it," I said. "He could have been a double."

"But the voice was the same. I think . . . no, I'm sure of it."

"He could have been mouthing a recording," Aunt Jemma

said. "Like singers do sometimes. There are many people who do that these days."

"Why would Dr. Brinkman use a body double?" Holly asked.

"I don't know," I said as we pulled into the parking lot. "But I bet we're going to find out."

"No, I bet *you* are going to find out," Holly said as I walked her to her door. "As for me, I think I'm done with all the guru stuff."

"I think that's a good thing," I said and watched as she opened her door and turned on the light. "Are you going to be okay here alone tonight?"

"I'm sure I'll be fine," she said. "It's simply awful to have two murders in the county. I thought I lived in a safe place."

"So did I," I said. "I guess wherever there are people, there's a chance for murder."

Chapter 16

The next day, I had no tours. That was pretty typical for a Monday. Most people wanted wine tours during the weekend, and Thursdays and Fridays were popular because of longer weekends or vacations. Since it was starting to get colder, there weren't a lot of people vacationing much now.

That meant more time to work at Aunt Jemma's tasting room and to plan for my own tours. It also meant there was time for me to think about what had happened last night. I poured myself a cup of coffee from my small kitchenette.

My puppy, Millie, sat bathing in the sun at my feet. Clemmie was lounging on the top of the couch. I loved my fur babies, and after a night of murder and mayhem, it was nice to be home with them and simply breathe the cool, fall California air. I reached for my phone and texted Tim:

Are you home?

He didn't respond right away. So I texted Holly:

Are you going to work today?

She texted back:

Yes, I work 10 A.M. until 6 P.M. There's a new artist at La Galleria. You should come in for a viewing if you're bored.

I texted back:

Not bored, wondering how you were doing after last night.

Okay, she texted. *Nothing went bump in the night. Have you heard from Tim?*

I tried texting him, but no answer. I'll contact Patrick and see what he knows, I responded.

Keep me posted, she messaged back.

I called Patrick. I pulled up a memory of his handsome face as I dialed.

"Hello, Taylor."

"Hi Patrick, how are you?"

"I'm fine. I would be better if I'd heard from you sooner. I heard you had quite the adventure last night."

"I'm sorry—I didn't think I needed a lawyer."

"I was hoping you'd have called just to talk."

I winced. "You should have called me."

"I heard you found another dead body last night," he said, his voice low and interesting. "Do you want to talk about it?"

"Not much to say," I said. "Tim was there."

"I know."

"Are you representing him? Is he okay? I tried to reach him today, but he's not answering his phone."

"So you called me to check on Tim?"

I felt the heat of embarrassment on my cheeks. "Yes?"

"Well, at least you're honest. Were you honest when I asked you for drinks and you said you were interested?"

"Yes."

"And you were—what? Waiting for me?"

"Yes?" I winced again.

"Then I'm asking again. Are you busy tonight?"

"No," I said and felt my heartbeat pick up. "I'm not. Tonight would be nice. Where do you want to meet me?"

"I can come and pick you up."

I looked out at the pool. If he picked me up, it was a real date. I thought about Sheriff Hennessey. He hadn't asked me on a date since my exoneration. Maybe it was time I gave that little crush up. "Okay. How should I dress?"

"We'll keep it to just drinks," he said. "We can talk about anything but your friend Tim and my law practice. Okay?"

"Okay," I said with a smile. A real date. It had been awhile since I'd had one of those.

"Good. Now that we have that out of the way, Tim might be in jail for a while. The evidence against him isn't good. He had the doctor's blood on his hands."

"He was checking on the body," I said. "I bet Mandy had just as much blood on her. She rolled the body over and exposed the knife sticking up."

"They have Tim's fingerprints on the knife."

"How? He never touched it," I said. "Besides, doesn't it take time to process evidence?"

"They did a spot-check on the site," Patrick said. "And they have a witness who says that Mandy was having an affair with Dr. Brinkman. That means Tim had motive."

"He didn't do it," I said and felt my hands shake.

"How do you know that?" Patrick asked me.

"I just do," I said. "Besides, I distinctly remember someone saying that Dr. Brinkman was cold. That meant he'd been dead awhile. Surely Tim wouldn't have killed the man and then stood over the body and waited for us to find him. That's a bit of a reach, don't you think?"

"I think I'm representing Tim, and I really can't talk about the case with you," Patrick said, backing off.

"But you just did."

"I haven't told you anything that won't be in the news tonight. The sheriff is calling a press conference. I'm sorry, Taylor. This time I doubt they'll let Tim out on bond."

"But there's a killer on the loose. If they keep Tim in jail, it means they won't get the real killer, and he may kill again."

"How do you know it's a 'he'?"

"I don't," I said with a frown. "Why are you being so combative?"

"Sorry," he said. "Habit of being a lawyer."

"Let me talk to Tim," I begged. "I want to hear his side of the story. I'm sure I can help."

"Tim will spend the day in interrogation processing," Patrick said. "I'll be with him. I'll let him know you called and you care."

"Tell him I'm looking for the killer."

"Taylor, please, stay out of it. I don't want you to end up hurt or worse—dead by sticking your nose where it shouldn't be."

I paused. "'Sticking my nose where it shouldn't be'?"

"You know what I mean."

"Do I? Because that sounded condescending and mean. I'm only thinking of my friend here. I know what it's like to be in jail. It's not nice and it's not fun, and he's innocent."

"I'm sorry," Patrick said. "I only meant that you should stay safe."

"I think maybe we should get drinks another time."

"Taylor."

"Goodbye, Patrick. Please tell Tim I'm thinking of him." I

hung up, hopping mad. Why did he think he could say things like that to me? It only made me more determined to figure out what was going on. Tim was innocent, and I was going to prove it.

I dialed Chelsea.

"Hey, Taylor," she said. "What's up?"

"Did you hear about Dr. Brinkman's murder?"

"Yes," she said. "I've been doing some more research into the guy."

"Well, I was there when the body was discovered. In fact, I called nine-one-one."

I could hear her smile over the phone. "I'll be there in about an hour."

"Good," I said. "I think we need to do a little more digging into what is going on here. It seems that someone is trying to frame Tim and is doing a believable job of it."

"So maybe we should start with who has the motivation to frame Tim."

"That's a great idea. I was thinking that maybe it was a serial killer and Tim just happened to be a convenient person to blame."

"No, serial killers are too self-important to try to frame someone," Chelsea said. "They are all about getting away with something. Or manipulating other people."

"Framing someone isn't manipulating them and the cops?"

"Not in the way most serial killers think," she said.

"You've studied up on the subject?"

"I'm into true crime. I've been thinking about writing a book—that's why I'm into reporting the crime beat. I'm certain that someday there will be a crime that goes national. Then I'll be there to figure out who did it and write the book that makes the bestseller lists."

"Now that's a great goal. Okay—I'm at the poolhouse. I've got some chores to do for Aunt Jemma, and then I'll meet you at the auditorium."

"You think that they'll let us into the building?"

"Maybe, maybe not." I shrugged. "We can certainly try. And I want to see those women from my tour again—I know where they're staying, and they were there last night. They might have seen something."

"I'll meet you in front of the auditorium."

"See you soon."

I hurried through my chores, ensuring that Clemmie was fed and petted, and Millie was walked. I left Millie with the tasting-barn personnel. Then I got into the van and headed into town. It was a bright, dry fall day, so I rolled the windows down and inhaled the scent of the vineyards. It was the dry, dusty smells of mulched leaves and the end of grapes that had all been harvested.

I loved living in Sonoma. I didn't tell Aunt Jemma, but it would take a lot for me to go back to the hustle and bustle of the city. Cities are where the real crime is. I suppose that was why Chelsea lived an hour away in North San Francisco. Maybe she should move to Sonoma. We seemed to be having a crime spree.

In my mind, by definition a serial killer was someone who killed more than one person. So whoever was framing Tim was most definitely a serial killer if you used that definition.

But Chelsea was right. This person seemed to be targeting Tim. It was like they were trying to ruin his name and reputation, and make him suffer through a trial and a possible lifetime in jail. Who would hate a man so much that they would do such a thing?

A jilted lover?

As far as I knew, Mandy was Tim's long-time girl. Tim was clever and funny and super smart. He could cook, but he was also difficult and picky. He didn't date around.

Had he said something to the wrong person? No, surely saying something mean wouldn't cause someone to react this severely.

Then what could Tim have done to deserve this?

I parked across the street from the auditorium. The place was deserted. There was a police tape across the door to the building. I peered into the glass-fronted lobby. No one seemed to be around.

"Are you looking for someone?"

Startled, I turned to see a man in his thirties, wearing all white, behind me. I hadn't heard him come up. "Hello."

"I saw you looking inside," he said. "The place is closed until further notice due to last night's incident. Are you looking for someone?"

"You look familiar. Do you work here?"

"I work for . . ." he frowned. "I *worked* for Dr. Brinkman. Wait—didn't I give you tickets to come to the lecture?" He looked around. "There was another woman with you, pretty with brown hair?"

"Holly," I said. "That's right. Your name is Bruce . . . Bruce Warrington?"

"Yes," he said, nodding. "I was stopping by to see if we had access to our equipment and such."

"Oh, I'm sorry for your loss," I said and held out my hand. "I'm Taylor O'Brian."

"You said you were here last night. Did you become a follower?" he asked as he shook my hand.

"Not really," I said. "I was on my second lecture last night, but I still didn't get it." I shrugged. "Three times is the charm? I guess we'll never know."

"Ah, so his message wasn't for you."

"What do you mean?" I tilted my head and squinted up at him.

"Dr. Brinkman was a gifted man. He'd done a lot of research on the subject of proper messaging and life-altering realities, but what he discovered is that it only works on eighty percent of the population." Bruce studied me. "If you still weren't sure after your second lecture, then you are an outlier. The messaging wasn't for you."

"Huh," I said.

"Dr. Brinkman was a man of science. We've done many research studies on the effects of his message. As I said, eighty percent had real positive benefits in their lives. The rest . . ." He shrugged. "Nothing works on every person."

"Were any of the outliers angry enough at Dr. Brinkman to want to kill him?" I asked.

Bruce blinked at me a moment. "Why would you think that Dr. Brinkman was murdered?"

"Because I was there last night. I found the body. I saw the knife. You can't un-see that, you know."

"I see," he said and took a step back. "I'm sorry. The police told us to keep quiet about the details of what happened last night. We released an official statement that Dr. Brinkman had died and that his death was under investigation."

"I was backstage. There were a lot of people around, but it

seemed that everyone had access badges. Did Dr. Brinkman have security?"

"He didn't think we needed security, but with the kind of fame he had, we convinced him to at least lock down the back-stage area. You see, he trusted that people would either under-stand his message and follow him or, like you, be an outlier. The outliers generally got their money back. We had a thirty-day guarantee. Customer service was one of his passions. Dr. Brink-man felt that there was enough negativity in the world, and good customer service was an easy way to spread more positivity."

"Yes, my friend Mandy said he was all about the light."

"Oh, you're a friend of Mandy's?"

"Yes," I said. "Why?"

"I'm surprised," he said and folded his arms.

"What surprises you about my friendship with her?"

"She doesn't seem the type to be friends with an outlier. I'm going to have to talk to the council about that."

"Gee, you make it sound like I'm in some sort of dystopian novel."

"I'm sorry if my language bothers you," he said with a per-fectly straight face. "Precision of language is important to our happiness. If you weren't an outlier, you would understand."

Would I?

Chapter 17

Things were getting weirder by the moment. Bruce left me to my own demise. He seemed quite put off by my status as a nonbeliever. The reaction made me wonder yet again what was really going on.

"Taylor!"

I saw Chelsea wave as she crossed the street. "Hi," I said and gave her a welcoming hug. "You got here quickly."

"I'm always fast when it comes to a good crime story. What happened?"

"Oh, that's a story for when we get coffee," I said. "I'm curious to look over the crime scene, but the building is closed."

"Let's do a walk-around. We can check out entrances and exits, look for cameras that might have picked up something on tape."

"Don't you think the police already did that?"

"Of course," she said with a grin, "but they think they have their suspect, and we're still open to other possibilities. Right?"

"Right."

"Then let's take a look around." We wandered around the outside of the large art deco building. The corner stone said it had been built in 1934, and it had tall, elegant clock tower. The building itself was painted beige, and the vintage marquee stood out over the town square. Aunt Jemma had told me that the theater held a supper club as a fundraiser. She went once a month to have dinner with friends and watch a vintage movie.

The front had two main doors and a box office. There were vintage buildings on either side, and so the only entrances were in the front and the back. Behind ran an alley and a small area for a few cars.

"It really is a lovely old building," Chelsea said and snapped a few pictures of the back and alley with her phone. "It looks like the entrances are covered by security cameras."

"I think Dr. Brinkman entered through the back," I said. "Mandy will be able to tell us more."

"Do you think the killer came through the back or entered the front of the theater and then came around to the back dressing areas?"

"I'm not sure," I said and tapped my fingers on my chin. "What I know is Dr. Brinkman was stabbed. Whoever killed him slipped into the room, stabbed him, and left. Why wouldn't Dr. Brinkman call out for help? I mean, it was violent, but only one deep stab wound." I motioned with my arm. "He should have come stumbling out to be found right away."

"Unless the killer knew what he or she was doing. If they thrust up and twisted the knife into the heart or lungs, he could have fallen in place and drowned in his own blood."

"Yuck," I said and made a face.

"Our killer was most likely a man who may have been a hunter. A hunter would know how to kill with one knife blow."

"Or a butcher," I said thoughtfully. "Or someone in the military."

"And is your friend Tim any of those things?"

I laughed softly. "No. Anyone who meets Tim can tell he's not exactly the hunter-killer type. Although he is a trained chef, so they might say he knows how to butcher meat."

"But chopping up a chicken is very different than slicing into a person."

"Yes. That's why I'm so certain he's innocent. The problem is that I saw his girlfriend Mandy kissing Dr. Brinkman just the night before. They think they have cause for a crime of passion. The thing is, I don't see Tim as much of a crime-of-passion type."

"So what if it is a crime of passion, but not your friend Tim? Who else might Dr. Brinkman have angered?"

"That's what I was asking. There was a guy who saw me looking into the lobby right before you got here. His name was Bruce Warrington. He was surprised I knew Mandy. Maybe there is more going on here than we think." I looked at Chelsea. "He called me an 'outlier' because I didn't get passionate about Dr. Brinkman's lectures and ideas of self-improvement. You went to the first lecture. Did you get a feel for what it is that has Mandy and Holly all worked up?"

"I didn't really get it," she said and shook her head. "I sent the tea off to the lab for analysis. It can't be the scent in the air because it would have affected us both."

"Maybe it only works on some people."

"Maybe," she said with a shrug, "but highly unlikely."

"So let's say Bruce is right. That there are no drugs in the tea. The scent is simply essential oils. Maybe I simply don't understand the message."

Chelsea shrugged. "Maybe he was just a charismatic speaker."

"With a doppelganger," I said. "We should talk to Mandy.

The body was found in her dressing room. And if Dr. Brinkman was dead, then who gave the lecture?"

"Wow, that is weird," Chelsea said. "Maybe he was a twin."

"I never thought of that. You looked into his background, right?"

"Yes," she said as we walked back to the front of the theater. "Dr. Brinkman didn't exist two years ago. So there's no telling who the man really was."

"Oh, there's that Bruce guy," I said. Bruce had walked out the front of the theater with a box in his hands. "Maybe he can tell us more."

We hurried toward Bruce.

"Excuse me," I said. Bruce turned toward me and sent me a gentle smile. "Bruce?"

"Yes," he said.

"This is my friend Chelsea. She's helping me look into Dr. Brinkman's death."

"Are you police?"

"No," we both said at the same time.

"I'm a journalist with the *North San Francisco Chronical*," Chelsea said. "We understand that Dr. Brinkman might have been dead while he was supposed to be lecturing last night."

Bruce's gaze shifted left and right. "Oh."

"I was backstage," I said. "I didn't get a close look at the man lecturing. Who was it?"

Bruce moved closer. "Look, I'm not supposed to talk out of turn."

"Off the record," I said quickly.

Chelsea made a noise of protest, but I put my hand on her arm to stop her.

"Off the record?" Bruce asked.

"Yes," we both said.

He shifted the box in his hands. "Dr. Brinkman was training a few of us to evangelize other counties. That's why we all dress the same and wear the same headgear. The more like Dr. Brinkman we look, the better. It's a brand thing."

"So who was speaking last night?"

"Harvey Winkle," Bruce said. "We were surprised Dr. Brinkman was even in the building."

"Why?"

"He doesn't like to be around when one of us is giving the lecture. That way his secret is harder to uncover."

"Wait. With Dr. Brinkman dead, you all just lost your jobs."

"Not really," Bruce said. "You see Dr. Brinkman set up an employee-owned corporation. When we joined, we gave our money in exchange for stock. Last night the board of directors had an emergency meeting. We've decided to move forward after a period of public mourning. We'll simply lecture using the Dr. Brinkman Method."

"Well, isn't that convenient," Chelsea said.

"No, no, don't take it that way. Dr. Brinkman was a brilliant man who was always looking out for others. He set up the corporation this way on purpose. He really believed in the communion of souls."

"Communion of souls?" Chelsea asked.

"Yes, you know—community. All for one and one for all."

"I see," Chelsea said. "And what about the killer? It seems there was someone who didn't like the communion of souls."

"That's the thing. We can't imagine who would do such a thing. Everyone loved the doctor."

"Literally?" Chelsea asked.

I looked at her quizzically.

She shrugged. "Some people take community to a whole new level, and you did see Mandy kissing him."

We both looked at Bruce.

"We're not that kind of community," he said. "Besides, Dr. Brinkman was married."

"What?" I asked.

"I didn't see that in his background check," Chelsea said.

Bruce shrugged. "He wasn't a formal contract kind of guy. He and his wife, Alycia, were handfasted."

"What does that mean?"

"They had a ceremony of commitment, but no government license."

"Oh, what about Mandy?" I asked. "I saw her kissing him."

"I doubt that," Bruce said. "Where did you see it?"

"Two nights ago, I came back to look for Mandy after the lecture, and I saw her in her office, kissing him."

"No, it couldn't have been him," Bruce said. "I happen to know that Dr. Brinkman was sick that night and stayed home."

"So the first lecture I went to wasn't given by Dr. Brinkman?"

"No," he said. "That was Harvey, too. He's good, though, isn't he?"

"Very," Chelsea said and took notes. "Where's Harvey now?"

"Last I saw him, he was at the house last night. He's on the board of directors."

"Where's the house?" I asked. "We should probably go see Harvey."

Bruce looked nervous. "No press. I've said enough, and it's

off the record." He turned on his heel and crossed the street, walking quickly away from us.

"That was interesting," I said.

"Off the record or not, this gives me more things to look into," Chelsea said.

"Do you think someone killed Dr. Brinkman because of something someone else did?"

"I don't know," Chelsea said. "But I think we should try to find out."

Chapter 18

We sat in The Beanery at a small table near the front windows. My chai tea latte steamed in front of me. Chelsea was on her phone, searching the Web.

"This makes more sense," she said and blew out a long breath. "Harvey Winkle is thirty-two years old. He went to Berkeley and studied psychology. He likes blonds and long walks on the beach."

"How do you know that?" I asked, perplexed.

She showed me her phone. "Social media."

"Oh, huh," I studied the picture. "You know it could have been him that I saw Mandy kissing. All I saw was the back of the guy, dressed in white with the signature headdress. I guess I just assumed it was Dr. Brinkman."

"Hey, girls, what's up?" Mandy said as she entered the coffee shop. "I got your text. What did you want to meet me about?"

"Come join us," I said and patted the chair seat next to me. "I'm buying."

"Thanks. I'll go order and be right back." She left to put in her drink order. It only took a moment, and she was back at the table, taking her seat. "I'm glad you texted. It's been rough with Tim in jail. I could use some girl time."

"Are you staying out at the winery?" I asked.

"No, I'm in town with my mom. I can't go out there, knowing a guy died there. It's super scary to be alone out there."

"You're not a fan of the quiet country life?" Chelsea asked.

The barista came over and put a frothy cup of cappuccino in front of Mandy. She wrapped her hands around it. "No, not really. I always thought it would be romantic to live out on a winery, but it's just a farm." She blew on her drink and sipped. "Besides, my mom won't let me go back since Tim got arrested twice." She shrugged.

"I texted because I was worried about you after Dr. Brinkman died," I said.

"I know, terrible, right? I mean I have no idea why Tim would kill anyone, but to suddenly find out he's a serial killer is super creepy."

"Oh, I don't think Tim did it," I said.

Chelsea put her hand on my wrist in a sign not to go down that path. "What about your job with Dr. Brinkman? His death must have put you out of work—and your dream job too."

"I still have my new opportunity," she said and sipped her drink again. "Dr. Brinkman's company is employee owned. He wanted everyone to be invested in the company. I heard we're going to call it the Dr. Brinkman Method of Soul Truth."

"Wow," I said. "That's—"

"Great, right?" Mandy interrupted. "It means his good message will go on and on."

"As long as the money lasts," Chelsea said as she took a swallow of her latte.

"Oh, there's no worry there. We're a thirty-million-dollar company and climbing." Mandy leaned forward. "Followers just hand their money over to learn more about Dr. Brinkman's method."

"Sounds . . . strange." I wiggled in my seat.

"If you get it, you get it," Mandy said smugly. "It's clear you don't."

"I'm glad you're going to be okay," I said. "Still it's terrible about Dr. Brinkman. Do you know who might have wanted him dead?"

"Well, the police are saying Tim did it, silly."

"Right," I said.

"Do you know why Tim would have killed Dr. Brinkman?"

"I think it's because he was jealous of Dr. Brinkman taking all my time. It's why I'm thinking of breaking up with Tim. I can't have that kind of negativity in my life. I'm just waiting for the right time. Like if he gets out of jail. Break-ups are hard, you know?"

"Probably for the best," Chelsea said. "Do you think anyone else didn't like Dr. Brinkman?"

"Oh no, everyone loved him . . . well, everyone who got him." She gave me a side eye.

"Were there a lot of people like me?" I asked.

"Not many," she said. "Outliers are about twenty in every one hundred, and then we try the message three times before we don't include them in it. That's why I was paying special attention to you. You see, if I got an outlier into the fold, I would have gotten promoted to top producer. But"—she shrugged—"after finding Dr. Brinkman dead, we're pretty sure you won't come for a third lecture."

"I heard that Dr. Brinkman wasn't supposed to be there last night," I said.

"Who told you that?"

"We know that he was training other guys to give the talk," Chelsea said. "People like Bruce Warrington and Harvey Winkle."

I studied Mandy closely to see how she reacted to Harvey's name.

"Oh," Mandy said. I think she blinked a couple of times. "Well, yes, Dr. Brinkman thought we could better serve the global community if there were others who could give the speeches. But I thought Dr. Brinkman was scheduled to talk last night. It's why I wanted you to go backstage and meet him. I wouldn't have taken you back if I had known one of the others was speaking in his stead."

"And he didn't usually come when someone else gave the lecture, so people wouldn't get confused," Chelsea surmised.

"Exactly," Mandy said. "It's why I didn't take you backstage after the first lecture."

"So maybe it's not that I'm an outlier," I said. "Maybe it's because I never actually met the real Dr. Brinkman."

"That was my argument," Mandy said. "They told me if you didn't get it after two lectures, then I was to bring you to Dr. Brinkman's talk next."

"Did Dr. Brinkman or anyone in the group get angry emails? Bad reviews? I mean, it's a social world."

"Oh yes, there are a few people who are unhappy, but we return their money right away. It's a serious one hundred percent happiness quota. We can't afford bad press of any kind."

"What do you do if they are unhappy?" I asked.

"Well, Dr. Brinkman would bring them in himself and speak to them for an hour-long session. If they were still unhappy, he would give them their money and walk them out of the building."

"How many unhappy people actually came back to the fold after he spoke to them?" Chelsea asked.

"Most," Mandy said. "At least that's what I heard. Dr. Brinkman is very persuasive."

"Was," I said.

"Poor man," Mandy said.

"You spent a lot of time out on Tim's winery before all this happened, didn't you?" Chelsea said.

"Oh yes, I lived with Tim, and then I helped in the tasting barn. He can produce a gorgeous wine, very full bodied and tasting of berries and chocolate." She smiled dreamily, placed her elbows on the table, and rested her chin in her hands. "I loved doing wine tastings. There was no money in it, but I did it for the people and the wine, of course."

"Not for Tim?" I asked.

"I supposed at first I did it for Tim, but he was more impressed with his wine than with anything I did."

"Did you ever help with the winery?" I asked. "Like cleaning out the barns or turning the must or picking grapes?"

"Oh gosh, no," she said and waved her fingers. "That kind of work would damage my manicure."

"Did your boss go out to Tim's place on a regular basis?" Chelsea asked.

"What? My boss? Dr. Brinkman? No, no," she said and shook her head.

"No, not Dr. Brinkman," Chelsea said. "The realtor, Jeffery Hoag."

"Oh, Jeffery, I had no idea that he had come out to Tim's. I mean, I know he was looking at property out in the area, but as far as I know, he didn't have any intention of meeting with Tim." She shook her head. "Last I knew, they weren't speaking to each other."

"You said Jeffery was looking at property in the area. Do you know why?"

"I think he was trying to put together new zoning or something. Whatever it was, I think it had to do with politics. I'm not so much into that."

"What do you mean?" I asked with a tip of my head.

"Well, you see, Paul Sutter ran for the senate, right? So, he wanted the wineries to back his campaign. Some of them chose not to, and, well, he won. So the first thing he did was pull some strings and have the zoning commission take a hard look at the wineries that didn't back him."

"That's terrible."

"I know, right? Tim told them where they could put their request for political backing. Jeffery told me that was why Tim's was the second winery on the list to be reviewed."

"What was the first winery?"

"Alan Clove's place," she said. "Alan was quoted in a story that exposed Paul Sutter as a misguided entrepreneur."

"What does that mean?"

"It means he invested in some pretty shady things a few years back. According to Tim, Senator Sutter tried to cover up that fact, but Alan never liked Sutter. Alan made it his mission to expose the truth."

"So Alan tried to tank the race and instead got caught in a revenge plot," Chelsea said. "That's a pretty interesting story."

Mandy shrugged. "Not as interesting as what Dr. Brinkman said about Paul."

That caught my attention. "What did Dr. Brinkman say?"

"He said that the Senator was an outlier and not to be trusted."

"Because he didn't understand the message?" Chelsea said. "Or did he do something else?"

"Personally, I think it was more than the Senator not understanding the message. Dr. Brinkman didn't like the man. I don't really know why. Dr. Brinkman loves all people."

"Maybe we should look into the reason why," I said to Chelsea. "There might be a real motive there."

Chelsea nodded and took notes. "Politics are crazy. Maybe Dr. Brinkman was involved in the senate race somehow."

"Maybe Senator Sutter has more enemies than friends."

Chapter 19

Mandy had to meet her mom at the yoga studio, and I left Chelsea to do some digging into Senator Sutter. I was to meet Aunt Jemma at La Galleria to check on Holly. Neither one of us had seen her since the good doctor's death, and I had a feeling she might need an intervention. She had gotten attached pretty quickly.

"Taylor!" Aunt Jemma called my name. My sweet aunt was wearing a turquoise-blue caftan and a white turban. She smothered me in a hug. "I know we live on the same winery, but I feel as if I haven't seen you for days."

"It's been a busy day," I said. "Thanks for meeting me here."

"Of course. I understand that Holly might need some help?"

"I haven't seen her since the murder, and she was so into Dr. Brinkman. I'm afraid she might be in mourning or something."

"She seemed a bit shocked last night, but not enough to jump off a cliff," Aunt Jemma teased me. "I'm sure she's just fine."

"She's my best friend. Let's make sure, okay?"

"Of course. I wanted to talk to Holly's boss, Miss Finglestein. I have a friend coming up from San Diego. She paints the most vibrant watercolors. All flowers, and they are so sexy. It would be great if I could get her a showing."

"Who is your friend? Have I met her?"

"It's Blake Kastor. I'm not sure you've met her. She has the warmest laugh. I've known her for years. We went to Berkeley together. I married my dear Anthony and came to Sonoma while she met her Michael and moved to San Diego." Aunt Jemma shook her head. "We were so ambitious. We were going to change the world."

"You have changed the world," I said with a squeeze. "Perhaps not as grandly as you had hoped, but you changed *my* world."

"You're sweet, dear."

I opened the door, and the soft scent of flowers rushed out. The art gallery was cool, the white walls and skylight windows highlighted the latest collection of California art. This week was pop art with bright colors and whimsical shapes.

"Welcome, my dear," Miss Finglestein called as she came around the corner. Holly's boss was in her nineties. She was skinny and dressed like an Audrey Hepburn character. She had short, gray hair, and wore large, round glasses. Today she had on a pair of capris and a pale blue sweater set. "Jemma, it's been a few weeks."

"I'm sorry—I've been busy with harvest and then blending the right grapes for this year's wines." They kissed each other on both cheeks in a dramatic European fashion.

"Is Holly around?" I asked.

"Yes, of course—she's in the back."

"Thanks. You two catch up. I'll be right back." I walked through the paintings to the tiny door in the back and opened it. The soothing music faded as I walked into a room with tall industrial ceiling and tables with stacks of shelves and wooden crates. "Holly?" I called.

She popped her head out from behind a shelf. "Taylor, what brings you here?"

"I was checking on you," I said. "Are you okay? We didn't get a chance to talk last night, and I hadn't heard from you." I pulled out my phone and wiggled it to emphasize that she was usually a mere text away.

"Oh yes, I'm fine," Holly said and stepped out into the aisle. "I'm sorry. I dropped my phone last night, and it hasn't been working well. I planned to take it to the store later today."

"I'm glad you're okay. I was worried after yesterday night. I know you really were into Dr. Brinkman."

She hugged her waist. Today Holly wore over-the-knee boots and a floaty dress with peekaboo sleeves. "That was terrible, wasn't it? I mean, we bought tickets, thinking we were listening to the actual Dr. Brinkman speak, and here it turns out it was not Dr. Brinkman at all."

"I know—that was odd," I said and narrowed my eyes. "How did you know about the body double? I thought Dr. Brinkman's group was keeping that a secret."

"It's on the website," she said.

"Seriously?"

"Yes. I checked the website at noon today to see if they had any information on when the memorial would be, and there was an announcement about the guys trained in the Brinkman Method. I mean, it's nice that they are going to continue his great work, but I thought we were listening to the real deal. It turns out Dr. Brinkman hasn't lectured in over a year."

"I'm sorry you're disappointed."

"I'm not the only one. It's causing quite the uproar."

"I imagine a lot of people are feeling duped right about now."

"What about Mandy?" Holly asked. "Did she know?"

"She did. And I'm pretty sure it wasn't Dr. Brinkman I saw Mandy kissing."

"Oh, you think she's sneaking around with one of the doubles?"

"I didn't have the guts to come out and ask her," I said and frowned. "I wanted to see if she knew anything about who might have wanted the doctor dead. If I'd accused her of cheating on Tim, she might not have talked to me."

"Did she know anything?"

"Just about the doubles, but I guess everyone knows about them now. They arrested Tim for Dr. Brinkman's death."

"I heard," Holly said. "You don't think he did it?"

"I really don't. I mean anyone could have found out about the doubles and been angry enough to kill Dr. Brinkman. Tim is not a murderer."

"You talked to Mandy, right?"

"Yes, she had some interesting things to say about Senator Paul Sutter. It seems he might have had a connection to both Jeffery and Dr. Brinkman. Chelsea is looking into the Senator now."

"It's all a big mess," Holly said. "And then my phone gets messed up, and to top it all off the water in my apartment has been turned off."

"What? Why?"

"There was a water-main break, and they cut the water for the next day while they fix it."

"That does it: you're coming home with me." I took her hand

and pulled her out of the back room and over to Aunt Jemma. "We need another girls' night, don't we, Aunt Jemma?"

"Oh, I'll bring the wine," Aunt Jemma said. Her pale blue eyes twinkled.

"I know," Holly said, brightening. "Let's have a séance and see if we can't contact Dr. Brinkman. Wouldn't it be cool if he could tell us who killed him? Or why?" Her eyes widened with delight. "Can you schedule your psychic to come and help us with the reading?"

"It would be last minute," Aunt Jemma mused and tapped her chin. "But it would be worth it if we can gain insights and help Tim."

"I'm in," I said and pulled out my phone. "Can I invite Chelsea?"

"Of course," Aunt Jemma said. "The more, the merrier. We can make a huge salad and grill steaks. I love a girls' night out." She rubbed her hands together. "Now, let me see if I can't get a hold of my psychic friend, Sarah. Frankly, it would be good for her to come out to the winery, if for no other reason than to do a general cleansing. Things have been a bit dark lately."

"This is great," I said, "but keep in mind we can't stay up too late. I have a tour in the morning."

"Where are you touring now?" Holly asked as she gathered up her things and waved goodbye to Miss Finglestein.

"I've got a group of ladies from New Jersey who are out for a weekend of wining and dining. I called The Timbers and spoke to Jeremy."

"Isn't he a doll?" Holly said with a twinkle in her eye.

"Yes, I worked out a deal with him for my tour groups and

got rooms at The Timbers. He said they were prepping for the grand opening and could use a few dry runs with having guests. The restaurant wasn't quite ready, but the ladies got a deal for being test subjects. They want a full day of Sonoma hospitality. I'm going to take them on a short hike and then off to the sculpture gardens, three wineries, and a meal in town at the best restaurant."

"Fancy," Holly said. "Are you sure they want to tour around in your VW van?"

I laughed. "Yes, they want the full experience, from funky to outdoors to fine dining."

"And you are the perfect woman to give them the experience," Aunt Jemma said. "The only thing missing is a séance."

"I think one night full of ghosts is good enough."

"I'll go get my overnight case and meet you back at the winery," Holly said. "Thank you both for taking such good care of me." She gave Aunt Jemma a squeeze and blew her air kisses. Then she hugged me and hurried down the street to her apartment building.

"I'm going to see what I have to do to bribe Sarah into coming out for the séance,' Aunt Jemma said. "I'll meet you at home."

"I'll see you in a bit." I texted Chelsea as I crossed the road and looked up when a car honked. "Sorry!"

"You should be more careful," Bruce said from behind the wheel of his black Toyota. "Outliers," he shouted and drove off.

My phone vibrated, and I waited until I was safely inside my car to check it.

I'll be happy to come, Chelsea texted. I have some interesting information on the Senator.

Anything we can use to save Tim? I texted back.

Not sure. We'll talk soon, she responded.

I studied the sleepy streets of Sonoma. "A senator, a guru, and a realtor walk into a bar . . ." I muttered. "There's a joke in there somewhere." I started up the van and pulled out into the road. Whatever the joke was, I don't think Tim was laughing.

Chapter 20

"Sarah will be here in an hour," Aunt Jemma said and handed me a glass of zinfandel.

I was out on the patio, grilling fish. Holly had arrived a few minutes earlier, and I put her to work making the fresh salad. "Do you still have the table set up in the den?"

Millie barked as if to answer my question. She ran around the patio chasing whatever caught her attention. Clemmie sat on the cushion of the outdoor settee and licked her paws. She had her eyes on my salmon, and I knew I'd slip her a morsel or two once it was cooked. It was a ritual. We both pretended that it wouldn't happen and then that it didn't happen. I loved my pets in all their silliness.

For all Aunt Jemma complained of Clemmie, I'd seen her sneak the cat a bit of chicken on occasion. So the curmudgeonry about my cat was all for show.

"Yes, everything is still set up in the den," Aunt Jemma said. "I did a sage smudge to cleanse it of any residual energy from the last séance."

"You mean your fake-out," I teased.

"It wasn't fake to the group," Aunt Jemma said airily, and

picked Clemmie up and placed her on the ground. Then my aunt draped herself across the settee and basked in the fading light of a cool California fall day. She sipped her wine. "I do my research, and Sarah has taught me a thing or two."

"She won't be playing tricks with us tonight, will she?" I asked, waving the metal spatula around. "I'm serious about figuring out how to get Tim out of jail and keep him out."

"You are a good friend," Aunt Jemma said.

"Tim's not a bad man."

"I heard you questioned Mandy today."

"I asked her a few questions. But nothing hardball," I said. "I want her to think I'm on her side. That way she might confide in me."

"They say you catch more flies with honey than you do with vinegar. It's something more people should understand. The world would be a better place."

"I've got salad," Holly said as she came out onto the patio, carrying a large wooden bowl full of colorful fresh veggies. Holly's salads were to die for. I asked her once to teach me how to make them. She said you simple reproduce the rainbow. Start with deep green things like spinach and kale, and then add romaine and cucumbers, green peppers and green onions. Then you go to red and chop in radishes, red peppers, and red onion (if you didn't put in scallions). Next is orange peppers and then yellow peppers. White was mushrooms, and then you finished with black olives. Literally as many colors of the rainbow as you could place in a single bowl. Then she tossed all of that and drizzled it with red wine vinegar and olive oil.

All I could say was "Yum!"

Chelsea came walking through the living room and out

to the patio. "Hello! I rang the bell, but no one answered, so I came in."

"Millie didn't even bark," I said, and I looked down at the puppy, who was bouncing around Chelsea's legs. "Some guard dog you are."

"You really shouldn't leave your door unlocked," Chelsea said. "Not with a killer on the loose."

"I suppose you are right, dear," Aunt Jemma said. "We do have people coming in for our tasting hours. We should lock the house doors."

"Grab a plate—the salmon and salad is ready," I said. "Aunt Jemma is pouring the wine."

We all filled our plates, then sat around the brick fireplace and ate while we watched the fire pop and snap in the hearth. "Okay," I said as I sipped wine, "Chelsea what did you find out about the Senator? Is he as evil as Mandy made him out to be?"

"It's true that Senator Sutter had the zoning commission looking at the wineries around Tim. But I can't connect that to who supported his campaign. It looks like he had some real estate thing going on, so we really can't say he was targeting only certain wineries."

"Hmm," I said. "Aunt Jemma, did you get any zoning commission inquiries?"

"Oh, heavens, not recently," she said. "In fact I was surprised that the commission was looking at any property in the county. We're pretty traditional here. Old families and old wineries. It's rare that the zoning commission does anything but rezone areas for highways and such. Wait—they aren't considering a highway, are they?"

"No highway improvements that I could tell," Chelsea

reassured her. "I do think Senator Sutter is up to something, but not murder."

"What about Senator Sutter's feud with Dr. Brinkman? Did you find out anything there?" I asked.

"The only thing I found was that Dr. Brinkman petitioned to have some land zoned for multiple housing. The Senator turned him down. There is a document that said the Senator did not want communes in his district."

"I don't think the guru was going to have a commune," I said doubtfully.

"Oh, he was trying to raise money to start a retreat house," Holly said. "It's in the brochure I got from Mandy."

"I don't see why the Senator would protest a retreat house," Aunt Jemma said. "It sounds like a nice thing. I bet it would bring in tourists from around the country."

"The brochure said it would bring in people from around the world," Holly said.

"But the Senator stalled the permits," Chelsea said. "Something about water rights on the property."

"What did Dr. Brinkman do about it? Do you know? Did he threaten him or something?"

"There's no record of any threats," Chelsea said.

"We should check Dr. Brinkman's social media pages," Holly said. She grabbed her phone. "I think they are still up. We can't see private messages, but we might see comments."

"That's a good idea," I pulled up my phone and checked for Dr. Brinkman. The guru had a lot of social media pages. It was clear he was social media savvy.

"I didn't see anything on his main page," Chelsea said.

"You know, girls, you can simply call people and ask them," Aunt Jemma said. "I know it's old-fashioned, but it does work."

"Who could we call?" I asked.

"I know Elsa Smith in the permits department for the county. I also know Mary Persimmon, the realtor who handles those kinds of properties. Then there's Sarah."

"The psychic?" Holly said and drew her eyebrows together in confusion.

"Yes, the psychic," Aunt Jemma said. "Sarah is really plugged into the community. She knows everything that's going on. People tend to confide in her, you know."

"Of course," I said and leaned back. "You didn't invite her here just for a reading."

Aunt Jemma smiled.

"Well, let me get you some more wine," I said and stood. "You deserve it." I took my plate and the other empties and brought them into the kitchen. Then I grabbed a new bottle of wine. I glanced outside and saw that a car had pulled up. Sarah got out. You would think a psychic would dress like Aunt Jemma, all robes and turbans and flowing clothes. Not Sarah. She dressed in a simple black sheath dress and sandals. Her black hair was pin straight and flowed in a curtain to the middle of her back. Her olive skin was flawless, and her brown eyes filled with empathy and expression.

I opened the door before she could knock. "Hi, Sarah," I said. "Come on in. Everyone's out on the patio. I grilled some salmon, and there's one of Holly's fantastic salads, if you're hungry."

"Hi, Taylor—I'm good," she said. "But a glass of wine would be nice."

"Perfect. Go on out and I'll get you a glass."

Sarah was in her early forties but looked ten years younger. She always made me feel somehow not quite up to snuff.

I grabbed a glass and went out to the patio. Sarah had pulled up a chair next to Aunt Jemma and was laughing with the girls. I handed her a glass and then uncorked the bottle and poured wine for everyone. "Cheers."

"Cheers," everyone said before sipping.

"That is wonderful," Sarah said and settled back. "Now, I understand you all have questions. Do you want a séance, or can we simply talk over wine?"

"Oh, I was hoping for a séance," Holly said. "I love all the mystery and such. I mean, you can't just talk to dead people without the whole ceremony, can you?"

"Of course you can," Sarah said. "The whole dark room and table and hands touching is to help people get in the right mood to receive messages. If I simply walked up to someone on the street and said your grandmother is worried that you spend too much time alone, the person would think I was a kook. But if they come to you, and you light a candle and close your eyes and ask for their grandmother to come, well, then they are completely ready to receive the message."

"Oh," Holly said, her eyes wide. "So can you talk to my grandmother?"

"What would you like me to say to her?"

"I guess I would like to know that she's okay and happy."

"She says she is," Sarah said. "She also says she's disappointed with your brother's recent girlfriend."

"Oh, right, Valerie is not all that into Ethan," Holly said. "We all told him he should be with someone who really cares about him. But he's smitten." She paused. "Wait—we just met. You wouldn't know that unless . . ."

"I was talking to your grandmother?" Sarah asked gently.

"Okay, I'm sold," Holly said.

"We're looking into the recent murders," I said. "Do you know anything about them?"

"Which ones?" Sarah asked. "Sadly, a lot of murder victims come around looking for help."

"Oh," Holly said, "that's terrible."

Sarah shrugged and sipped her wine. "I have to tell some of them I can't help them. So they go find someone else who can hear them."

"It must be crazy with all those people in your head," Chelsea said.

Sarah turned to her. "It's sort of like sitting in a crowd all the time."

"Like a concert?" Holly asked.

"Exactly," Sarah said. "You learn to shift information to what's relevant and let the rest go as noise."

"We're interested in who killed Jeffery Hoag on my friend Tim's winery," I said.

"We want to know if there is a connection between Jeffery's death with the recent death of Dr. Brinkman," Chelsea said.

Sarah closed her eyes. "I'm not getting anything from a Jeffery. Wait . . . he drowned?"

"I'm not sure if he drowned," I said, "but he was found floating in a vat of wine must."

"Ah," Sarah said, "he thinks he's in darkness, and that has him confused."

"Does he know how he got there?" I asked and leaned forward.

Sarah frowned. "No, he's not sure where he is . . . I told him he was found floating in a vat."

We all sat in silence and waited on her next words.

She kept her eyes closed as if concentrating on a faraway sound. "I asked him what he last remembers. He said he pulled up to the wine-tasting building. There was a woman there."

"What did she look like?" I asked.

"Blond and pretty," Sarah said. "But there was also a man. The two were making out on the bar. He thought they were tasters, but then he realized the woman was . . . Amanda?"

"Tim's Mandy?" I asked. "It had to be her. Was she working that day? Did Jeffery see her kissing Dr. Brinkman?"

She paused. "Paper. He said he liked the old-fashioned paper and pencil because he was often in places where there was little cell service, and his notebook and pen were always in his pocket."

"Wait, what does that have to do with anything?" I asked.

Sarah shrugged. "It must mean something to him."

"They didn't find a notebook on him," Chelsea said.

We looked at her, and she shrugged. "I read the police report."

"There's a report?" I asked.

"Sure," Chelsea said. "The police have to keep track of evidence."

"He had to have seen Mandy kissing someone who was not Tim," I said.

"But the man could have been Tim. That wasn't ruled out," Aunt Jemma said.

"Why would it matter if Tim was making out with his live-in girlfriend?" Holly asked.

"Unless it wasn't Tim," Chelsea and I said at the same time.

"So it could have been someone else?" Holly said. "Someone like . . . who?"

"Harvey Winkle," I said. "We think that's the guy who she was making out with at the lecture. The one I thought was Dr. Brinkman, but I only saw him from behind."

"Now I'm confused," Holly said. "Are you saying that Mandy was possibly seeing another man while living with Tim?"

"It could be that Jeffery Hoag stumbled onto something he wasn't supposed to see," I said.

"But there's no way Mandy could have killed that man and dumped him in the vat. He was at least twice her size," Holly said. "I work out with weights, and there's no way I could lift a dead man over my head and put him in the vat."

"Maybe Harvey Winkle did it," Chelsea said. "I haven't done a lot of research into the man."

"It seems odd that Jeffery's car was never found," I said. "Sarah, you said he drove up to the winery, right?"

"Yes," she said. "He said he drove a four-door sedan . . . beige. He seems like a very . . . careful person. Everything in its place. The car keys were in his pocket."

"No keys were ever found," Chelsea said.

"Well, he certainly had keys," Sarah said. "Find the car and the notebook, and you will find your killer."

Chapter 21

"Do you think Sarah was right?" Holly asked as we walked out to our cars the next morning.

"She did seem to have some interesting insights," Chelsea said. "I'm going to check on this Harvey Winkle."

"I've got a full day of tour guiding," I said, "or I'd help."

"I know a guy who lives down by Tim," Holly said. "I'm going to ask him if he knows the best place to stash a car."

"Seems like they would have looked for it," I said as I unlocked the van. "Chelsea, did they do a search by helicopter? For all we know, the car could be sitting out in the middle of a nearby field."

"I'll check," Chelsea said. "But first I have to go into my office. They need a story by this afternoon."

"What are you going to write about?" Holly asked.

"I'm going to pitch the story of the Senator and the wineries and upcoming rezoning. I've got a nice start to it. I wouldn't mind digging deeper into the new senator."

"Holly, do you know if they have water restored to your apartment yet?"

"I got a text that it's still out," she said as she got into her car. "I'll be back tonight if it doesn't get fixed. I hope that's okay."

"As long as you make a salad like you did last night, I think it will be just fine."

Aunt Jemma came out as I got into my van. I started it up and rolled down the window.

"Where are you off to?" I asked.

"I have a full day, sweetie," she said. "There's a meeting with the coffee club this morning, lunch with the seniors at the center, and then an afternoon meeting with the wine appellation. I've got Julio working today as it's time to strain the wine and put it into the fermentation glass."

"Don't you want to be here to supervise that step?"

"No," she said. "Julio is my winemaker. I trust him to do a good job. He wants to buy up the nearby wineries, and that means his wine has to be premium to continue to grow his business. He won't risk his future."

"Sounds like you picked the right man for the job. Will you be home for dinner?"

"Of course," she said. "Bring your girlfriends back. I like having people in the house."

"I will if they want to come." I rolled up my window, waved goodbye, and headed to town. I was meeting my group at The Timbers.

This particular tour group was made up of five women who had flown in from St. Louis to get the full Sonoma experience. Mae Bramble was the leader of the group and had coordinated everything from the hotel to my tour, to the flights.

"Hi ,Mae," I said as the ladies walked out of the hotel. They were dressed for a causal tour in sundresses, sunglasses, and walking shoes. This morning's hike would be more of a stroll. They were holding mimosas. I knew it was going to be an interesting day.

"Welcome, ladies, to Sonoma. I see you have drinks already."

"This wonderful tour lady was giving away mimosas this morning. We couldn't resist," the first woman said. She had short blond hair and blue eyes. Her silk tee shirt had a palm tree on it that was the same color as her capris.

"Tour lady?" I asked.

"Oh, yes, I think her name was Bridget something or other," Mae said. "She had a logo hat with a cute pink bus on it. Do you know her?"

Quirky Tours . . .

"Yes," I said slowly and tried to smile. "Did she say why she was here giving out mimosas?"

"Something about working with the resort owner to bring Quirky Sonoma Tours to life," Mae said. She shrugged. "Whatever, I'm only in it for the drinks. We already have our tour guide. Right, ladies?"

"Right," they answered.

"Let us introduce ourselves properly. I'm Helen," a smiling woman with a strawberry-blond bob lifted her drink. She had brown eyes and freckles. "And this is Josie in the palm tree shirt, and this is Karen and Rachel."

"Hi, ladies," I said and tried to regroup as best I could. "Welcome to Sonoma and Off the Beaten Path tours. We have a full day ahead of us. Let's load up the van and get started."

I was helping the ladies onboard when my phone rang. "This is Taylor," I said when I didn't recognize the number.

"Taylor O'Brian?"

"Yes."

"I have your Aunt Jemma."

"I'm sorry, what?"

"I have your Aunt Jemma."

"Is she all right?" I asked as a spike of fear went down my spine.

"For the moment," the man's voice said.

"What do you mean?"

"You have one hour." He hung up.

I stared at my phone, not knowing what he meant or what to do.

Josie stuck her head outside the van. "Is everything all right?"

"I'm not sure," I said. "I need to make a phone call."

"Can we help?" Rachel asked behind her.

"Oh, I'm sure I'll be fine. It will only be a moment." I put on a brave face. The last thing I needed was to lose my tour to Bridget. "If you want, I'll have the hotel bring out another round of mimosas."

"Don't worry, honey," Karen said. "I'll get it. I need to use the little girl's room anyway. Better to be safe than sorry, I always say."

The ladies laughed and piled out of the van. I stepped to the side of the hotel and called Aunt Jemma. She didn't pick up. Instead, I got her voicemail. I tried three times, and not once did she answer, and each time my worry deepened. Where had she said she was going? To the coffee club. They met at The Beanery. I gathered up the ladies once more and got them settled in the van.

"If you don't mind, I'm going to make a quick stop at the local coffee shop," I said. "The Beanery is a few blocks up and quite popular with the locals. I suggest the Americano after a couple of mimosas. Can I get you all one? Cream and sugar?" I parked the van, took their orders, and hurried to the shop. The sound of the bells jangled as the door closed behind me.

"Hey, Beau," I said to the barista.

"Taylor, what can I do for you?" Beau was a skinny guy with long, curly blond hair and green eyes. He was about six or eight years younger than me and worked the morning coffee shift on a regular basis. In the afternoon, he played his guitar on the corner of Main Street for the tourists. He was quite good.

"I need these six drinks to go," I said as I looked around for Aunt Jemma and her group. "And cream and sugars, sweeteners, and such."

"Got it," he said and studied my list. "Is this for a tour group?"

"Yes," I said. "They want the full local experience. Listen, I thought Aunt Jemma's coffee group was meeting here this morning."

"Oh, Elise and Sarah came in. They waited about thirty minutes, but when your aunt didn't show up, they left."

"Aunt Jemma didn't show up? Not even after?"

"No," Beau said as he made the coffees. "The ladies were disappointed."

"I'll call Sarah." I dialed the psychic's number. She picked up immediately.

"What's wrong?"

"Hi, Sarah," I said. "I'm looking for Aunt Jemma."

"She didn't show for coffee club," Sarah said. "I found that odd since she said she would after our meeting last night."

"That's the thing," I said and winced. "When she left this morning, she said she was going straight to the coffee club. I tried to call her, but she isn't picking up."

"I think something's wrong," Sarah said. "I've tried contacting her too, but she didn't answer. Elise went to the library to see if she went there for a meeting with the garden club."

"Sarah."

"Yes, dear?"

"I got a strange phone call from a man a few minutes ago. He said he had my Aunt Jemma. What does that mean?"

"Oh my goodness, she's been kidnapped," Sarah gasped with conviction, and I felt a cold chill in my veins. "So you have his number?"

"Yes," I said. "He called my cell phone."

"Did he say what he wanted?"

"No. He didn't demand anything." I tried to think about the conversation. "He didn't ask for anything. Are you sure she was kidnapped?"

"You have to call the police," Sarah said. "This is bad. Very bad."

"I'll trust your judgment. I'm going to hang up now."

"Wait!"

"What?"

"I need to be with you. There might be something I can help with."

"I've got a tour group. The ladies are kind, but I'm not sure what will happen if I back out of the tour."

"Oh goodness, where are you? The least I can do is entertain your group while you get this figured out."

"I'm at The Beanery," I said. "I was looking for you."

"Of course you were. I'm a few blocks away. Don't go anywhere."

She hung up, and I turned to see Beau putting the drinks in cardboard drink trays. "Is everything all right?"

"I'm not sure," I said. "You're the second person to ask me that this morning." I paid for the drinks.

"These are all marked with names from your list," he said.

The extra cup has cream in it, and the smallest cup is filled with packets of sugar, raw sugar, and other sweeteners."

"Thanks, Beau," I said and picked up the drinks.

"Do you want some help with the door?" he asked.

"Yes, thanks." He opened the door, and we both had a full view of the van. The ladies were snapping pictures of Main Street and generally laughing and talking and having fun. I was glad. They'd paid for a tour, not my personal problems, no matter how unusual.

I opened the door and held out the coffee trays. "Thank you for your patience, ladies," I said. "There's been a bit of trouble in my personal life."

"Oh no—I thought maybe something was up," Josie said. "What can we do to help?" She distributed the coffee cups.

"I've called in a friend who is going to take over the tour," I said. "You will love her. She is California through and through. Plus, she's a psychic. So you can ask her anything, and she can steer you in the right direction."

"Oh," Karen said, "I've always wanted to meet a psychic. Can she talk to dead people?"

"Yes," I said. I glanced down the street to see Sarah power-walking my way. "There she is."

"I came as fast as I could," Sarah said and stopped to give me a quick hug. "What's on the agenda?"

"Well, I was going to take them to the botanical gardens for an hour walk, but no one is really dressed for hiking . . ."

"No problem," she said and stuck her head into the van. "Hello, ladies, I'm Sarah. How would you like to tour the Schultz Museum? They have all the Peanuts characters."

"Oh, that would be wonderful!" Josie said.

"You read my mind," Karen said.

Sarah looked at me.

I shrugged. "I told them your profession."

"No problem, I can use the endorsement. I see the keys are in the ignition. I've got this—go figure out how to save Jemma."

"Thank you." I hugged her. "Goodbye, ladies. I'm leaving you in good hands."

"Bye, dear," they said.

Sarah climbed into the driver's seat and drove off. I grabbed my phone and redialed the number of the caller.

"What took so long?" the male voice asked.

"I had to know that Aunt Jemma was truly missing," I said and walked with purpose toward the sheriff's office. "I want to speak to her."

"You are in no position to make demands," the voice said.

"What do you want?"

"I want you and your friends to stop digging into Dr. Brinkman's death."

"Why?"

"Let's just say I have a vested interest in seeing that the police do the job."

"I want to speak to my aunt," I said. "She has a heart condition. I need to know she is all right."

"We've made her comfortable," the man said. "I suspect we will need to keep her for a while to ensure you aren't investigating any further."

"I want you to put her on this phone right now," I said as I stormed toward the station. I was going to get Sheriff Hennessey to trace the call and get this guy. "If you so much as harm a hair on her head—"

He hung up on me. I felt anger boil inside me as I redialed the number.

"I said no cops." He hung up again.

Frustrated, I stopped in front of La Galleria and studied the roads. There didn't appear to be anyone watching me or even following me. I dialed the number again. "I haven't called the cops." Which wasn't a lie. "If you want money, it's going to take me some time to raise anything substantial."

"Taylor?" Aunt Jemma sounded scared.

"Aunt Jemma, are you all right? What happened? How did they get you? What can I do?"

"I'm fine," she said in a shaky voice that told me she was far from fine. "Be careful."

"He said he would keep you for a while. I can't have that—"

"I can't have you investigating," the man said again. "I want you to call your friend the reporter and tell her to stop investigating. Then I want you to go home and wait for further instructions."

"I can't tell Chelsea not to investigate."

"You can and you will if you want to see your aunt again."

Then all I could hear was the dial tone.

Chapter 22

I might have said something dark under my breath as I stared at my phone. I called Chelsea.

"What's up?" she asked in a cheerful voice.

"Please tell me you haven't pitched any stories about Dr. Brinkman's death yet."

"I might have. Why?"

"They've got Aunt Jemma."

"Who? Why?"

"I don't know who," I said. "All I've got is a phone number and a man's voice." I started to shake from head to toe, so I found a bench and sat down.

"Do they want money? Can you get money?"

"He says he wants us to stop investigating Dr. Brinkman's murder."

"That's it?"

"Yes. Weird, right? He didn't ask for ransom. Does that mean he's keeping Aunt Jemma? I mean, he has to know that as soon as we get her back, we're going to be looking into this. Do you think he will ask for money? I don't have any . . ."

"Have you called Sheriff Hennessey?"

"No," I said. "I was on my way over to the police station when the guy called and said no cops. I don't know how he knew I was going that way, but he seemed to know."

"They must be watching you."

"I don't see anything," I said and looked around again. "Listen, can you meet me?"

"Where?"

"I don't know . . ." I glanced around. "How about La Galleria?"

"I can be there in forty minutes."

"Great." I hung up and walked over to the art gallery. It wasn't open yet. I glanced at the time. It was only nine forty-five. It felt like it had been the longest day of my life. I texted Holly:

Where are you?

She texted back immediately. *I stopped in to Safeway. Why?*

I'm at the gallery, I texted. *Aunt Jemma has been kidnapped.*

OMG! What can I do?

Can you meet me at your work? I want us to stick together.

On my way.

A sheriff's patrol car went by, and I felt a fission of panic like electricity down my back. All I could think was, "Don't stop! Don't stop!" I didn't want to make things worse for Aunt Jemma. The car slowed and turned down the next street. I took a deep breath.

This was nuts. I called the number again. This time there was no answer. I didn't know what to do. I guessed there wasn't anything I could do but wait.

"Taylor."

I looked toward the sound of my name and saw Sheriff

Hennessey standing in the alleyway out of the line of sight of the street. "Go away!" I said in a stage whisper.

"Taylor." He only said my name, but there was a wealth of meaning in it.

Frowning, I looked around and then walked to the alley. "I'm not supposed to talk to the police."

"The gallery's back door is open. Go in, and someone will meet you inside."

"How did you know?"

"Chelsea," he said. "Now go inside. We're here to help."

His tone was no-nonsense. I pulled my sweater around me and walked through the alley and to the back of the gallery. Trying the door, I discovered he was right. It was open. "Hello?" I called.

"Come in, dear," Miss Finglestein said. She sat at one of the tables and unboxed a canvas. "Chelsea called Sheriff Hennessey. He called me and asked me to open the back door."

"I think the kidnappers are watching. They'll see him come in," I said. "I don't want to do anything to jeopardize Aunt Jemma's life."

"It's going to be okay," she said and came over and smothered me in a Chanel-scented hug.

"Is it?" I asked. "They aren't asking for a ransom. What does that mean? Will they kill her or keep her for months? How can I deal with that?"

"The front is clear," Deputy Bloomberg said as he walked through the door. "Hi, Taylor."

"Oh," I said as I realized what had happened. "Of course. You came in while I was out front."

"As far as we can tell, no one's following you," he said.

Holly rushed in through the back door. "Taylor, are you all right?"

"Yes—no." I shook my head. "Sort of."

"Deputy Bloomberg?" Holly said as she turned to me. "Taylor, did you call the sheriff's office?"

"Chelsea did," I said.

"Okay, what's going on?" Holly put her purse on the table and then her hands on her hips.

I took a deep breath and relayed the entire story. Deputy Bloomberg took notes on a notepad. Holly looked horrified, and Miss Finglestein looked boiling mad.

"How dare they!" Miss Finglestein exclaimed. "Why, I'm in a mind to pummel this person. Poor Jemma, what must she be going through?"

"I don't understand the lack of ransom," I said. "What does it mean? They can't keep her forever."

"You said she has a heart condition," Deputy Bloomberg said. "Perhaps they are trying to scare you to keep you out of the investigation."

"Oh, they've scared me, all right," I said and hugged myself.

"Whoever took her is most likely local and must feel they are able to take her again at any time," Deputy Bloomberg said. "That threat is most likely what they are trying to accomplish. If they hadn't taken her, would you be this worried?"

"No," I said and frowned. "I wouldn't take any threat that seriously."

"Then I'd say they accomplished their mission," the deputy said. "Let's try to stay calm and see if we can't get your aunt home."

"I'll make us some tea," Miss Finglestein said.

"You said that you talked to your aunt?" Deputy Bloomberg asked.

"Yes, but not for long."

"Then she is still alive. Try to relax a little bit. It is most likely they won't harm her. As I said, the only advantage they have over you is the threat of harming her. They have to keep her alive to do that."

"Why no ransom?" Holly asked. "Is it really all about not investigating?" She looked at me. "You or Chelsea must have been close to figuring things out."

"That must be true," I said. "But what part of our investigation was close? We will never know now, because I need my aunt back in one piece."

"We get paid to put our lives on the line, Taylor. You and your friends never should've gotten involved," the deputy said.

"I was trying to help Tim," I muttered and sat down hard in the nearest chair.

"Listen, we can't know what the kidnappers are thinking," Holly said and patted my shoulder. "It seems to me that they didn't think it all the way through when they took her, or they would have asked for ransom."

"Oh, dear," Miss Finglestein said as she brought in two cups of tea. "It sounds like our kidnapers are a bit rash." Her mouth made a thin line as she handed me a teacup and the second one to Holly. "There's no knowing what a rash person will do."

"Miss F!" Holly said and gave her a look that said she was worrying me.

"Just saying." The older woman shrugged. "Can I get you some tea, Deputy?"

"No, thank you," he said. Miss Finglestein went out to make

herself some tea, and the deputy's expression grew more serious. "She's right. While it's encouraging to think that they won't hurt your aunt because they will lose their leverage, there's no predicting what will happen."

"I don't know how they could have taken her without being seen."

"Would she have stopped somewhere on the way?"

"I don't know. I don't think so. She didn't say she needed to stop anywhere, and The Beanery is pretty much a straight shot into town."

"Was her car in the parking lot?"

"Gosh, I didn't really look." I frowned. "I don't think so, or her friends would have thought she was there. I called Sarah, and she said that Aunt Jemma never showed."

"Okay, we'll assume Sarah is right, and your aunt never made it that far. That means either she stopped somewhere, or the kidnappers somehow got her out of her car. Would your aunt have stopped to help someone at the side of the road?"

"Maybe . . . but we all came down the same stretch of highway. I turned just outside of town to go to The Timbers to pick up my group."

"I went the opposite direction in town to go to Safeway," Holly said.

"Chelsea didn't turn into town because she was headed back to North San Francisco."

"Then your aunt's car must be in town somewhere," the deputy surmised. He got on his radio and put out a notice for the squad cars to be on the lookout for my aunt's little red MG.

"The Beanery isn't too far into town," the deputy said. "She had to have stopped somewhere else first or run an errand."

"I just don't understand. She didn't say she was going to do anything like that," I said and put the untouched tea on the worktable. I hugged my waist and chewed on the inside of my cheek. "They could have called her cell phone and gotten her to go somewhere besides town. Wait! Her cell phone . . . can you do a GPS locator and find her?"

"We need permission to ping her phone," he said.

"I give you permission," I said quickly.

"It's not that easy." He frowned. "There are procedures that have to be followed. If you'll excuse me, I need to make some calls."

Holly gave me a big hug. "I'm so scared."

"Me too. What if Aunt Jemma has another heart attack? This is terrible."

Miss Finglestein came back with her teacup and Chelsea.

Chelsea rushed to me and gave me a big hug. "I hope you are okay with the fact that I called Sheriff Hennessey."

"It was smart," I said. "I'm glad you did."

"What's the word? Is there any?" she asked.

"Nothing," I said. "I could call the number again. But the last time I did they didn't answer."

"Don't call it," Miss Finglestein said. "We don't want to provoke whoever is doing this. If they feel backed into a corner, there's no telling what they will do. Rash personality, remember?"

"It's the killer, isn't it?" Chelsea said. "I think the killer is rash. Neither of these murders felt planned."

"What do you think triggered them to take Aunt Jemma?" I asked. "We must have gotten too close in our investigation." I frowned. "But we weren't that close. I mean, we really have no idea. Plus, how would they know what we were doing?"

"I ran a story about Dr. Brinkman's death," Chelsea said. "In it I did speculate that the two murders were connected."

"But that's not news," I protested. "The police have arrested Tim in connection with both murders. What would make the killer desperate enough to take Aunt Jemma?"

"Maybe there wasn't anything you did," Miss Finglestein said and took a sip of her tea. "Perhaps the person is simply insane. There's no predicting how insane people will act."

"They certainly didn't think this through," Holly said. "Tim is still in jail. They have now pretty much handed him reasonable doubt."

I studied Holly for a moment, mulling that point over. "They could twist that and say Tim orchestrated Aunt Jemma's kidnapping."

"We have to stop speculating," Chelsea said. "Let's all go over what we know from the beginning."

We all moved to the kitchen and sat down around the table.

Miss Finglestein took away my teacup and made me a fresh cup. The cup was warm, and I wrapped my hands around it. "What happened last night?" she asked.

"Chelsea, Holly, Aunt Jemma, and I had Sarah over to see if we could figure out who the killer was," I said and sipped the tea.

"Who else was there?"

"No one," Holly said.

"Who did you talk to about last night?" Miss Finglestein asked.

"I didn't talk to anyone. I was concentrating on today's tour group."

"I contacted that guy I know," Holly said. "The one with a

winery near Tim's. I left a message and asked him what he knew anything about the Senator and the zoning commission."

"What time did you contact him?" I asked.

"Right before I went into Safeway," Holly said.

"I don't think it's connected. Aunt Jemma was taken early."

"Chelsea, did you talk to anyone?" Holly asked. "Maybe last night? Did you email anyone at the paper?"

"No," Chelsea said.

"Then it probably wasn't part of last night's meeting," Miss Finglestein surmised. She drummed her fingers on the table. "What about yesterday?"

"I spoke to a guy named Bruce about Dr. Brinkman," I said. "And then there was Mandy, of course."

"Bruce told us that it was Harvey Winkle who was having an affair with Mandy," Chelsea said.

"And Sarah said that Jeffery Hoag caught Mandy making out with a man at Tim's—what if this Harvey Winkle is behind everything?"

"Why would he take Aunt Jemma? How would he know to do it?"

"Maybe Bruce told him what he told you. Brinkman's team seems pretty close. Even an off-handed comment about you thinking that Mandy was sleeping with Dr. Brinkman might have set off Harvey."

"Where's Deputy Bloomberg?" I asked.

"He's in the office."

I got up and went to the office to find the deputy on the phone. "Excuse me," I said.

"Yes?" He covered the phone's receiver.

"Can you tell Sheriff Hennessey to look into a man named Harvey Winkle? We think he might be involved."

The deputy wrote down the name. "What makes you think that?"

"It's a long story."

"I'm all ears."

I sighed and walked into the room and sat down. I relayed our thinking to the deputy.

"Have you ever met Mr. Winkle?" he asked.

"No."

"Has Mandy ever told you anything about Mr. Winkle?"

"No."

"I hate to say it, but this is all conjecture. I can't send police over to talk to a man who has no real connection."

"Then talk to Mandy," I said. "She's got to be connected."

"We'll do what we can."

"Have you found out anything about the number the guy called me on?"

"As best we can tell, the phone was bought at a big box store, and the number was registered to John Smith. The address was a post office box number. We haven't been able to trace it to a real person. Has he called you back?"

"No. Should I try to call him again?"

"Probably not a good idea," the deputy said. "He's most likely ditched the phone."

"What about Aunt Jemma's phone? Were you able to trace it? Or her car?"

"The phone takes time. We have to go through proper channels, and we're working with her carrier service right now."

"What about her car? It's pretty distinctive."

"We haven't found the car yet."

"Can't you do a "find my phone" app?" I asked. "Wait! I can do it." I pulled out my phone. "I set up the 'find my phone' app on my phone the last time Aunt Jemma lost hers." I thumbed through my apps and pressed the button. Nothing happened. "I don't understand."

"The phone could be dead," he said. "Let me see that." I handed him my phone, and he fiddled with the app for a moment. "Yeah, no signal. The phone is either dead or turned off."

"Darn it." I stood. "I can't just sit here and wait for something to happen. Aunt Jemma could be having a heart attack."

"The best thing you can do is sit here and wait," the deputy said. "We have officers out throughout the county, looking for your aunt. It's best if you let us do our job."

"I want to talk to Sheriff Hennessey," I said.

"I can get him on the line for you, but every moment of his that you take up is a moment lost in finding your aunt."

"Put him on anyway."

Chapter 23

"Hennessey."

"Hi, it's Taylor. What are you doing to find Aunt Jemma? She has a heart condition, you know. Have you found her car? Pinged her phone? What am I supposed to do? I can't just sit here and do nothing."

"Taylor, calm down."

"Don't tell me to calm down. My aunt's life is at stake. She is probably with the murderer. You know, the one person you haven't put in jail."

"Taylor, I need you to sit tight."

"This is not about what you need, Ron."

"Okay." He was calmer than he should have been. I imagined he had his flat-eyed, cop face on. "Taylor, sit down."

"What?"

"Find the nearest chair and sit."

I did what he said out of instinct more than anything; the tone of his voice was commanding.

"Good," he said. "Now, we still haven't found your aunt's MG. That means there is most likely more than one person involved. You talked to her yourself, correct?"

"Yes, but—"

"She's a strong woman, and you know that. I've got every man in our county and two adjacent counties out looking for her. You need to stay safe."

"But—"

"Don't let Chelsea or Holly out of your sight. There's safety in numbers. Also, stay away from the winery."

"But Millie and Clemmie are there."

"I called Juan. He and Julio are watching out for your pets. I've got Deputy Bloomberg there with you for a reason. Can you stay there? Can you be a part of this? Can I count on you, Taylor?"

"Yes," I said with a sigh. "We think it might be Harvey Winkle."

"Who?"

"Harvey Winkle. This guy, Bruce Warrington, from Dr. Brinkman's group said that they all took turns giving the lectures and acting like Dr. Brinkman. That night I saw Mandy kissing Dr. Brinkman, it was actually a man named Harvey Winkle. I'm certain if you find Harvey, you will find my aunt."

"I've written that down," he reassured me. "Do you trust this Bruce guy?"

That stopped me for a moment. "Sure, why would he lie to me?"

"Taylor, what do you know about him?"

I thought about it for a moment. "I guess nothing other than that he works for Dr. Brinkman."

"Listen, I'm going out to the Brinkman headquarters right now. I'll see what I can find out about this Harvey guy and this Bruce Warrington. I'll keep you posted if anyone knows anything about your aunt's whereabouts."

"Wait, you don't think she went out to Dr. Brinkman's compound, do you?"

He paused. "Why would she do that, Taylor?"

"I don't know," I said and frowned. "She should have gone straight to The Beanery, but she didn't. Maybe she went out there to investigate."

"I told you ladies to leave it to the professionals."

"Ron, don't lecture me right now. I need you to focus on finding my aunt. Deputy Bloomberg tells me that the number that called me is untraceable. Can I call him back? I did before."

"No," Ron said. "No, let him call you. My guess is that he's dumped the first phone and is getting a second."

"What do I do when he calls again? It's not like he's asking for money. All he asked for was for us to stop investigating. I don't know how to prove that we've stopped. I don't know how to get my aunt back."

"Listen to me, Taylor. When the kidnapper calls back, I want you to get Deputy Bloomberg. Put the man on speakerphone. Try to keep him talking, and we will try to trace the call."

"How will you trace the call? Is there something you need to put on my phone?"

"Deputy Bloomberg took your phone, right?"

"Yes, but only for a minute. I thought he was writing down the phone number."

"When you gave your permission, he put a tracking app on your phone. I've been working through the process to get the courts to allow us to find the phone that calls you. We can track them as soon as the court order comes through."

"What if they call me before that?"

"Listen, I know this is hard. I need you to trust me. We're

doing our best while working through the system," he said. "That said there are a few apps you can use."

"I'm going to do a search and download some now."

"Don't do anything questionable," he said. "We want to catch this guy and make the charges stick."

"I'm calling Patrick."

"That might not be a bad idea. Is there anyone else we should contact about your aunt? Any cousins, siblings?"

"No, no, just me. She needs to be found, and soon. She has a bad heart."

"We're doing everything we can, Taylor," he said, his tone patient and calm. "I'm going to let you go now so I can get back to work. You have to trust me that I'm doing everything I can. You have to trust Deputy Bloomberg. Can you do that?"

"I'm trying."

"That's all we can ask right now. I know this is high stress. We'll find her." He hung up the phone, and I stared at it a moment.

"Feel better?" Deputy Bloomberg asked.

"I suppose." I pulled out my phone and went to the app store and searched for call tracing apps. There were so many. I stood. "I'm going back to the break room."

"Just don't leave the building without letting me know," he said. "I've got a few more things to handle, but I'll be back the minute we get permission to put a tracer on your phone."

"Okay, thanks." I left the office and found the ladies in the break room. Chelsea was on her iPad. "They can't put a tracer on my phone until they get a court order. If this guy calls before that, I want to be able to track him. There are several apps. Do you have any idea which one is best? Sheriff Hennessey said I needed to stay within the bounds of the law."

"Here, give me your phone," Chelsea said. She bent over it and quickly swiped though a few things.

"They have phone number tracing apps?" Holly said.

"Yes, but not all of them are legal," Chelsea said. "There are laws in some states that don't allow you to track who is calling you. The family and friends app will let you see where the other person is."

"Oh, that's a little crazy," Holly said.

"It can be abused," Chelsea said and handed me my phone. "I once did a story on a guy who watched everywhere is wife went. She didn't even know he was doing it."

"Did he catch her doing something?"

"No actually, he was the one who was doing bad things. He didn't want to get caught."

"How did she figure it out?"

"One day she forgot her phone and showed up without it. Caught him in the act with another woman."

"Oh, man," Holly said.

"I used several examples of abuse of that app in my story. People still use it. They think they can trust their family with knowing exactly where they are."

"It might be useful if you are in an accident and run off the road or something, and no one can find you," Holly pointed out.

"True," Chelsea said, "but with knowledge can come abuse of power."

I paced around the kitchen, studying my phone.

"Taylor, you should sit down."

"I can't sit. Everyone keeps telling me to sit. I'd rather be taking action. There must be something we can do."

"I've been doing some research on Harvey Winkle," Chelsea said. "The man is eighty-five years old."

"What?" That news made me sit down. "I'm pretty sure Mandy would *not* be sleeping with an eighty-five-year-old man. Are you sure he doesn't have a son or grandson?"

"Not in California," Chelsea said. "In fact, Mr. Winkle is in a nursing home in North San Francisco. There is no way he could have been having an affair with Mandy."

"Bruce lied to me."

"Or someone else is lying to Bruce," Chelsea said and shrugged. "Without any pictures or fingerprints, we can't tell if Bruce made Harvey up or if someone else is playing Harvey Winkle."

"I told Sheriff Hennessey to look into Harvey Winkle. He's going to go over to the Brinkman compound and talk to Bruce and Harvey."

"Good luck finding Harvey," Chelsea said.

"So if Bruce made up Harvey, is Bruce the guy Mandy is sleeping with?" I had to ask the question.

"I think only Mandy can answer that," Chelsea said. "Do you think Bruce is connected to Aunt Jemma's kidnapping?"

"I don't think so," I said and frowned. "I think I would have recognized Bruce's voice. I've talked to him a couple of times now."

"So we're back to square one," Holly said and put her elbows on the table and tilted forward so her head was in her hands.

"I hate waiting. I especially hate not knowing."

"Well," Chelsea said, "the good news is we are all here and safe. Also it would seem that Tim is safely out of this since he is currently incarcerated."

"I'm calling Patrick," I said as I suddenly remembered my lawyer.

"Why? What can he do?" Holly asked.

"I don't know, but he might know something. At this point, I'm hoping for any help at all." I dialed Patrick's number.

"Taylor, what's up? Are you still mad at me?"

"Hi, Patrick. I have a problem. Someone has kidnapped Aunt Jemma."

"That's not good."

"I've got Sheriff Hennessey working on it, but I need to know. Is there anything else I can do? They tell me just to sit tight."

"Where are you? Are you safe?"

"I'm at La Galleria with Holly, Chelsea, and Miss Finglestein. Deputy Bloomberg is here as well, although I can't tell if it's to keep us safe or keep us captive."

"Okay, you're safe." He blew out a long breath. "Are the kidnappers asking for money? Do you need cash?"

"No," I said. "Not yet anyway."

"What are they asking for?"

"They want Chelsea to stop investigating. Me too. I can't imagine that's all they want."

"Are you waiting for another call? Listen, I'll clear my schedule and come down there."

"Thanks, Patrick, but I'm not sure there is anything you can do here."

"Taylor, why did you call me?"

"I don't know. Because Sheriff Hennessey said I needed to not do anything that might jeopardize the case against the kidnappers once they are caught."

"He has a point."

"I know. I thought you could advise me."

"Then I advise you to stay put and let the professionals do their job." He took a breath. "But you don't listen to me, do you?"

"Patrick, please don't chastise me. I need a friend."

"I'm your friend, Taylor," he said, his voice low and serious. "I've always been your friend."

I sighed. "I know. Listen, thanks for listening. I'm waiting for the kidnappers to call me back. Chelsea is ensuring I use a legal app to record and trace incoming calls."

"Good," Patrick said. "That's a good start. I'll cancel my appointments for the day and come down and keep you company."

"Please don't," I said. "As a friend, thank you, but there's nothing we can do but wait, right?"

"Yes."

"Well, I've got people here waiting with me."

"I'm a quick phone call away," he said. "Seriously, if you need me, I can be there in two minutes."

"Thanks, Patrick."

"Are you okay if they demand money?"

"I don't know," I said. "I guess I'll cross that bridge when I come to it."

"If you need money, I can get it for you. You let me know."

"I will, thanks." I hung up and looked at the three women in the room. "What do I do if they ask for money?"

"We'll take care of it," Miss Finglestein said and patted my hand. "Jemma has a lot of friends in the community. We'll get whatever you need."

I rubbed my face with both hands and tried to remember to breathe.

"I say we all get in my car and go down to the Brinkman compound. Someone there has to know something," Holly said. "And to think, I almost gave them my life savings."

"We don't know if it's them at all," Miss Finglestein said. "We really don't have a clue."

"I've been digging into the Senator," Chelsea said as she looked up from her iPad. "His political contributors have to be listed online. It looks like Dr. Brinkman was a significant contributor."

"Wait, what? I thought they didn't like each other."

She turned her screen toward us. "He gave the Senator ten million dollars."

Holly whistled.

"That's a lot," I said. "The feud must have happened after the Senator was elected."

"My guess is our guru went to visit the Senator and ask him for a favor," Chelsea said.

"Maybe it was a favor the Senator couldn't grant," I pointed out.

"Or maybe he didn't want to grant it," Chelsea said. "It would certainly cause bad blood."

"Then this is about real estate, right? So who was the realtor or developer who was involved?" I asked and leaned toward Chelsea's screen.

"The land that Brinkman wanted was near Tim's winery," Chelsea said. "In this petition for zoning, it lists it as a two-hundred-acre ranch. They wanted to develop hiking trails and horse trails as well as off-roading trails for bikes and four-wheelers."

"So who stood to gain besides Dr. Brinkman?"

"The property is owned by a trust . . . Oh, boy."

"What?" we all asked Chelsea at the same time.

"The trust belonged to Harvey Winkler. He inherited the land from his grandfather, but he left it in trust."

"Does Harvey have any heirs who might inherit?" I asked.

"I'll have to do more digging."

"Things are pretty twisted up," Holly said. "My head hurts just thinking about it."

Patrick came into the back from the front area. "Hello, ladies," he said. He was a handsome man with dark hair and blue eyes. "Dreamy" was the best word for it. Today he wore a navy suit with a white shirt and a blue and red striped tie. His presence filled up the room. He came straight to me and gave me a hug and a kiss on the cheek. "Are you holding up?"

"I'm certainly trying," I said. "I thought I told you not to come."

"Taylor, I care about you and Aunt Jemma. There's no way I wouldn't be here."

I hugged him again. "It's been two hours since I heard anything from the kidnappers."

"What exactly are they looking for? You said they didn't ask for money."

"They want us to stop investigating Dr. Brinkman's murder."

"Okay, and how is that going to get your aunt back?"

"That's what we've all been asking all morning."

"We think the person who took her didn't think it all through," Holly said. "Deputy Bloomberg told us that they are likely to keep her alive or they lose their leverage."

"But I think the person is acting rashly and might just dump her," Miss Finglestein said.

My heart squeezed at the idea. "We don't know how they

took her," I said, trying to change the subject. "We all left the winery at the same time this morning. She never showed up for her first appointment—coffee with her social group."

"How long ago was this?"

I looked at the time. "Nearly four hours."

"And you know she's still alive?"

"I spoke to her." I stood. "There's got to be something we can do. Maybe we should be out looking for her car. I tried her cell phone but got nothing. I even tried locating the cell phone with the family app, but it's off or something."

"Was she driving her MG?" Patrick asked.

"Yes," we all said.

"That should be easy to find," Patrick said. "There aren't a lot of vintage red MGs out there anymore."

"Sheriff Hennessey assures me they are looking for the car, and he'll let me know when it's found, but they never did find Jeffery Hoag's car," I said. "Whoever is doing this knows the area enough to stash cars where even the cops can't find them."

There was a deep rumbling sound from outside, and we all got up and went out the back door to look.

"They've called in a helicopter search," Deputy Bloomberg said from just inside the door. "Like I said, they're taking this very seriously."

Chapter 24

My phone rang. I was concentrating so hard on the helicopter that the sound startled me. I didn't recognize the number.

"Who is it?" Holly asked.

"I don't know."

"Let's go inside before you answer," Patrick said.

I hurried inside, afraid they would hang up and not call back. "This is Taylor," I said.

Deputy Bloomberg motioned for me to follow him.

"I said no cops," the man's voice said. His voice sounded different, as if he were using a machine to change it.

"You changed phones," I stated.

"You were calling too much. It was annoying."

"I'm worried about my aunt. I want her back. What can I do to bring her safely home?"

"Stop investigating," he said.

"Okay, we've stopped. Can I come pick up my aunt?"

"It's not that simple," he said. "I know there's a story set to be printed in the *North San Francisco Chronicle* this afternoon. I want the story pulled."

"There's a story? We didn't write a story . . ."

Chelsea shook her head.

I shot her a stink eye. "Okay, the story won't run," I said. "When can I get my aunt?"

"I want the cops called off."

"I didn't call them."

"Someone did, and they need to back off or else."

"If you hurt a hair on her head, I'm going to hunt you down and do whatever you did to my aunt to you. So I'd be very careful what you do to her. If this nonsense does anything to her heart, I will find you and pull *your* heart out of your chest and squeeze it myself."

"Threats don't bother me," he said. "Your aunt is sedated and resting comfortably . . . for now. Call off the search party."

"Any other demands?" I asked as Deputy Bloomberg motioned for me to keep him talking.

"More will follow," he said. "Don't call me back or else." He hung up.

"Were you able to trace it?" I asked.

"We have it pinged between two towers, but we really need three to get a good read on it."

"Let me check my apps," I said and quickly opened the app Chelsea had installed. I looked at the finder map. "It says they are in Sonoma County. That's good, right? We don't have to worry about jurisdiction or something."

"Did you recognize the voice?" Patrick asked from the doorway. He must have followed Deputy Bloomberg and me.

"No," I said. "In fact, he sounded different this time."

"He could be using a voice-changing app," the deputy said. "There are several out there."

I turned to Chelsea. "Pull your story."

"I don't think I can."

"Please," I said.

"How did he know about that story?" she asked. "Only my editor and the printer know about it."

"The kidnapper must have ties in the community," Deputy Bloomberg said. "He may very well be closely tied to you."

"What?" Chelsea asked and pointed at herself. "I'm not tied to anyone in Sonoma besides Holly."

"And Aunt Jemma and me," I said.

"But I didn't tell any of you about the story."

"That's true," Holly said. They had all followed me into the office and now hung out in the hallway. "But you did tell your boss, and others on the paper staff had to know. Who's on the staff?"

"There's Cary, Adam, Frank, and Ted." She counted them off on her fingers. "They wouldn't do anything to jeopardize a story."

"Who else?" Patrick asked. "There has to be someone else. Anyone in the mail room, an intern, someone who sells ads . . ."

"It's a small newspaper," she said and rubbed her chin thoughtfully.

"What about their wives and family?" Miss Finglestein said. "Wives can be active in other things."

"Cary's wife is a second-grade teacher. Adam's wife is a stay-at-home mom," Chelsea said. "Frank's wife is a mover and shaker at the country club. She has her own real estate company. Then there's Ted's wife. She's an artist with a small gallery on the coast."

"Check Frank's wife," Patrick said. "There might be a real estate connection."

"Got it," Chelsea said and sat down to do some research on her tablet.

"We still need to find out the developer for the proposed Brinkman retreat," I said. "Could it be so simple that it's Frank's wife?"

"Maybe there's a connection with the Winkle trust."

"Hmm, according to Frank's wife's website, she's big into investor properties. There are pictures of her with some local celebs . . . wait—here's a picture of her with Dr. Brinkman."

"There's our connection," I said. "But the caller wasn't a woman."

"You already said they could have used a voice changer," Holly pointed out.

"I'll get Sheriff Hennessey to check out Frank's wife," Deputy Bloomberg said. "What is the last name?"

"Reddington," Chelsea said. "Frank Reddington is the publisher, and his wife is June Reddington."

"I'll make the call," the deputy said.

I motioned for everyone to leave the office, and closed the door. "There's got to be something we can do. I don't want to just sit here. Chelsea, can you call Frank and ask him to pull the story? Tell him that Aunt Jemma's life is at stake. If he won't pull it altogether, ask him to hold it for at least twenty-four hours. That way the kidnappers will see that we are doing all we can."

"Right." Chelsea walked away and dialed her phone.

"What are you thinking, Taylor?" Patrick asked. His eyes narrowed in concern. "I know you want to act, but we need to remain as calm as possible."

"I'm thinking I want to strangle whoever is doing this, that's what I'm thinking. But I can't. So next is to follow the breadcrumbs. We can't go to the Brinkman compound ourselves.

Sheriff Hennessey is taking a team out there. But maybe we can all go to Frank's house and pay him and his wife a visit."

"They live in North San Francisco," Holly said. "Do you really want to leave Sonoma while your aunt is being held hostage?"

"Not me," I said. "Patrick and Chelsea."

"What?" Patrick said. "I don't know . . ."

"I think it's a good idea," Chelsea said as she walked back. "I couldn't get a hold of anyone at the paper. They must all be at lunch. So I tried Frank's home phone. He didn't answer. I left a message, but it's the perfect reason to go track him down."

"Patrick, I want you to go with Chelsea. I don't think any of us should be alone. Can you do that for me?"

"Fine," he said.

"Come on, hot stuff," Chelsea said, linking her arm through his. "Let's take your car. I'm sure it's a comfy ride."

"Thank you!" I called after them as they went out through the front of the gallery. The bells on the door rang again right after they left, and I looked at Miss Finglestein.

She shrugged. "It could be a customer. We do have those on occasion, you know. Hang tight." She disappeared out front, and it was just me and Holly left. We went back to the break room, where there was more space for me to pace.

"Do you think they are giving her food and water?" I asked. It was past noon.

"They have to keep her alive," Holly said and stopped my pacing to look me in the eye. "They lose any advantage if anything happens to her."

"What if something happens and they cover it up? We might not know for hours, or even days."

"Okay, let's not go down that path. Let's do something constructive. Come with me." She pulled me to the back room.

"No, I don't want to work on art."

"Don't be silly," Holly said. She unfolded an easel and then put a large pad of paper on it. "Here's a marker. Let's draw a diagram of what we know. Let's start with the murder of Jeffery Hoag." She made a line across the paper. "Now, Jeffery was murdered, and his car is missing." She drew lines out to show the missing articles. "Next we learn that Mandy is mixed up with Dr. Brinkman. She drew another circle on the time line. "We discover Mandy is having an affair with Dr. Brinkman."

"Who isn't Dr. Brinkman at all," I said.

"Right." She drew a line up from the Dr. Brinkman circle and then out on a parallel path. "We assume it is Harvey Winkle because Bruce told us it was."

"Then we find Dr. Brinkman dead." I got into the game by marking an X on the original time line. "And Tim is arrested and jailed for both murders."

"Right," Holly said. "Now, who did we talk to besides Chelsea?"

"Well, Mandy," I said, "and Bruce and now Patrick, Sheriff Hennessey, and Deputy Bloomberg."

"Also Sarah and Aunt Jemma."

"Okay."

"We don't know who Sarah or Aunt Jemma talked to," Holly pointed out.

"What about the guy you know who lives south of Tim's winery? Did you talk to him?"

"No, I just left a message."

"What did your message say?"

"Only that I wanted to ask him about the zoning commission and Senator Sutter. He's usually up on the gossip in the area. I offered to buy him coffee and pick his brain."

"So none of us actually talked to Senator Sutter," I said and wrote his name on a list at the side of the board. "But we think he's connected because of the legislature that was pulled that would allow the Brinkman retreat compound to be built. And Jeffery Hoag was involved in zoning meetings shortly after Senator Sutter took office."

Holly stood back and studied the sheet. "There doesn't seem to be a connection to any of this."

"There has to be somewhere," I said. "Let's start at the beginning. What do we know about Jeffery? He was a local realtor, of course, and he might have been influenced by Senator Sutter."

"Right." She pulled the first sheet up and over and started on a blank one. "Let's say Sonoma is here." She made an X and circled it. "The Brinkman compound is here." She made another X on the bottom of the page toward the left. "The top is north, the bottom south, left is west, and right is east. The Brinkman compound is small, but in the southwest. Tim's winery is also small, but in the southeast."

"The Winkle trust is a nice chunk of prime grape-growing area south of Sonoma, but north of Tim." I made a big circle. "Wait, it looks almost adjacent."

"We should ask Tim if anyone was asking to buy him out lately."

I frowned. "Tim said that he was looking for investors. I don't see him selling out. He loves his place, but a fresh cash flow might have been good."

"So maybe Tim knows who the developer is. Maybe they approached him before the zoning got cancelled."

"That could be," I said. "It would be reasonable for the developers to meet with the closest wineries and try to win support for the zoning. The thing is, I happen to know Tim hates people. The idea that tourists would be staying so close to him and coming and going all the time. That probably didn't sit well."

"Plus the road is a two-lane, twisty highway out here. Can you imagine the fuss if it became the world-class destination that Dr. Brinkman's group wanted?"

"Tim must have been having a fit."

"Maybe he got enough neighbors stirred up to put pressure on the zoning commission to not push the zoning through. Enough voters can trump any push from a senator."

"Well, we'd certainly like to think so," I said. "I can see how Tim might be involved, but how was Jeffery Hoag involved? Was he part of the group trying to run the winery owners out so they could buy the land?"

"We don't know that much about the guy, other than what Sarah told us, and that was her talking to the dead, and we know that won't hold up in a court of law."

"True," I said. "Jeffery Hoag didn't have any family. We really don't know anything about him other than that he had a local office and that Mandy worked for him. There really is no proof that the two murders are connected."

"But I bet it's no coincidence that Dr. Brinkman was killed so soon after Jeffery. I mean, Tim was free on bail when Dr. Brinkman died. The timing is not good for Tim."

"Maybe they weren't connected other than that Dr. Brinkman's killer took advantage of Tim's situation to kill the man and frame Tim."

"That's creepy," Holly said.

I studied the piece of paper. "It seems like there are a couple things we really don't know about. We need more personal information on Jeffery. Who would want him killed? And then who else lost money in the lack of zoning? Was it one of the wineries around Tim? Maybe his neighbors thought their wineries would be worth more money if the zoning went through . . ."

"I say we go to the courthouse and do some digging."

"The courthouse?" I asked.

"Yes, they would have public records on all of the zoning commission meetings and the developers of the retreat."

"Plus, who's going to hurt us in the courthouse?" I grabbed my purse.

"Should we let Deputy Bloomberg know where we're going?" Holly asked.

I picked up the marker, switched sheets of paper, and wrote: *Gone to the county courthouse.* "There, now he knows."

"What if they call you back with more demands?"

"I've got that tracker app on my phone," I said. "I'll keep them talking, and maybe we can pinpoint where they are keeping my aunt. In the meantime, I think we need to do our best to figure out who killed Dr. Brinkman and why. They have to be the ones who have the most to lose if the *Chronicle* publishes Chelsea's story."

Holly put her arm through mine. "Come on—the biggest danger will be when we walk from here to the courthouse, so let's stay together."

"I think we'll be safe. The last place they will expect us to go is the courthouse."

Chapter 25

Two hours later, I got a call from Chelsea. "Hello?"

"Hey, Taylor, I got Frank to agree to hold off on publishing the story."

"Wonderful," I said. "How was meeting his wife?"

"She wasn't home. She was at an investment seminar, which is a bit odd, don't you think?"

"Did he know anything about her involvement with the developers and the proposed Brinkman retreat?"

"He knew that his wife had lost a venture, but he wasn't clear on the details. He said that usually he learns about her dealings after they are successful. Those that don't succeed she doesn't talk about."

"So he didn't know who the developers were?"

"No."

"Are you heading back to Sonoma?"

"Yes," she said. "Patrick has been very helpful."

"Oh, good. Well, Holly and I have been at the courthouse."

"The courthouse?"

"Yes, looking through public records," I said. "It turns out the developers had over a million dollars invested."

"That's a lot of money," Chelsea said.

"They had several people buy in and pool their money. Almost all of the buyers were from Sonoma County."

"Local people beating on the local economy," Chelsea surmised.

"Yes, except it still didn't get zoning, so not as much local influence as we might think."

"You think there were only a few who bet big?"

"Yes," I said. "The group was incorporated in the county, so we're looking into who was a part of that."

"What banks were involved?" Chelsea said. "Following the money is always a good way to look at it."

"Holly is doing that right now. We did learn something else that was interesting."

"What is that?" Chelsea asked.

"Jeffery Hoag was an investor."

"Wait—what? Hmm . . . I suppose it makes sense. He would have had friends on the commission and in the area. A lot of local realtors are developers and involved in politics."

"His political influence might push the wineries to choose to give in to the pressure of the developer and sell. There were several deals on the table to buy adjacent wineries."

"He would have to have had some powerful influence," Chelsea said. "Maybe he had something to blackmail them. There's a story in there somewhere."

"One you can't write about until we get my aunt back. I'm going to call the kidnapper and let him know the story was pulled, and we're not investigating."

"But you are investigating," Chelsea said.

"How will he know that?"

"You know that tracker app you have? He might have one on your phone number."

"Are you saying he knows where I am?"

"He could."

I studied my phone and suddenly felt as if it might have betrayed me. "That's creepy."

"Welcome to the digital age," Chelsea said. "Where shall we meet you?"

"Meet us back at the gallery," I said. "We should know more by then." I hung up and my phone immediately rang. I didn't recognize the phone number. "Hello?"

"Taylor O'Brian?"

"Yes."

"Deputy Bloomberg. I asked you not to leave the building without letting me know."

"We left you a note."

"I saw it." He did not sound pleased. "Where in the court-house are you?"

"In public records," I said.

"Do I want to know what you are doing there?"

"It depends. Are you trying to find my aunt?" I asked, my chin raised in defiance. "Because that's what we are doing. By the way, Chelsea called. They got the paper to hold off printing the story. I want to call the kidnapper and let him know that we have met his demands."

"You should be here when you make that call," he said.

"We're heading back now," I said.

"I'll head that way and walk with you."

"No! Stay where you are," I said. "As far as we know, the

kidnappers don't know about you yet. If you come here and escort us, you will blow that. Holly is with me. We'll be fine."

"I'd feel better if you stayed on the phone with me while you walk."

I frowned. "Fine, I'll call you back when we leave. Can I call this number?"

"Yes."

"Good. I'll talk soon." I hung up the phone and looked at the records we had spread out in front of us. "We're busted. Deputy Bloomberg wants us back at the gallery now. What can we take with us?"

"I've got a few notes on who to look into," Holly said. "Jeffery had to be up to more than investing into the Brinkman project."

"Let's make some copies of stuff and get out of here. Chelsea is on her way back. She might have more insight into what we're looking at."

"Fine, I'll take this pile, and you take that one," Holly said. "Make what copies you can, and then we'll go."

It took us nearly thirty minutes to make our copies and return the originals to the desk. When you looked at public records, you had to leave an ID at the desk. It took the clerk awhile to sort through what we had and give us back our stuff. Deputy Bloomberg called me every five minutes. I quit answering after the fourth call.

When we left the courthouse with our arms full of papers, I dialed the deputy. "Okay, we're on our way over. Is there any news from Sheriff Hennessey?"

"He said to tell you that he's disappointed that you chose to leave the gallery. Frankly, my bum is on the line because of it," Deputy Bloomberg said.

"We went to the courthouse. We were safe and are still safe," I said as we walked down the sidewalk toward the gallery. "Is there any news on my aunt?"

"We think we found her car."

My heart rate sped up. "That's great news, right? Where did they find it?" Holly looked at me and mouthed, "What did they find?"

"Her car," I said.

"That's good, right?" Holly asked.

"It's good, isn't it, Deputy?"

"It's a lead," he said.

"We have some leads as well," I said.

"I'm listening."

"No, you have to wait until we get there."

"I was looking over your time line."

"Our time line?"

"The one you wrote on the paper," he said. "It's interesting. You believe the two murders are connected."

"Well, so do you," I declared. "You arrested Tim for both murders. But we've done some research into Jeffery Hoag."

"And?"

"And did you know that he invested in the development group that was trying to get Dr. Brinkman's retreat zoned and developed in Sonoma county?"

"What?"

"Yes, we think he was pressuring the wineries into to selling to the developer. The more land the developers had, the more they could plan trails and such from the retreat house. There's a copy of the proposal at the courthouse. It was quite illuminating."

"I'll have the deputies look into it."

"Don't bother. We have a copy," I said. Suddenly a car screeched around the corner and stopped in front of us, blocking out way. "What?"

The door opened, and Bruce stepped out. "Come with me." He took my arm.

"No," I said.

"No," Holly said and grabbed my other arm. "You can't have her."

"I want to take you to your aunt," he said.

"What's going on?" Deputy Bloomberg asked on the other end of the phone.

"It's Bruce. He wants me to go with him," I said.

"Who are you talking to?" Bruce asked as he looked around.

"A deputy," I said. "He knows that you have your hands on my arm."

"Oh, geez, hang up the phone," he said and grabbed my phone to switch it off. "You can't trust anyone. Especially law enforcement." He tugged me, and I stumbled toward the car. "Come with me."

"No!" Holly dropped her papers and grabbed me with both hands. "You take her, and you have to take us both."

"Fine. Bruno," Bruce called. A second, larger man stepped out of the passenger side and helped stuff both me and Holly into the back of the car, leaving our papers scattered on the pavement along with my phone.

"I'm going to scream," Holly said and tried to roll down the window. Bruno grabbed her hand.

231

"Just listen."

"What?" I asked as we hurtled out of town. "Where are you taking us?"

"There are people in the sheriff's office involved in your aunt's disappearance," Bruce said.

"You know about my aunt? Where is she? Did you take her?"

"We didn't take her," Bruno said. "Listen to Bruce."

"The cops will be after you," I said. "They know you took us."

"We're not kidnapping you," Bruce said.

"That's exactly what you did," I countered.

"Listen, we're taking you out to the compound."

"Why?"

"Because there are things you need to know."

"Like what?" I asked.

"Like who we think might have your aunt."

"You know where my aunt is?" I asked. "Tell me. Tell me now."

"I can't."

"We know you're involved," Holly said.

"In what?" he asked.

"In Dr. Brinkman's murder," I said. "You told me Harvey Winkle was the guy lecturing the night I saw Mandy kissing the guru. We know that Harvey Winkle is an old man with a trust fund. A trust fund that owns the land Dr. Brinkman wanted for his worldwide retreat."

"Mr. Winkle is in a nursing home," Holly said. "So we know he wasn't the one kissing Mandy. You lied."

"I didn't lie," Bruce said as we swerved around a corner and bounced down a rough road. "I didn't know that Harvey wasn't really Harvey Winkle until a few hours ago."

"So you had nothing to do with my aunt's disappearance or

Dr. Brinkman's death? Because you sure look like a good suspect."

"I had no idea," he said. "But I know who does know."

"Who?"

"Harvey Winkle."

"I told you, he is in a nursing home."

"Maybe, but his grandson was at the Brinkman estate."

"Did he take Aunt Jemma?" Holly asked as she continued to try to open the door of the moving car.

"No one at the compound has your aunt. You have to believe me," Bruce said.

"Why?" I asked and crossed my arms over my chest. "Why do we have to believe you?"

"Because I'm trying to help you," he said.

"By bringing a bouncer to ensure we get in your car?" I waved at Bruno, who continued to move Holly's hand away from the door lock.

"Bruno is here as my bodyguard," Bruce said. "What I'm doing could get me badly hurt."

"You? Why? Are you afraid the police will hurt you?"

"Just let us take you out to the compound. We're almost there."

The driver turned us into the gated compound. Holly slapped at Bruno as we waited for the gates to open. They did slowly, and soon we were driving down the long and winding road of the compound that was the Brinkman empire.

The car stopped, and Bruno got out and opened the door. Holly stumbled out and started to run back down the driveway, but Bruno went after her. I gave Bruce the stink eye as I got out. "What are we doing here?"

"I think I know where your aunt is," Bruce said as he climbed out of the car.

"And you couldn't just tell us?"

"No," he said. "You were talking to Deputy Bloomberg, weren't you?"

"Yes."

"I hate to tell you this, but he's in on your aunt's kidnapping."

"What? No—"

"Yes," Bruce said. "Come inside and I'll explain."

"Let me go!" Holly shouted as she squirmed and pushed against Bruno. He had her around the waist and physically carried her in behind us. The inside of the compound was quiet. There was a huge foyer like the kind you saw in the movies, with a large staircase and doors to rooms on either side. I hadn't seen so much marble in my entire life.

"Put me down!" Holly shouted, and Bruno covered her mouth with his hand.

"Please stop it," I said to Bruno. "Put her down."

"She can't go running off," Bruno said. "It's not safe."

"Let's all go into the parlor," Bruce said. "We can have some tea and calm down."

"You calm down," Holly said as she squirmed. "I don't like being forced into cars."

"Fine," Bruce said. "Bruno, put her down."

He did as Bruce asked and Holly stopped, adjusted her top, and took a deep breath. "Thank you."

"Are you going to run off?" Bruce asked.

Holly gave him a stern look. "I need to know that I can leave any time I want."

"You can leave any time you want," he said. "Now, please come in to the parlor. Let's have some tea and talk."

The parlor was decorated white with pops of orange and turquoise and had large glass windows and mid-century modern seating. I took a seat on a Danish couch. Holly sat beside me. Bruno went into another room and came back with a bar cart with a tea service.

"That was fast," I said.

"We always have tea ready for visitors," Bruce said. He took a cup and poured liquid in it and handed it to me.

"Is this the tea you serve at the lectures?" I asked and sniffed the cup.

"Yes," he said. "It's a special brew that Dr. Brinkman created. It's quite soothing."

"I think you should drink it first," I said.

"Oh, sure. I understand your reluctance," he said and sipped from the next cup he poured. "You've had a hard day. I want to prove to you that you can trust me." He sipped some more. "See? Please, it will help."

Holly took a cup from Bruno and shrugged. "I like the tea. It's good."

"Fine," I sighed and sipped. What could possibly go wrong?

Chapter 26

"You said that Deputy Bloomberg has something to do with my aunt's kidnapping." I said as I put down my cup. I had taken a few sips of the tea that tasted of ginger and cinnamon and warmed my tummy.

"Yes," Bruce said. "He is Harvey Winkle's grandson."

"Deputy Bloomberg?" I asked. "But wait—you were the one who told me that Harvey Winkle was the man who gave the lecture the night I saw Mandy kissing Dr. Brinkman."

"Right," Bruce put down his cup and pinched his nose. "Right. Okay, things are a little complicated. Let's start from the beginning. Dr. Brinkman came to visit Sonoma last year and fell in love with the area. He met with a realtor named June Reddington. She told him that Harvey Winkle was on his deathbed, and his family was looking to sell the vineyard. They toured the space, and Dr. Brinkman loved it. He wanted to set up a retreat house, so he got a developer who knew about local politics and who could get us more land and the proper zoning."

"So you lied about the guy Mandy was kissing being Harvey Winkle."

"No." He shook his head. "I thought he *was* Harvey Winkle.

You see, Dr. Brinkman went to Harvey Winkle's family and offered to buy them out and let Harvey spend his final days in comfort and peace. Well, his grandson said if they were going to invest in his family's land, he wanted to be a part of the organization."

"So why change his name?"

"He said it was to honor his grandfather, but I think it was to keep his involvement in the group secret from the rest of Sonoma society." Bruce sighed. "We all knew him as Harvey. He was really interested in all parts of the Brinkman community and soon became Dr. Brinkman's right-hand guy."

"If you all bought his family's land, then he stood to gain."

"Only if the permits went through," Bruce said. "You see, the contract to buy the land was contingent on the proper zoning. Dr. Brinkman thought it would be easier to get all the proper permits if the locals had a stake in the profits."

"And Deputy Bloomberg?"

"He had all of us but Dr. Brinkman convinced he was Harvey Winkle and the owner of the property. We treated him like our number-one guru next to Dr. Brinkman."

"But then the zoning didn't go through," Holly said. "Wait— was he working as a deputy the entire time he was with Dr. Brinkman?"

"Apparently," Bruce said. "We thought he was evangelizing in Washington State. Only he and Dr. Brinkman knew who he really was."

"Except Mandy," I pointed out. "Mandy knew who he was."

"He's the one who brought Mandy into the fold," Bruce said. "He convinced Dr. Brinkman to train her for the West Coast moderator position."

"I can see why he knew about our investigation," I said. "We've been pretty honest with Sheriff Hennessey. But I don't understand why Deputy Bloomberg would kidnap my aunt."

"Bruno and I have a theory," Bruce said.

"And?"

"Well, when you told Sheriff Hennessey about Harvey Winkle, he went to Deputy Bloomberg to look into it."

"But Deputy Bloomberg didn't have to look into Harvey Winkle. He was Harvey," I said. "He went after us instead."

"Yes," Bruce said. "We think so. When I heard that your aunt had been kidnapped and the kidnappers weren't asking for ransom, I thought about Harvey. I did some digging myself and discovered he was a deputy. Bruno and I went to get you as soon as I realized the connection."

"You could have called," Holly pointed out.

"You wouldn't have believed me," Bruce said. "In fact, you *didn't* believe me."

"But you don't know for sure he has Aunt Jemma," I said, "unless you saw him take her."

"We didn't see anything," Bruno said and put down his teacup, "but we found out that Harvey was really Deputy Bloomberg."

"Then, when Sheriff Hennessey came by earlier today, it wasn't a big leap to figure out who would do such a thing. Think about it. Wouldn't your aunt go with a deputy? Who else would you trust?"

"Plus Harvey, er, Deputy Bloomberg," Bruno interrupted, "would be able to hide the car. He grew up in the area, owns over two hundred acres south of here. Go check out the outbuildings on his property. I bet you find the car."

"But Deputy Bloomberg told me that they found my aunt's MG," I said.

"And you believe him? Did you call Sheriff Hennessey?" Bruce asked.

"You left my phone on the street," I pointed out. "I didn't have time to call."

"My point is that you wouldn't have checked, would you?"

"You must think that Deputy Bloomberg killed Dr. Brinkman," I said. "Why else would he be the first one you thought of to take my aunt?"

"I saw Harvey leaving Mandy's dressing room earlier that night," Bruno said. "I was working the door. He seemed upset and wouldn't turn when I called out to him." Bruno shrugged. "I didn't think anything about it until later. Harvey always treated the bodyguards like second-class citizens. He rarely acknowledged us unless he wanted something. Then it was 'Bruno do this. Bruno do that.'"

"We need to call Sheriff Hennessey," I said and grabbed Holly's phone. "If you think Deputy Bloomberg killed Dr. Brinkman, the Sheriff should know."

"He won't believe us," Bruce said and pulled the phone away from me. "Trust me, we tried."

"How did you try?" I asked and drew my eyebrows together in question.

"When he asked about Harvey Winkle, we told him that Harvey Winkle and Deputy Bloomberg were the same person. He looked at us as if we were making stuff up. Then he dismissed it with 'You must be mistaken.'"

"He was protecting his own," Bruno said. "It happens."

"Okay, let's say for one moment that Deputy Bloomberg is

involved. That he killed Dr. Brinkman for some reason, and he doesn't want us to investigate. Why would he take my aunt?"

"You said so yourself that you were starting to look at connections. He knew that you told Sheriff Hennessey about Harvey. It would only be a matter of time before he was found out."

"But taking my aunt made this worse," I said softly, "didn't it?"

"He might think he's protected by his status as deputy," Bruno said. "Sometimes bad guys get involved with local law enforcement. It's an easy way to stay on top of the investigation."

"I bet he volunteered to help you with this, didn't he?" Bruce piped in.

"I don't know," I said. "Chelsea called the sheriff's department, and when I went into the gallery, he was already there."

"If he was involved, he might have volunteered to be the inside person," Holly said.

I blew out a long breath. "Arguing about whether he's involved doesn't get me any closer to finding my aunt. She has a heart condition. I need to find her and get her home. If you can't help me with that, then there is no reason for me to be here." I stood. "Please take us back to the gallery."

"We think we know where your aunt is," Bruce said.

"Why didn't you say that in the first place? Let's go!"

"We can't," Bruno said. "Deputy Bloomberg is a member of our board. We can't have anyone think we know anything about this."

"That's ridiculous!" Holly said. "You're already involved. Deputy Bloomberg knows you took us."

"Tell me where she is, and I'll take care of it," I said and took back Holly's phone.

"Who are you calling?" Bruce asked.

"I'm calling an Uber. Tell me where you think she is, and I'll go get her."

"There is a small farmhouse and numerous outbuildings on the Winkle property," Bruce said. "We feel there's a good chance she's there. It's relatively secluded, and there are places to hide cars."

"Come on, Holly," I said. "Let's go check it out."

"We can drop you up the road," Bruno said, "but that's as far as we can take you."

"Let's go."

Holly and I got back in the car. Bruce stayed behind as Bruno drove us out of the compound.

"How are you going to explain taking us?" I asked.

"Deputy Bloomberg is going to know we were here," Holly said. "There are cameras." She pointed at the cameras on the gate.

"I'm part of security," Bruno said. "I'll see that no one asks questions."

"And tossing my phone?" I asked. "How are you going to explain that?"

"A misunderstanding," he said with a shrug.

"I hope it's that simple."

He dropped us off at the corner of Main Street, where I'd dropped my phone. It was still on the side of the road. "My phone's still here," I said and swooped down to pick it up. "That means that Deputy Bloomberg didn't report us being taken. Or maybe he didn't come looking for my phone."

"Let's go to my apartment complex and get my car," Holly said. We were careful not to be noticed by the police, and got into her car and drove off. My phone rang just as we headed out of town. "Hello?"

"Where are you?" It was Sheriff Hennessey. "I've been trying to call you, and you haven't answered. Deputy Bloomberg tells me you left the gallery and haven't returned. He can't leave, in case the building is being watched."

"We had an interesting conversation with Bruce from the Brinkman compound," I said and encouraged Holly to drive faster.

"You saw Bruce? I asked you not to talk to anyone."

"Well, he had a theory about who took Aunt Jemma, and Holly and I are following up on it."

"What's the theory? Where are you going?"

"The theory is that someone in the sheriff's office is involved," I said. "So I am not sure I want to share where we think she is. If you tell the wrong person, they could move her."

"Taylor, where are you going?" His voice got low and fierce.

"We are heading out of town," I said. "I'll let you know when we get there. My phone is being tapped. Remember?"

"Taylor—"

I hung up and looked at Holly, who was concentrating on getting us down the winding country road as quickly and safely as possible. "Who was that?"

"Sheriff Hennessey," I said.

Holly glanced at me and then back at the road. "If Deputy Bloomberg is listening in to your phone, then he knows we are on to him."

I chewed on my bottom lip. "He also has my phone tracked, so I imagine Sheriff Hennessey is looking up my GPS coordinates as we speak."

"Then we'll have to go faster," Holly said and stepped on it. The car zoomed. I was glad we had seatbelts on and hung on to the sissy bar at the top of the door.

"Is that a siren?" I asked and looked behind us.

"No," she said. "It's the radio." She turned down the music, and she was right: blissful silence.

"How far out are we?"

"Another ten minutes of normal time," Holly said. "I can make it in five."

"As long as we make it in one piece."

Holly grinned at me. "I live to go fast."

The scenery zipped by. I looked up at the rolling hills and acres and acres of rows of vines. "We're getting close. You'd better slow down or we'll miss the entrance."

"Right." Holly slowed, and the property we came up on had a large "For Sale" sign out front. The entrance was rather hidden. It was clear the property didn't have a tasting barn, and it had been awhile since anyone had lived here. The drive was about three quarters of a mile from the road. The grapes were well tended and trimmed up for winter. "Somebody must be still caring for the vines," Holly said as we slowly rolled up the drive.

"They can rent the acres," I said. "Sell the grapes to other wineries. Aunt Jemma sometimes buys from others and mixes grapes for a variety of flavors. Stop here."

Holly slowed way down and pulled to the side of the drive. The road curved ahead of us, but we were not within viewing distance of the buildings. "Are you thinking we should get closer on foot?"

"Yes—pull over under that tree."

Holly pulled the car over to where I pointed, and we both got out. She locked the doors, and we walked up the rest of the drive. It was quiet and smelled of fall and cut-back grape vines. The first building was a barn. We crept up to it and peered into the dust- and dirt-coated window. It was dark and difficult to see. I put my finger to my lips, but there was no sound except for the rustling of the dead brush against the peeling paint of the wood building.

I looked around the corner. There was a door, but it was in the line of sight of the farmhouse. I frowned and Holly waved for me to follow her around the back. There was a hole in the wood that used to be a knot. Holly looked inside. "A car!"

"Shush," I said softly and motioned for her to let me see. I glanced inside, and the dim light from the grimy window shone off a beige sedan. It didn't look very dirty, so it hadn't been parked in there long. I looked at Holly. "Do you think that's Jeffery's car?"

"Or someone from the Winkle family is living here and is going to call the cops on us for trespassing," she whispered.

"We need to find Aunt Jemma's MG."

"And Aunt Jemma."

I took a deep breath and blew it out slowly. "There's a shed and then the farmhouse," I whispered. "Let's see what we can find out."

"And if they catch us?"

"We can say we're looking for our dog."

"What?"

"Shush—we tell anyone we run into that our dog ran away and we are looking in the bushes for it."

"Huh. Okay."

We glanced around the side of the barn. The shed was angled behind the house, but beside the barn. We hurried to the shed. It didn't have any windows, and like the barn, the main door was in the line of sight of the house. If anyone was watching out the window of the farmhouse, they would see us. The shed was made of metal, so there was no chance of a hole to peer into. That left just the house on the top of the hill.

It was a two-story farmhouse that looked as if it had been built in the 1800s and added onto. It had once been painted white but now was mostly gray. The windows were tall and narrow. We made a fast dash to side of the house and ducked under a window.

I sneaked a peek. The inside of the house was sparsely furnished. Someone sat in a settee that had its back to the window. I could see that the person sat sideways, her legs and feet handing off the side—at least, they looked like a woman's legs. From the spiky heeled boots on the feet, I knew it wasn't Aunt Jemma. A sense of disappointment filled me.

The person got up, and I caught a glimpse just before I ducked down out of sight.

"What?" Holly mouthed.

"It looked like Mandy." I said in a low voice.

Holly looked as confused as I felt. "Why would she be here?"

"I don't know," I said. "I didn't see anything else."

"We can't do anything until we know for sure your aunt is here. We need some tangible proof."

"I know."

We heard the back door open and froze. We were at the side of the house and out in the open. All Mandy had to do was look around at the side of the house, and we would be caught. I didn't think the lost dog story would work on Mandy.

"Honey, I'm telling you she doesn't know who we are," we heard her say. "The blindfold is tight. There's no way she knows where she is. No, there's no way anyone knows. I haven't talked to anyone." We heard her pacing on the back porch, and we hunkered down closer, our backs pressed to the siding.

"No, no one's come up the drive. I promise I've been watching. There is no television here and no Wi-Fi. It's just me and the old lady." She paused. "No, I've not been streaming things on my phone. For goodness sakes, I know what's at stake here."

I looked at Holly, and she looked at me. I went to stand up and confront Mandy, but Holly grabbed my arm and stopped me. She shook her head. I sent her a fierce frown. All I could do was imagine my aunt tied up and blindfolded.

The door slammed shut and all was quiet. Mandy had gone back inside.

Holly took my hand and pulled me away from the house to the shed, and then the barn, as we retraced our steps to the car. She unlocked it, and we climbed inside and locked the doors.

"She has my aunt. Mandy has my aunt. Mandy has been in on this from the start. Think about it! She worked for Hoag. She was conveniently gone when he died. She was there when Dr. Brinkman died. For all we know she is the killer, and she has Aunt Jemma!"

"We need to call the sheriff," Holly said emphatically. "We can't confront Mandy alone. There is no way a conviction would stick. It would be your word against hers, and she has a deputy for a boyfriend."

"Well, I am friends with Sheriff Hennessey."

"And you were under suspicion for murder just a few months ago."

"Fine!"

"Good!" She said.

There was a knock on my window, and we both screamed.

Chapter 27

"Get out of the car."

I looked into Sheriff Hennessey's face and unlocked my door. "When did you get here?"

"I wasn't far behind you two when we talked on the phone." He straightened. I saw Deputy Hanson standing near the squad car that had stopped on the drive behind where we parked.

"Oh, thank goodness you're here," Holly said. "It's Mandy. She has Aunt Jemma in the house."

"How do you know?" Sheriff Hennessey asked. He crossed his arms over his beefy chest.

"We heard her talking," I said and mirrored his stance by crossing my arms over my own chest. "She was telling someone on the phone that there was no way the old lady knows where she is or who took her because she is blindfolded."

"That sounds suspicious, right?" Holly said. "Go and arrest her."

"It's not that simple," Sheriff Hennessey said. "We have to have cause."

"We just gave you cause . . ."

"What I can do is go and knock on the door and see if

anyone is home," he said. "You stay here. Hanson, make sure these ladies stay put."

"But what if she doesn't answer?" I asked. "What if my aunt is in there and dies of a heart attack because Mandy refuses to answer the door?"

"Let's cross that bridge when we come to it," he said. I watched as he strode up the drive and out of sight.

"Does Deputy Bloomberg know you are here?" I asked Deputy Hanson.

"Most likely," he said. "We let dispatch know we were heading out this way. Why?"

"That's why he called Mandy," Holly said.

"We think he's involved and was spying on us," I said.

"Why would you think that?" Deputy Hanson asked. "Bloomberg is a straight-up guy."

"Really?" Holly said and put her hands on her hips. "Did you know he was one of the inner circle of the Brinkman group?"

"He was trying to sell this place to the Brinkman group to develop it into a fancy retreat house for self-helpers," I added.

"Bloomberg? Why would he do that?"

"His grandfather is Harvey Winkle, the owner," I said. "People will do amazing things for money."

"You need to go find out what is going on with Sheriff Hennessey," I said. "He might need backup."

"Against a young woman? Did you see anyone else when you were up at the house?"

"No," I said, "but we suspect the murderer is Mandy. If she can kill Jeffery and Dr. Brinkman, there isn't a lot keeping her from killing Sheriff Hennessey."

"I think Hennessey can take care of himself."

"Well, I don't," I said and headed up the drive.

"You have to stay put," Deputy Hanson said.

"You can't stop us both," Holly said and followed after me.

"I can," he said and pulled his gun. "Stop or I'll have to shoot."

"I'm going to bet you won't," Holly said. "Run!"

We raced up the hill. I glanced back to see Deputy Hanson swear and put his gun back in its holster before chasing after us.

I got up to the barn and raced straight to the front door of the farmhouse. Sheriff Hennessey was nowhere in sight. I banged on the farmhouse door. "Let me in, Mandy. I know you're in there. I want my aunt and I want her now!"

Holly was beside me and banging as well. The door opened and Sheriff Hennessey stood there. "What are you doing?" he asked.

"I'm sorry, I couldn't stop them," Deputy Hanson said behind us. He was winded and bent over, putting his hands on his thighs, to catch his breath.

I pushed past the Sheriff. "Aunt Jemma! Aunt Jemma, it's me. Where are you?"

Mandy stopped me as I began to climb the stairs. "What are you doing? Your aunt isn't here."

"She is and I'll prove it," I said and raced up the stairway. "Aunt Jemma?" There was a center hall with four doors. I opened the first. It was an empty, old bedroom. I opened the second. A dirty bathroom. I opened a third. Nothing. I went for the last one as Mandy came up the stairs with the Sheriff behind her. "Aunt Jemma!"

There was a cot in this room, and it looked as if it had been slept in. I searched the room and saw a closet. I reached for the closet door as Mandy grabbed me. "Stop!" she said.

"I will not stop," I said. "Shame on you. Shame on you for hurting and scaring an old woman with a heart condition." I pulled the closet door open and peered inside. It was empty.

"I told you she wasn't here," Mandy said.

"I'm checking the basement." I tried to push past Mandy and Sheriff Hennessey, but he stood in my way.

"You need permission to check," Sheriff Hennessey said softly, "or you are trespassing."

"Fine." I turned to Mandy. "The only reason you wouldn't give me permission to check the premises is if you have something to hide. Do you have something to hide?"

"No," she said, her eyes narrowing.

"Good. Then I'll be checking the basement." I hurried down the stairs, calling my aunt's name. I checked the parlor, the small kitchen, and the pantry. I opened every door until I found the basement door and turned on the light and went downstairs into the cool musty air of a cellar. Multiple wine barrels were stored down there. The floor was dirt. "Aunt Jemma?" I called her name and thought I heard something.

"She isn't here," Mandy said from the top of the stairs. "Stop this nonsense."

"Shush," I said and put up my hand. "I heard something." It was dark in the back of the cellar, so I turned on the flashlight on my phone and peered into the darkness behind the barrels. There was a wooden wardrobe the size of a closet. I pulled the door open and found my aunt sitting on the floor of the closet. Her eyes were covered with a cloth, and she had a cloth stuffed in her mouth. "Aunt Jemma! She's here! Call an ambulance!"

I heard scuffling behind me as Mandy tried to run. Sheriff Hennessey must have taken care of her. I didn't pay attention to what was going on. I was fully focused on my aunt. I gently pulled the rag out of her mouth. "Aunt Jemma, it's me. It's Taylor. Are you okay?"

"Water," she said in a harsh voice.

"Someone get some water!" I called to the people behind me. I untied the binding on her eyes and carefully helped her out of the closet. She was cold and stiff and had trouble standing.

By the time I got her up, Sheriff Hennessey had passed Mandy on to someone else and came back to help me get her my aunt up the stairs and onto the settee.

I gave him a stern look. "I told you she was here."

Aunt Jemma put her hand on mine. "I knew you would come for me."

"How did they get you?" I asked. "You were on your way to the coffee club and then didn't show up."

"I was stopped by Deputy Bloomberg," she said. Her voice was shaky. I sent Sheriff Hennessey another look that said, "I told you so."

Sheriff Hennessey had his notepad out. "Did he pull you over?" His tone was flat and severe.

"Yes," she said. "I was surprised because I didn't think I was going too fast, but then I was just tootling along, so I wasn't sure." She shrugged. "If a police officer pulls you over, you stop."

"Then what happened?" he asked.

"I don't remember," she said and looked confused. "He asked for my license and registration. I got it out of the glove box and turned toward him to show him. The rest, well, is fuzzy."

"Did he hit you?" I asked and looked for bruising or a knot on her head.

"I don't know."

"Don't worry," Sheriff Hennessey said. "The EMTs will check her out thoroughly. What's the next thing you remember?"

"I couldn't see anything, and my hands were tied in front of me. I think I was on a chair or a bed. I sat up startled, but couldn't see. I felt the bindings on my face and wondered if I'd been hurt somehow."

"Were you alone?" he asked.

"I called out, and there was someone there. A woman, I think. She had an odd whispery voice. Then the voice changed again, but I swear there was only one person." She looked at me confused. "Can a person change their voice?"

"If they use a voice app," I said. "She must have recorded her voice and played it back."

"The next thing I know, she handed me a phone. I thought I heard you, Taylor."

"Yes," I said and held her hand. "I asked for proof you were alive, and they gave me the phone."

"I only spoke briefly before I smelled something sweet, and then the next thing I knew, I was woken up, and the woman was demanding I get up. She kept shouting at me and jerking me downstairs. So many stairs. Then it was cold, and I was told to sit and stay quiet. She shoved a rag in my mouth."

Holly brought in a glass of water, and Aunt Jemma thanked her and took a few sips.

"I always thought I would be difficult to kidnap. I'm a fighter. I fight back." She started shaking.

"It's okay," I said and put my arm around her. There wasn't a blanket, or I would have tucked her into one. The sound of the ambulance could be heard as it pulled up the drive.

"Did you recognize the woman's voice?" Sheriff Hennessey asked.

"No," she said and shook her head, frowning. "Should I?"

"It was an extreme stress," he said carefully. "Most likely you wouldn't recognize the voice."

She looked at me. "Did you have to pay a lot of money?"

"No," I reassured her. "No."

"Oh, good." She held her head. "Good."

The EMTs came in and took over, pushing me out of the way. They put a blanket around Aunt Jemma and took her vitals.

"I'm going to have to get a statement," Sheriff Hennessey said.

"I hope you've arrested Deputy Bloomberg," I said.

"My team has him at the station," he said, his mouth a grim line.

"Mandy was at Tim's the night Jeffery went missing. There's a beige car in the barn. It looks like it hasn't been there very long. I think it might be his missing car."

"My guys will take care of it."

"Mandy was at the theater the night Dr. Brinkman was killed too. He was killed in her dressing room. She must have killed him, cleaned up, and then come back to get me as her alibi."

"I said, we'll connect the dots."

"I'm just so angry," I said and rubbed my forearms. "What was she thinking? Why take Aunt Jemma?"

"We'll get the truth," he said. "You should not have come out here. You put yourself and Holly in danger."

"You wouldn't have found my aunt if I hadn't," I said and tried not to accuse him of not doing his job.

"Miss, we're ready to take your aunt to the hospital," an EMT said.

"Can I ride with her?" I asked.

"Yes," he said.

"We'll be talking later," the sheriff said as I followed my aunt, on a stretcher, out.

"Holly," I called to my friend as I walked out. She was on the front porch, her face pale and her arms hugging her torso. "I'm going with Aunt Jemma. Are you okay to drive?"

"I'll be fine," she said and waved me on. "I'll meet you at the hospital."

More police cars arrived, filling the weedy lawn. People in uniform were everywhere, opening the barn door and the shed. I climbed into the ambulance and held Aunt Jemma's hand.

"You did it," she said and smiled weakly at me. "I'm so proud of you."

I smiled at her and patted her hand. I just wish I had figured it out before they took her. She suddenly looked her age for the first time since I'd moved back home.

Chapter 28

"I guess Deputy Bloomberg turned on Mandy," Chelsea said. "He pled guilty to accessory to murder and kidnapping."

"Tim is free," I said. I glanced at my phone. "He texted to say he's on his way over with a case of his best wine."

We sat in Aunt Jemma's living area. The sliding glass doors to the patio were open, letting in the soft evening breeze. A fire crackled in the center fireplace. Aunt Jemma was lounging on her pink fainting couch, her white, faux fur blanket tucked firmly around her. Chelsea sat in one flowered, wing-backed chair, and Holly and I were curled up on the big overstuffed couch.

"He owes me more than wine," Aunt Jemma said with drama.

"I can't believe they were able to drug you so effectively," Holly said. "Are you still feeling effects?"

"The doctor said it was propofol and it will be in my system for a few more hours," Aunt Jemma said.

"Where did they get the drug, I wonder?" Chelsea asked.

"Mandy is very manipulative," I pointed out. "It didn't take much for her to convince someone to help her. It turns out she was the one who put Dr. Brinkman and the Winkle family together."

"Here we all thought she was one of Tim's ditzy girlfriends," Holly said. "She really didn't seem that bright."

"I know," I said. "I guess we all just assumed there wasn't much going on behind those blank blue eyes."

"Turns out it was all an act," Chelsea said. "Mandy was also connected to the Senator. It seems she was busy manipulating many people in the county."

"Why did she kill Jeffery Hoag?" Holly asked.

"Deputy Bloomberg confessed to Sarah's assessment. Jeffery caught Mandy making out with Deputy Bloomberg. He knew she was also the Senator's mistress and threatened to tell him."

"Wait, she was the *Senator's* mistress? What was she doing with Tim?" I asked.

"Apparently, she targeted Tim with her helpless idiot routine to get him to sell so they could increase the size of the Brinkman estate."

"Well, she blew it then," I said.

"Yes, being caught with Deputy Bloomberg would have blown everything she had been working on," Aunt Jemma said. "She had to silence him."

"How did she kill Jeffery?" I asked. "I'm assuming Deputy Bloomberg helped put him in the vat with the grape must."

"He did," Holly said. "I heard that Mandy hit Jeffery in the head with a bottle of wine. He dropped dead instantly."

"She then convinced Deputy Bloomberg to help her put the body in the wine. She was hoping the fermentation would destroy all evidence," Chelsea said.

"She didn't know too much about wine fermentation, did she? I mean alcohol is a preservative," Holly said.

"Still, it was brilliant, framing Tim. No one suspected her," Aunt Jemma said.

"It was actually Deputy Bloomberg who drove the car off Tim's property and out to the Winkle barn," I added.

"And Dr. Brinkman?" Holly asked.

"The Senator pulled out of the deal after Jeffery died. He didn't want any connection to murder," Chelsea said. "When they lost the zoning backing, Dr. Brinkman told Mandy he was going to propose the group go south to Orange County. He had connections there for a beach retreat."

"Mandy didn't want that?"

"No, she had invested all of her money in the little winery beside the Winkle estate."

"She would have lost everything."

"Yes," Chelsea said. "Plus, Tim was free, and she needed him as the scapegoat."

"So she killed Dr. Brinkman, which got Tim arrested and put her on the board of directors of the Brinkman group," I said.

"Yes," Chelsea said. "She had convinced the board to put together a big donation to the Senator's campaign in an attempt to get him to back the zoning request this time."

"But then we started investigating the Senator," I said. "She couldn't have anyone point toward the Senator, or he would've shut everything down."

"She convinced Deputy Bloomberg to kidnap me," Aunt Jemma said.

"Actually, it was Deputy Bloomberg who suggested it. That's why it was so out of character. Mandy was a big-picture plotter. She had spent a year working on this deal. She wouldn't have kidnapped me without an end game. But the deputy took me, and she didn't have a choice but to go along."

"Everything began to unravel, and he called her to tell her we knew you were out at the farmhouse."

"So she stuffed me in the cellar closet. She would have left me there to die," Aunt Jemma said. "I'm so thankful you didn't give up."

"I knew you were there," I said. "I wasn't going to give up until I tore every inch of that place apart."

Millie barked and we all looked over as the door opened. "Hello, everyone," Tim said. "I've got the best wine you'll ever drink."

I got up and helped him through the door. "Welcome! How does it feel to be a free man?"

"Feels good," he said. "It will feel better once I get some wine in me." He put the case on the kitchen counter and went over to Aunt Jemma. "How are you, dear woman?" He kissed her cheek. "Thanks to you, I'm free."

"I'll be fine in a few days," she said. "Nothing some rest and pampering can't cure."

I uncorked the wine and poured everyone a glass. Holly helped me pass out the glasses.

"Here's to good friends, good wine, and lovely California evenings."

"Here, here!"

I sipped my wine and petted Clemmie, who'd jumped up on the arm of the couch. Sonoma was once again safe, and I was happy to know my friends and family were finally safe.

Recipes

Zinfandel is a very versatile wine that goes well with all-American classics like pizza, hamburgers, ribs, meatloaf, roast, and chili. So feel free to serve it with your family's favorites. For something more ethnic, here's a tandoori chicken recipe.

Tandoori Chicken

Ingredients:

2 lb of chicken—get a whole chicken, remove the skin, and cut
 it into serving sizes.

2 lemons—juice one and slice one

1¼ cups plain yogurt—I prefer nonfat Greek style (yes, I'm
 mixing cultures).

1 onion finely chopped

1 tsp salt

1 clove of garlic minced

1 tsp freshly grated gingerroot

2 tsp garam masala (hot spices). This is a classic Indian mix of
 spices and can be different. I recommend you go to a good
 Indian food store and ask to taste different varieties. Find
 one that appeals to your palate. I like mine with coriander,
 cumin, cardamom, black pepper, cloves, nutmeg, and
 cinnamon.

1 tsp cayenne pepper

2 tsp finely chopped cilantro—I am not a fan of cilantro, so I
 substitute parsley.

Directions:

The day before you want to serve it, take the cut-up chicken
pieces, and slice slits into them. Rub with salt and lemon juice,

and set aside for 15–20 minutes. Mix the yogurt, onion, garlic, gingerroot, and spices together in a bowl. Spread the mixture over the chicken, cover, and let sit for 24 hours.

The next day, fire up the grill. Grill chicken until it no longer is pink, and the juices run clear. Garnish with cilantro and lemon slices. Enjoy with long grain rice and your favorite zin.

Cheeses that go well with zinfandels:
When it comes to cheeses, the spicier the better!
Smoky mozzarella
Dry aged Jack
Blue cheese
Aged (over six years) cheddars
Chèvre
Roquefort
Provolone
Parmesan reggiano

Desserts that pair well with zinfandels:
Rich caramel pecan fudge
Vanilla pecan pie
Rich dark chocolate fudge with caramel and pecans

Fun and Easy Homemade Fudge

Ingredients:

3 c. dark chocolate chips
1 (14–oz.) can sweetened condensed milk
¼ cup butter
1 jar caramel sauce
1 cup chopped pecans

Directions:

In a heavy saucepan, mix chocolate chips, sweetened condensed milk, and butter. Stir on medium heat until the chips and butter are melted, and the mixture is smooth. Remove from heat and add pecans. Stir until well mixed. Pour into a greased 8" × 8" × 2" cake pan. Smooth the top of the fudge. Use a spoon to make small indents at regular intervals. Spoon caramel sauce into the indents. Drizzle remaining sauce along the top. Refrigerate until set. Cut into suitable sizes and enjoy!

Acknowledgments

I always say it takes a village to make a book, and that becomes more and more true with each book I write. Thanks to the Crooked Lane folks for the beautiful covers, fine editing, and patience with the writer. Thanks to my agent, Paige Wheeler, for finding me wonderful opportunities. Special thanks goes out to my family and friends for understanding that to get a book ready, I might have to take time away.

Thanks to my readers who are my dearest friends. Together we build stories and enjoy the characters in my head.